POLITICAL DEATH

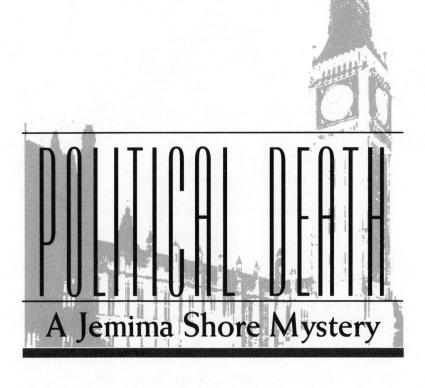

POLITICAL DEATH

A Jemima Shore Mystery

ANTONIA FRASER

BANTAM BOOKS

New York   Toronto   London   Sydney   Auckland

POLITICAL DEATH

A Bantam Book / March 1996

First published in Great Britain
by William Heinemann Ltd.

BOOK DESIGN BY GLEN EDELSTEIN

Library of Congress Cataloging-in-Publication Data

Fraser, Antonia, 1932–
Political death: a Jemima Shore mystery / Antonia Fraser.
p.   cm.
ISBN 0-553-09964-7
1. Shore, Jemima (Fictitious character)—Fiction.   2. Women
detectives—England—Fiction.   I. Title.
PR6056.R2863P65   1996
823'.914—dc20   95-37779
CIP

Published simultaneously in the United States and Canada

*Bantam Books are published by Bantam Books, a division of Bantam Doubleday Dell
Publishing Group, Inc. Its trademark, consisting of the words "Bantam Books" and the
portrayal of a rooster, is Registered in U.S. Patent and Trademark Office and in other
countries. Marca Registrada. Bantam Books, 1540 Broadway, New York, New York 10036.*

PRINTED IN THE UNITED STATES OF AMERICA

BVG   0 9 8 7 6 5 4 3 2 1

For Paul, Harold, Gawn and Doug

NO MAN'S LAND 1992–3

NOTE

This story is set in the spring of 1993.
There was, of course, no British General Election
in March of that year, nor a Labour–Liberal Alliance.
All these political happenings, like the politicians
involved in them, are imaginary.

CONTENTS

POLITICAL DEATH

CHAPTER 1

A RADICAL SOLUTION

ILLIE SWAIN WAS IN HER DRESSING-ROOM READING THE EVENING
paper and thinking how rotten the government was, when the
telephone rang. With a sinking heart, she knew that it was her
sister. Olga was married to a Conservative MP, known to his
sister-in-law as Holy Harry, but Millie did not imagine that
Olga was calling her to discuss politics. If only she were! Millie
would bait her about the government's record, and how they deserved to lose the election, which would be enjoyable. As it was,
Millie Swain was filled with dread.

"She's done it again. Madre of course. Today of all days. I could
kill her. And so could Harry." Olga's voice was crisp, but even so
Millie could detect the note of resentment towards herself. "Your
turn, Millie," Olga's voice was saying to her.

"Where?"—defensively—"You know I'm just about to—it's the
last preview—"

"I know. I looked it up in the paper. To get the number." More
resentment. This time the voice was saying: "You haven't arranged

for tickets for us for the first night. And I had to look up your telephone number."

In the large mirror opposite her chair, Millie could see herself already dressed in the velvet trouser suit and frilly shirt in which she was about to play a sixties Viola. She had grown her short dark hair so that it could be cut to resemble that of a fashionable young man of the period, curls brushing the collar of her shirt. An enormous plastic Pop mackintosh and hat for the opening scene hung on a hook in her open cupboard. She must not let herself be distracted by Olga.

To stop that unspoken voice of complaint, Millie decided on a policy of sisterly warmth. "*Where*, darling? Yes, it does matter. Perhaps I can help this time. You know I want to. This *Twelfth Night* is not a long version," she went on, "many, many cuts, I'm happy to tell you. That means you and Holy Harry—all right, *Harry* then— will love it, won't you? It starts at seven thirty. And I can be out of the theatre pretty sharply. At least the West End, if a desert, is a convenient desert." Millie hesitated. "Olga, you say this time it was worse . . ."

But could anything be worse than last time, Millie wondered. "Last time" referred to the occasion when Madre had gone to Harrods, bearing an ancient evening dress, shell-pink and heavily beaded, in a Safeways bag. She had then decided to exchange it for a new one on the grounds that there was a stain on it—true enough, there were in fact a good many stains. She must have pulled it out of one of her terrible cupboards. With a kind of dreadful plausibility, the precise dress Madre wanted in exchange—Versace, Christian Lacroix, that sort of thing, costing thousands—had similar bead-work to the remnants on the ragged pink object on the chair beside her.

"Actually it did have a very dirty label in it, something like 'Christian Dior–Harrods'," reported Olga. "No doubt that was what aroused the manager's respect." It was naturally Olga who'd had to cope with all this. (Millie was in rehearsal and could not be reached.) Olga found herself summoned to Harrods by a house manager or some such functionary who was, under the circumstances, amazingly polite. Perhaps that was part of the Harrods' training course: how to pacify middle-aged ladies bringing in ancient dresses to exchange them for something new?

"Lady Imogen was rather distressed," he began, "but fortunately she had your number written in her diary under the words 'Next of kin'." The manager coughed discreetly at what such a phrase might otherwise suggest. "So it seemed wise to summon you."

Olga tried to match the manager's own delicacy. "I'm afraid my mother does get a little distressed from time to time. Confused is probably the right word." Olga thought she had better broach the unpleasant subject. "Did she by any chance try to pay for the dress by putting it on her account?"

"I don't think you quite understand." The first hint of something less bland beneath the manager's composed surface. "Lady Imogen didn't try to *pay for it* at all—"

"Yes, yes," stumbled Olga, "How stupid of me." Just as well, she thought, since the account had long ago been closed: one of the many facts her mother found impossible to accept.

"As a matter of fact Lady Imogen seemed to think that the original dress had been a present," went on the manager with a tactful cough, blandness restored. But Olga knew better than to pursue that one. She knew from experience that this could be lethal. She could imagine only too well who was supposed to have given her mother the dress, probably *had* given it to her, dammit.

"Come along, Madre," Olga said bracingly—but not too bracingly, she hoped. Past experience again: too much bossiness, the nanny's touch, tended to make things worse. "Let's go home."

"But my pretty dress." Lady Imogen spoke up suddenly in that breathy little-girl voice which became that much breathier on these occasions. "I need it for tonight. The Barracloughs' ball. Teresa is coming up from the country. As you can imagine, rather a fraught occasion. But Burgo has promised, you know, *my* Burgo—" More coughs but this time from Olga, as she resolutely interrupted her mother. She simply could not allow Madre to keep introducing that name. It was so terribly recognisable! The manager sounded nice and was certainly helpful, but the Press were everywhere. With the election coming (it had finally been announced for March 18) politicians were more in the news than ever, and if the story got repeated . . . what on earth would poor Harry *do* about it?

Her mother was sitting quite docilely on a gilt chair brought by the thoughtful manager; she had the unhappy air of an abandoned child. It was indeed extremely irritating to Olga that her mother, a woman in her sixties, for heaven's sake, could from a distance be mistaken for a girl. It was partly the sheer littleness of her. Imogen Swain was no more than five foot one, a tiny fairy of a woman, and even the absurd high heels she insisted on wearing, on which she balanced so precariously, hardly took her to average height. Both Olga and Millie had inherited the more robust physical appearance of the father they could not remember.

Of course when you saw Madre close, no slimness could make up for the fact that here was a wrinkled, no, an *extremely* wrinkled woman, who would never see sixty again—might indeed be seeing seventy quite soon. The huge blue eyes (Olga and Millie both had eyes like black olives) were surrounded by lines, which the spiky mascara on the sparse eyelashes only emphasised, and lines dragged down the wide mouth with its slightly-too-bright lipstick. Raddled was probably the right word for Madre's appearance. Olga's daughter Elfi, an only child with an unfortunate gift for accuracy, had once observed, "Nonna looks like a very old doll, doesn't she, like a doll you find in the garden when it's been left out in the rain?" It was still true that neither Olga nor Millie could be mistaken for dolls.

Now, as Millie Swain sat in her dressing-room in her velvet suit, waiting for the latest report from the distressing maternal front, her gaze fell again on the evening paper. It would happen that there was a picture of the Right Honourable Burgo Smyth at Heathrow beneath a report of the latest poll on the outcome of the election (still a dead-heat). That in itself was hardly unusual: a Foreign Secretary was always at some airport or other. BURGO FLIES OUT was a familiar headline as the photogenic Foreign Secretary headed towards the latest crisis. In this case Burgo was flying in: he was calling, she noted, for a radical solution to something or other, some place or other. Millie had long ago trained herself not to tremble with agitation every time she saw a picture of Burgo or caught sight of him on TV. But this afternoon's picture was different.

By a fluke of shadow as he bent down, Burgo's magnificent head of silvery hair—his most characteristic feature—looked black again. This was once more the young man who—but Millie would not let herself continue. She had to think of Madre now, not Madre then, not Burgo at all. For a long time as children they had not been allowed to mention his name. The topic had been cut off, just like that, with bewildering suddenness. In the same way Burgo himself—marvellous generous teasing huggable bear-like Burgo—had vanished mysteriously and suddenly from their lives. Questions to Madre had met with a blank stare of those huge wide-open blue eyes, so famously beautiful, so free from lines around them. And there would be silence as though the question had simply not been asked. Questions to Nanny Forrester had met with a sharp reproof and, if repeated, a sharp slap. So Millie had learnt to divorce the public image of Burgo Smyth, politician, from the private man she had once known. Most of the time she genuinely felt nothing.

Millie in the theatre firmly turned the paper over: "Go on, Olga, tell me all," she said encouragingly.

"It was worse this time. Worse than Harrods, the rest of it." A significant pause. "Madre went to the house in Westminster Place."

"Christ!" Millie sat up, reached for the paper and instinctively started to crumple it, as though to obliterate the handsome threatening image. Then she relaxed. "But surely *he* wasn't there. I mean, he's been in Turkey, according to the paper, but in any case I read somewhere that he finally sold the house. If only Madre had done the same! Anyway, doesn't the Foreign Secretary have a residence? Which *we* of course pay for. Ridiculous and unnecessary extravagance," Millie couldn't help adding.

But Olga did not rise. She allowed herself the luxury of quarrelling with Millie about politics only on occasions (like family Christmas) which could do with a little heightened blood pressure. This was not one of them.

"No, *he* wasn't there. But someone was. Someone who took Madre in, someone who found the 'Next of Kin' note in her Asprey's diary—one day, Millie, don't you think that you might . . . ? Especially when Harry really needs my help, with his tiny majority. Ah well, perhaps not, the Bohemian life and all that—as I was saying, someone who telephoned me. Someone who got me just as I was going to see Elfi in her school play. 'Your mother seems rather confused.' The usual story."

"Olga, please. I'm on stage in twenty minutes. I know it's dreadful you had to cope once again. But for God's sake, who?"

"Mack McGee, that's who. He's bought the house, it seems. And Mrs. Mack McGee. A nice woman, by the way. Madre was sitting with them both when I got there. Sipping tea and telling them all about it."

"*All* about it?" asked Millie faintly. "Wait, tell me first, what happened about Elfi?"

"I rang Harry's secretary at the House and she found Harry in the constituency. So he went. In spite of his commitments. He's very good in that way." Millie did not comment. Holy, *Holy* Harry, she thought.

"And being *your* daughter—," continued Olga (it was an old joke between them and signified that Olga had, for the time being, forgiven Millie), "as your daughter, she screamed and had hysterics at my non-arrival offstage, and then gave a brilliant performance."

"OK. Now for the bad news."

"It's pretty bad, I'm afraid, Millie."

"Surely the McGees must have known? It must have been pretty well known at the time. Think of the McGee Group and its papers. Surely people knew about things like that, even if they couldn't print things the way they do now."

"I'm afraid Mr. and Mrs. Mack McGee were still in Aberdeen in those distant days. If they did own papers, they were respectable Scottish ones. But, Millie, they surely do know now. You see, Madre had another of her famous Safeways bags with her. Only this time, instead of a grungy dress it contained one of her Diaries. And she was reading from it when I arrived. Luckily, it seemed to be about some dreary round of fifties parties rather than anything worse. In between sips of tea."

There was a short silence. Millie broke it. "That's it," she said briskly. "This time there's got to be what's known as a radical solution. I'll come round after the theatre. I'll get a taxi. Can you be there? What about Elfi? *Au pair*? Babysitter? Or will Holy—will Harry be back?"

"One or the other. For obvious reasons, Harry will do anything—" Olga wanted to say, "This is pretty embarrassing for him too, an MP and the same party too and all that," but she did not want to test Millie further, given that her sister was officially on record as being fond of her brother-in-law (in spite of his politics). Even that stupid nickname, Holy Harry, could be seen as a tribute to his many selfless good works. The important thing was that the sisters were united again, as they had been throughout their forlorn and baffling childhood.

After Olga rang off, Millie continued to sit in her chair opposite the velvet-trousered image in the mirror until the theatre tannoy interrupted her thoughts. The voice of Hattie Vickers, the stage manager, called: "Act One, beginners please, Mr. Birley . . ." Normally Millie listened with amusement to the slight quiver in Hattie's voice when she pronounced the name of her beloved—at least Millie told Randall Birley that she heard a quiver. Tonight her thoughts were far away from Hattie and even from Randall. It was a measure of Millie's distraction that although she had been acting with Randall Birley for five months now, and they had been lovers for most of that time, she still thought she heard Hattie say "Mr. Burgo . . ."

She had promised Olga, promised herself, a radical solution. Should she call *him*, should she warn Burgo? And if the answer was yes, warn him against what? Surely Madre, having been silent for so long, could not seriously be thinking of going public now? Or could she? What could age, and let's face it, drink and loneliness, do to you . . . ? Millie sighed. Time to get ready. She cleared her throat.

"What country, friends, is this?"

The lines, which Millie had been saying for so long, suddenly had an ominous ring. What country were they all getting into after so long? She, Olga, Harry—for him it was indeed possible to feel sorry, MPs being what they were. And Burgo Smyth? What about *his* children, no longer children, of course, very much adults and political adults at that? Those twins. Sarah Smyth had been elected to the Commons last time, and Archie Smyth was standing at this election. And the rest of the politicians? Horace Granville, the Prime Minister? Now, were they all to be plunged back into this grim Illyria?

Millie, used to being the strong one to her younger sister, longed desperately for some dispassionate advice. She would hardly have time to consult Randall before she left for Hippodrome Square; besides, he always had so many visitors backstage (predominantly female). And she was treading cautiously there, didn't want to involve him too closely in her strange background. . . . Originally Millie had not been sure that their romance would outlast their season at the Addison. It was not so much the effect that Randall tended to have on women generally—Millie honestly did not believe that he encouraged poor Hattie—more that there was something so concentrated (or should one say ambitious?) in Randall. Thus Millie could not imagine him involved with an actress in a production other than his own. Now that they were at the Irving, she would have to see. Yet increasingly she knew that she was becoming desperate to keep him, could no longer easily bear the thought of losing him.

The fact that she was older than Randall—just a few unimportant years—was not the point. It was in any case impossible to tell the ages of the various bubbly blonde girls who crowded into the small

room (why always blondes? wondered fierce, dark Millie). But Millie had to admit to a certain jealousy about the women, invariably
pretty, who were said to be Randall's cousins, or else at Oxford with
him, in some cases both. Of course Randall was entitled to have
cousins, sacks of them: Millie knew that he came from a vast network of relations. She could also understand that Randall with his
glamour and success provided a focus for a series of people not
otherwise distinguished by anything but birth. But Millie's childhood had been different. If she had any cousins on either side, they
had never come forward to claim the Swain girls. And she had not
been to Oxford.

The transfer of this "sixties" version of *Twelfth Night* from the
Addison Theatre on the fringe to the Irving Theatre in the West
End had been, to say the least of it, unexpected. Millie was aware
that Randall's rising reputation as a romantic actor had been a prin-
cipal element—and he *was* very romantic, true sexiness on and off
stage, how the public loved it! Of course, let's face it, they also
loved the fact that Randall had not only been to a famous public
school although he was very very careful never to refer to it (thus,
in the opinion of his enemies, having it both ways). But it did
enable critics so minded to make knowing allusions. Of his Orsino
for example the *Daily Telegraph* noted, "A Duke in whom we can,
mercifully, for once believe . . ."

As for herself, her Viola turned out to be the part of which
actresses dream, the one that hiked her into another dimension. To
begin with, the costume suited her wonderfully. Her long legs, her
height, were natural advantages in a trouser suit. And Randall was
tall enough for the height, which had sometimes been a problem,
not to matter. Further than that, Millie knew that she was giving the
performance of her career. Even the linkage to Randall was helpful:
talk of the new Branaghs and "that kind of rubbish" as Millie put it,
still put no one off. Whether it was love for Randall, or just plain
sex with Randall, she knew that she had somehow flowered. Or had
done so in the limited arena of the Addison. Now she had to do it
again in the West End.

Madre could not be allowed to ruin this chance. She had ruined Millie's childhood; that was enough. Some radical solution must surely present itself. As Millie Swain headed for the stage, hampered by her voluminous Pop mackintosh, she remembered Olga's opening words: "Today of all days. I could kill her!" Yes, Millie knew the feeling.

CHAPTER 2

TRUE CONFESSIONS

T HE FIRST FLOOR DRAWING-ROOM OF NUMBER NINE HIPPODROME square was a handsome room, thought Jemima Shore—or rather it had once been a handsome room.

She was sitting opposite Lady Imogen Swain on a sofa which sagged heavily. The grime on its cover was so ingrained that Jemima could not imagine what the original pattern had been. The surface of the tapestry stool beside her, on which Jemima had gingerly perched her glass, had been reduced to threads. There were rugs which were covered with dark sticky-looking stains—Jemima shuddered to think where they came from. The curtains of the tall windows looking into the square, like the covering of the stool, hung in tatters. Had they been made of chintz or taffeta? Once again, impossible to tell. Naturally the window panes were filthy.

In a way, the walls were the worst of all. For one thing, large lighter spaces on the dirty paint indicated where pictures had once hung. And then there were the cracks.

"My God," thought Jemima, "look at those cracks, was there some earthquake in West London . . . this house is simply not safe." An enormous and grandiose marble mantelpiece—one of the few pieces that had defied decay—was the focus of the room. "I should *not* care for that to fall on me. The wind is terrible tonight, they say there's going to be a storm. It could blow the house down. And I'm on the first floor. How could anyone live like this? The daughters—how could they *let* her live like this?"

At that moment two huge black and white cats pushed their way into the room. One padded towards Imogen Swain, tore at her skirt with its claws as though for exercise, then settled plumply in her lap. The other cat looked up at Jemima with an imploring expression. It was the size of a small dog. It gave some long exploratory scratches at her hem (my Valentino! thought Jemima, never mind if it was bought in a sale) before settling in its turn in her lap. So there were the two of them, in this cold, filthy, ill-lit, high-ceilinged room with only two predatory cats to warm them.

Jemima noticed that Imogen Swain, unlike most cat owners (unlike herself for example), did not ask her visitor whether she minded a cat the size of a dog flumped on her lap.

"Joy and Jasmine," murmured Lady Imogen, "for my favourite scent and my favourite soap, rather sweet, isn't it? I've tried *washing* the girls in Jasmine but they didn't like it." The girls? What girls? Take a grip, Jemima, she means these vast felines. Lady Imogen started to stroke the cat which had a raucous purr commensurate with its size.

"You see, Jemima—I may call you Jemima? I feel I know you from television—" She leant forward, so that her little wrinkled monkey's face came alarmingly close to Jemima's. "You see, Jemima, I know all about it. Lots of naughty secrets. It's time for my side of the story. My true confessions at last. I know where the bodies are buried. Funny phrase!" she laughed. "Well, I really do know. That's why I'm telling *you*, Jemima. A lot of people would like to shut me up. But they can't shut me up, can they, once I've told you? I'll be safe."

It was not exactly what Jemima Shore Investigator had come to hear; the maudlin true confessions of a former society beauty who had once—a very long time ago—known some famous people. There were a few faded but extremely large photographs (of Imogen Swain) visible at strategic points in the room. Nothing demonstrated more the ephemeral nature of beauty. One showed her as a bride, huge eyes and rosebud mouth, ravishing even under an unflattering veil; another as a bewitching young mother with two dark-eyed rather sullen children. That woman was gone forever and should be allowed to rest. Really, in raising people's expectations of fame, the tabloids had a lot to answer for! Guiltily, Jemima Shore added to herself "and television too."

There had been a series of political scandals recently. The government, in calling a general election, had stoutly denied that there was any connection between these scandals and its decision to go to the country within a year of the previous election. The ostensible reason was the economic crisis and the swinging rises in taxation which had followed, contrary to electoral promises. All of this was true enough.

Nevertheless a nervous and (to outsiders) rather exciting atmosphere prevailed on the subject of political scandals generally. The most unlikely people seemed to have got the idea that they could get in on the act—be rich and infamous, if you like. At least, that was the politest interpretation of Lady Imogen's surprising behaviour. Another possible explanation would involve Alzheimer's disease, or some other form of senility. . . . For heaven's sake, what were her family up to, letting their mother ramble on like this? One daughter was married to an MP: *she* should have a sense of family responsibility, considering how politicians of all parties went on about the subject.

Should Lady Imogen be living here at all? Apparently she lived alone: that is to say, there were no signs of a companion, maid or whatever. No one had even come to answer the bell which Jemima had rung for a long time. The wind rustled the sparse leaves on the trees in the square and scudded across the doorstep. Jemima shivered. After a while, a skinny arm in a lacy sleeve, ending in a hand on which a ring glinted, had emerged from an upper window. Wordlessly, the invisible owner of the arm had thrown down a key which rattled on the steps at Jemima's feet. (It missed the basement area by a few inches.) For a moment Jemima felt she had strayed into some confused fairy story, where Rapunzel met the witch of the gingerbread house . . . then she wondered, more practically, at the trust of Lady Imogen (presumably) who had not even bothered to establish her identity.

Yet surely money could not be a real problem? If not an ancient parlour maid or a decrepit butler, there could at least be some kind of live-in help, an *au pair*, a student in need of accommodation, *someone*. Number Nine Hippodrome Square, admittedly extremely run down, was an enormous house. It must be worth a fortune, even if Hippodrome Square was not one of the fashionable West London squares, given that it lay north of Holland Park Avenue, closer to the upper reaches of Ladbroke Grove. But most of the houses had an air of considerable prosperity.

Jemima had parked her car in a space on the other side of the square, trusting it would not rain before she returned. As she walked around, she noted bay trees outside one palatial doorway—three houses had been discreetly adapted into a block of flats. Their pots had been secured by chains but they were bay trees for all that. A little way outside the square, in effect in Ladbroke Grove, there was of course the new and chic Hippodrome Hotel, another set of houses run together. Jemima's company, JS Productions, sometimes used the elegant small restaurant and its patio when the weather was hot and their finances were flourishing. Since the hotel was near but not too near, its presence must have a favourable effect on property prices, thought Jemima. There were also a few houses in the square with builders' boards up, where development was probably on the way. Yes, one way or another, Number Nine had to be worth a packet.

JS Productions was a company which Jemima had recently founded with her former PA at MegaTV, and now partner, Cherry

Bronson. (Cherry's consciousness had been permanently raised by seeing the film *Working Girl*: as an example of life imitating art, she now ran JS Productions with great energy; only her fabulous dipping necklines showed a certain lingering attachment to old-fashioned values, Jemima sometimes thought, although she was far too frightened of the New Cherry to say so.) The company had been founded to package the longstanding and successful series of social enquiries, *Jemima Shore Investigates*, and sell it back to MegaTV. How Cy Fredericks, Jemima's former boss at Megalith, had groaned!

"My little Jem, you too betray me . . ." His attitude was that of Caesar being stabbed by Brutus. In the subsequent negotiations it was Cherry rather than the more soft-hearted Jemima who had struck the right deal. She was helped by the fact that Cy insisted on treating her as an exotic stranger ("Your wonderful raven-haired Miss Bronson") and had somewhat lost his head over her at lunch at the Ivy at a critical moment in the negotiations—although Cherry had worked under Cy at Megalith for ten years.

The new series of *Jemima Shore Investigates* was considering various aspects of old age: one programme was, roughly speaking on the subject of "Memories". Lady Imogen Swain was among those who had answered an advertisement put out by Jemima for potential interviewees, hence Jemima's presence at Hippodrome Square. But Jemima had been unprepared for the flood of revelations—inventions?—now pouring forth from her hostess. Most surprising, and indeed disquieting, of all was the involvement of the Foreign Secretary. Jemima Shore had never met Burgo Smyth. But looking at him on television, she had found herself, like most women, susceptible to his distinguished-older-man's looks, his courtesy, and above all the vitality he exuded. It was difficult to connect him with this sad, vindictive little monkey hissing away about her memories in the wasteland of her ruined drawing-room, difficult to believe that they were only five years apart in age.

At the same time Jemima did not find Lady Imogen totally unappealing. This was against her better judgment. But the sheer outrageousness of what she was saying had a mad courage about it, although Jemima had no doubt it was the courage of the fantasist.

"You see," said Lady Imogen solemnly, "he was the great love of my life."

In the present political climate, how could Lady Imogen really hope to rake up a thirty-year-old affair with the Foreign Secretary—which is what she seemed to be intent on doing—and emerge without great humiliation on her part? The election was a mere two and a half weeks away. On second thoughts, even the tabloids might hesitate to run this one, given that Lady Imogen was certainly no bimbo offering enticing photo-opportunities.

It was now quite dark, and outside the lights of the square beckoned. She must get out of this depressing drawing-room, this house with its creaks and its rattling windows, make an excuse and leave . . . Imogen Swain interrupted this line of thought. She had by now manifestly drunk a great deal: whisky by the look of it, and not much water.

"No wonder they want to kill me," she said, with a slight giggle. "Because what I want to give you is the real story of the Faber Mystery."

"The *Faber* Mystery?" repeated Jemima. "But I made a programme—" She thought, "And Burgo Smyth turned down my request for an interview. Some pompous secretary replied, 'Mr. Smyth has for many years made it his practice to decline all interviews on this subject.' "

"Exactly!" Lady Imogen was childishly delighted, adding to the general impression of unreality. "And you got it all wrong. Everyone has always got it wrong. They were meant to get it wrong. But little me knows the truth, always did. And now I'm going to tell everyone all about it—on your programme. Then of course they won't kill me, because there won't be any point."

She hesitated, fluttered her eyelashes, and gave a smile which just lifted the corners of her curly lipsticked mouth; in spite of the garish lipstick the smile made Jemima realise what men must have seen in Imogen Swain. The connection with the old faded photographs of the society beauty was visible. "Burgo won't like it, my Burgo, will he? That pompous face! But when he comes round, I'll do just what he likes." What followed was quite a vivid description, slightly palliated by the soft voice in which it was delivered. Jemima felt deeply embarrassed.

"When did you last see Burgo Smyth?" she asked hastily. She might as well get that straight. If Lady Imogen was capable of telling the truth.

"Oh, Burgo, he came round last night." Imogen Swain stroked the big cat—Joy? Jasmine?—complacently. "Teresa's in the country. With the children." She made a little moue; like the cat, she was purring. Then Imogen Swain's expression changed. All the incongruous flirtatiousness had gone.

"No, no, that's not true, is it? Of course he didn't come round last night. He never comes here now. Someone came round. But it wasn't him. Someone's going to come round tonight. But it won't be him. I've got to live in the real world, that's what my daughter Olga says." She made it all sound very bleak. "Do you know my daughter Olga? Sometimes she's so cruel to me." The cat gave a plaintive mew as if in sympathy. "That's all a long time ago, isn't it? Teresa won, didn't she? She's got him forever now, hasn't she? Poor mousy Tee. Clever, clever Tee."

"Lady Imogen, when *did* you last see Burgo Smyth?" Jemima Shore, the practised interviewer, used her gentlest tone. Instead of answering, Lady Imogen fished underneath her dilapidated chair and took out a plastic bag.

"These are *my* Memories, *my* True Confessions," she said, "And I'm going to give them to you. My Diaries, his letters. All very secret. And then you'll know just what to ask me about on television." She flung the plastic bag rather clumsily in Jemima's direction, and some of the contents spilled. Jemima saw a couple of smallish navy blue leather books with gilt edges to the pages. The one at her feet was stamped in gold with the initials IMS. A letter fluttered out. The House of Commons crest set in an oval at the top was unmistakable, especially to Jemima Shore who had once had an unhappy affair with a married MP and had received letters on that paper. Her heart gave an irrational thump.

At that moment the telephone rang. Lady Imogen did not answer it, although it stood on the table at her side, the only modern artifact in the room. Jemima wanted to pick up the Diaries or perhaps the letter . . . it was tantalising. She could read the words "My beloved" and that was all. Instead she politely made a sign indicating that she would be prepared to answer the telephone (if only to shut it up, it had rung for over a minute). Lady Imogen nodded vaguely. The moment Jemima picked up the instrument a female voice began at her, "Madre, will you *please* answer the telephone? That's what it's for, you know, because someone wants to talk to you. Now listen, we're both coming round tonight to discuss things. And Madre, it's no good not answering the bell, I've got a key. No, I won't let out the bloody cats. That's all." The caller rang off.

Before Jemima had time to say more than, "A visitor tonight, your daughter I think," the telephone rang again. This time she let her hostess answer it. The other daughter? Regan following Goneril? But Jemima could not hear what was being said, not even whether the caller was male or female. What she did note was that Lady Imogen's eyes had filled with tears. As she replaced the telephone, Lady Imogen dabbed at her eyes with a handkerchief already visibly marked by her mascara. What on earth . . .

"I'm sorry, you'd better go, Jemima. There's something I must do. No, no, you can't help me. Just take the Diaries, take them, take them all, take them and keep them safe. I give them to you. They're yours. And the key—could you leave it in the bowl downstairs?"

Jemima hesitated. Finally: "I'll just take one of them." Even as she spoke the words, she had a feeling that she had made the wrong decision. But it was too late.

"It's yours. I give it to you. It's yours," Lady Imogen repeated like a puppet. Then she called after her in a slightly stronger voice, "Please be careful not to let the cats out. Jasmine is a really naughty

girl and she likes to wander. There's no cat-flap in the front. Poor
Jasmine might get locked out."

Jemima went down the staircase, still clutching the Diary which
had fallen at her feet, feeling her way on the banisters with her
other hand since there was either no light or no bulb. She felt one
of the cats—presumably Jasmine—slithering softly around her ankles. She took care to keep her inside the house and leave the key
in the bowl. Once in the square, Jemima looked back at the tall,
rather grim house above her head. She felt it must be rocking in the
wind: from an open window on an upper floor curtains were flying.
Nevertheless, the balcony windows of the drawing-room were open
and she saw Lady Imogen standing there. She appeared to be indif-
ferent to the storm. Jemima's last sight was of the small forlorn
figure gazing out into the night.

All of a sudden, Hippodrome Square seemed an eerie, haunted
place and Number Nine the most haunted house in the square.
Even a solitary man in a raincoat standing in the shadows by the
gardens had a sinister look about him. A burglar? You would not
have to be an accomplished burglar to rob the house she had just
left. No alarms, nothing. No guard dog; only two languid cats.

On the other hand, Lady Imogen manifestly would not be alone
tonight since she was expecting two visitors—"*we* are coming
round"—if not more.

CHAPTER 3

WOMAN'S WHOLE EXISTENCE

WHEN JEMIMA SHORE GOT BACK TO HER FLAT, SHE FOUND NO MES-sages on her machine. Instead, enormous bunches of white lil-ies—her favourites—filled the sitting-room. Every conceivable vase, and a plastic bucket as well, had been filled by Mrs. Ban-croft, her cleaning lady. There were two notes.

"Jemima," the first one read. "Hope you like my floral arrange-ments. Change of job??? Don't worry, that's a joke. Cheers. Mrs. B."

The second came with the flowers but was not quite so pleasing. "Darling," it ran, "Forgive me. Flying to Singapore now. Back soon. Love Ned." Forgive Ned Silver, her brilliant mercurial barrister companion, partner, lover, with whom she had such a wonderful, passionate semi-attached relationship, when he had to fly abroad on urgent business? Forgive him, of course she forgave him. Forgive him, *never*, vowed Jemima, kicking her new black suede boot so hard against a chair that the heel broke off.

That seemed to complete the sense of desolation she had felt ever since she left Hippodrome Square. Jemima had looked to Ned to cheer her up over dinner. They might also, perhaps, have discussed the Faber Mystery again; when making her programme on the subject, Jemima had enjoyed posing problems of evidence to Ned. He would surely be fascinated to hear of her encounter with Lady Imogen. They were also due that weekend to go to a country hotel in Dorset "to take a real break", something that had already been postponed twice due to professional commitments and was now presumably postponed again.

"Isn't it lucky that I live alone?" said Jemima aloud, "and isn't it lucky I am so thoroughly independent and have such a brilliant career? Otherwise I might be absolutely miserable."

The sight of her cat Midnight gazing at her with dignified reproach from the kitchen doorway—surely the first thing any decent person did was to feed a starving cat?—stopped this disloyal line of thought. "No, no, Midi, of course I'm not alone. You're never alone with a cat." And that of course took her thoughts back to one person who was undeniably alone, in spite of two enormous cats: Lady Imogen Swain. And the little blue leather Diary in her handbag which did or did not contain a clue to the Faber Mystery.

There was an odd aspect to all this, thought Jemima, as she opened a bottle of Chardonnay from the fridge with which to wash down the diary, as it were. When she had researched her programme about the Faber Secrets Case a year ago, she had simply not come across the name of Lady Imogen Swain. It was the last programme she had made directly for Megalith, so the mellifluous Byzantine presence of Cy Fredericks had made itself felt on her project. He had performed certain introductions for her, for example, including one to Burgo Smyth himself, even though she had not secured that particular interview.

Was it possible that Cy had headed her off? It was true that Cy had a notorious weakness for pretty women he could somehow regard as being society figures. Comparisons from Proust sprang readily to his lips, although the social standing of some of the women optimistically found to resemble the Duchesse de Guermantes might have astonished the author. As for Cy's *jeunes filles en fleur!* The range of age and experience of those Cy was still able to regard as maidens was indeed remarkable. (Jemima and Cherry, before they left Megalith, might be two examples of that.) Nevertheless Jemima did not really think that Cy had had a romance with Lady Imogen. It was of course hardly a subject on which anyone could be absolutely certain—including, she sometimes thought wryly, Cy himself.

Yet there had been a fatal air of loss about the house in Hippodrome Square with all its dust and neglect, of a past which had overwhelmed the present and negated the future. Lady Imogen herself was not only a clear loser (that unattractive but evocative modern phrase) but lost beyond rescue. Cy, the ever hopeful and buoyant survivor, thoroughly enjoyed the adventure of rescue (including rescuing himself when times were bad, which had happened more than once in Jemima's experience). But someone like Lady Imogen, so utterly desolate, no, Jemima did not think that chivalric Cy would have been tempted to roll his eyes in her direction.

The truth about Lady Imogen's seeming obliteration from the Faber Secrets Case saga was probably more to do with the unfulfilled nature of some women's lives in the previous generation, than anything more sinister. Jemima was reminded of the lines of Byron in *Don Juan* which always irritated her (although naturally she adored Byron):

> *Man's love is of man's life a thing apart*
> *'Tis woman's whole existence.*

Very much *not* true of Jemima Shore: look how well she had taken Ned's vanishing! She was now prepared quite happily to devote her evening to reading the Swain Diary with scarcely a thought for the reprobate. But perhaps the lines were true of Imogen Swain and Burgo Smyth.

"You see, he was the great love of my life." The words spoken in that forlorn house came back to her. What had happened to Imogen Swain since the time of her affair nearly thirty years ago? She had not remarried but she had brought up two daughters: one a rising actress and the other married to an MP—success stories of a sort if you liked. But Imogen Swain did not seem to enjoy very warm relations with them, if the sharp daughterly voice on the telephone was any clue. Jemima suddenly realised that the drawing-room had contained no recent photographs at all, not even one of her actress daughter at some moment of triumph. Weren't there any grandchildren? If so, they too were invisible. The daughters remained frozen in time as those dark sullen little girls, looking slightly reluctant in their pretty mother's arms.

Burgo Smyth on the other hand had risen up high from being a bright young MP, Parliamentary Private Secretary (in other words dogsbody) to the Secretary of State for a ministry long since abolished (perhaps because of its fatal connection to the Faber Secrets Case). In spite of the cloud which that whole affair had undoubtedly cast on his earlier career, Burgo Smyth had emerged as a junior minister in the new Conservative government of 1970. No doubt his strongly pro-European views had been helpful at that juncture. No doubt Burgo Smyth's particular kind of charismatic charm had been helpful too, as it always would be—or had been at least until the present time.

Nowadays Burgo Smyth, white haired, well preserved, elegantly tailored, manners as perfect as his suits, was surely the epitome of the British Foreign Secretary: unshakably courteous in the face of his country's enemies, implacably tough in his country's interests. Yet as a young man in the early sixties Burgo had exuded an air of vulnerability which appealed to Tory ladies of all ages. It went with a youthful English male's untidiness set off by his heavy build, his broad shoulders and the thick black hair which to a martinet's eye was never quite short enough.

How someone so handsome—and so ruthless, for in Jemima's opinion no politician rose to the top without ruthlessness—could really be vulnerable was another matter. As ever in politics, image was more important than reality. The Tory ladies, so vital to the party, had believed Burgo Smyth to be vulnerable, in need of loving care. That fact had probably saved him when their menfolk had been inclined secretly to hold his remarkable good looks against him. Those eyelashes! Unsuitable in any male over the age of five! From the press cuttings, Jemima had learned that Burgo Smyth had once been nicknamed the Tories' Elvis, an image he certainly did not suggest today.

She pondered once more on the Faber Secrets Case, or the Faber Mystery as it was popularly termed. The Faber Secrets Case could surely be ranked with the Profumo Affair, in terms of the damage to the Tory government of the early sixties. As a result the administration had to endure an embarrassing trial in early 1964. Maybe it was already moribund. Yet the unpleasant mixture of double-dealing and hypocrisy which the trial of Franklyn Faber had revealed, contributed strongly to the government's defeat in the autumn of that year, quite apart from the dramatic ending of the case itself.

Of course this Tory defeat was not a disaster for everyone. Various people had had their careers helped by that particular election, not just Harold Wilson, the incoming Labour Prime Minister. One of the others was thirty-one-year-old Burgo Smyth: he lost his seat, and was able to disappear out of the public eye for the next five or six years until he regained it in 1970. For an MP who had been a key witness in an official secrets case, there was a positive benefit to this obscurity.

The Faber Secrets Case! What a sinister, baffling affair it had been, thought Jemima. And the disappearance of Franklyn Faber—his presumed suicide at such a dramatic moment in his trial—meant that it would never be utterly resolved despite many books written on the subject (and programmes like her own). Had Franklyn Faber really passed on that secret list of armaments for money as the prosecution alleged? Or had he done so for idealistic reasons as the defence firmly stated? Just why did he kill himself—if indeed he had? His friendship with Burgo Smyth, going back to Oxford days, when Franklyn Faber had been an Oxford scholar, now what was the truth of that?

Jemima poured herself another glass of Chardonnay; somehow the bottle was emptying itself remarkably quickly, as though there were an invisible but drinking ghost beside her. Or perhaps just the spirit of Lady Imogen hovering over her Diary, no mean drinker she, determined to inject her presence into the Faber Mystery even at this late date. In all this, the name of Imogen Swain had never, so far as she knew, appeared. Yet here she was holding in her hand the Diary (with its chic initials) which purported to tell the truth of it all . . . Or rather one of the Diaries. She had left the others in Hippodrome Square for another occasion, and those letters on their House of Commons' writing paper as well.

Time to begin. It seemed appropriate enough, since she was to read of a woman's passion for a younger man, to put on the first act of *Der Rosenkavalier*. As Jemima began to read Imogen Swain's sprawling black handwriting, the sensual post-coital music of the Marschallin and Oktavian (Lotte Lehmann and Sena Jurinac, restored to life by CD) filled the flat. It was music which Ned also loved . . . But it didn't do to think about that . . .

The first entry in the Diary was fairly short. But for Imogen Swain and Burgo Smyth at this stormy moment in their lives, the background of *Der Rosenkavalier* did indeed seem well chosen.

"*February 3. Bur came round after vote. We had cocoa for hours. Then more cocoa. Bur* wonderful. *Ecstasy etc. (Tee in country,* good*)."*

Cocoa? Ecstasy from cocoa? Ah yes, lovers' code. All lovers had them. To Jemima, Lady Imogen's code had something rather pathetic about it, nursery talk. However, what would Lady Imogen make of *her*, Jemima's code . . . Let that thought drop too and back to the Diary.

"*Made stupid scene when he said he had to go. Said stupid things. Me: 'You don't like me as much. I'm getting old.' Cried. Bur: 'I've never loved anyone like I love you. Just remember that.' More cocoa. Ecstasy.*

"*Bur really had to go. In court tomorrow. Will get me a ticket but better if I go with Su. Girl friends more respectable. All that about F.F. is awful. Poor Bur. But can't worry too much when we're so happy. He's never loved anyone like me, not Tee, not* anyone.

Tee. That's just because he thought an MP should be married. I'm the first woman he's ever really loved. He never understood about loving women before he loved me. His shady past as we call it!"

Jemima skipped quickly over a less ardent day.

"Talk to Nanny about Mill and The Lies. Mill tells lies, then gets furious if she's caught out. N says Mill 'a little show-off'. Always wanting attention. Mill jealous of poor baby Ol, always so good and sweet, never any trouble. Even when Ol has one of her black clouds, she just doesn't speak. How unlike Mill! Me: 'Well, Nanny, give her plenty of attention then she won't tell lies.' " So that was how an actress was born, thought Jemima, out of a neglectful mother and an unpleasant Nanny, to say nothing of a jealous older sister syndrome.

"February 5. Bur in court giving his story. Looked so handsome. Heart swelled. Couldn't help thinking about cocoa—wicked with that awful old judge peering round. Not allowed to meet for lunch though. Bur: 'Unwise'. Promised to come round later for cocoa if Tee doesn't come up. (Typical Tee! Not interested in seeing Bur in court). Su maddening at lunch. So much for girl friends! Had forgotten about her old friendship with Tee (school). Told me quite unnecessary story about Bur and Tee being so happy together in the country."

But the evidence, thought Jemima. Ah, here Imogen Swain did get on to the appearance of Franklyn Faber in the dock. This was more like it:

"Bur says F.F. could ruin him. Political death, he says, if things come out. Always looks so sandy for a villain, hate white eyelashes in a man. Nonsense to say Bostonians are more English than American—that's what he thinks. Looked at him hard, willing him. Don't ruin my Bur. Otherwise, says Bur, boot could be on the other foot. Political death all round. Wore my navy-blue Dior which Bur—" But Jemima skipped quickly over the details of what Lady Imogen had worn.

Burgo Smyth had told his mistress that Franklyn Faber could ruin him. That it would be political death. What did that mean? Beyond the obvious fact that Franklyn Faber's evidence had been crucial to Burgo Smyth's survival as a politician. In the box, Faber had denied Burgo's fore-knowledge of the use to which he would put the document. They were old friends, but not conspirators. That was all.

" 'Otherwise'," says Bur, " 'boot could be on the other foot' " and " 'Political death all round'." A threat? Threatening someone with "political death," i.e., permanent exclusion from the world of politics, was hardly the same as threatening them with actual death, was it? Although some dedicated politicians might not agree. The scrappy Diary simply did not make it clear what had been meant.

Jemima flipped forward the light golden-edged pages. There were a great many details about interior decoration, fifties style. Lady Imogen's house was generally deemed to be ravishing ("pale pink swags in my bedroom a triumph" was a typical entry) and the houses of her friends rather less so ("Laura's dining-room dragged paint positively dull . . .") Poor Laura, lucky Imogen. Jemima passed over all this as quickly as possible, merely marking that the present dilapidated state of Hippodrome Square gave little clue to the fact that its owner had once been preoccupied by triumphant pink swags and positively interesting dragged paint.

A certain amount of the Diary was also occupied by the some-what tedious problems of Nanny, who sounded a real old-fashioned nightmare, with Bad Millie the little show-off and Good Olga the little angel (with occasional black clouds). There were children's parties to which Lady Imogen generally sent the nanny, but at one of these, to which she did actually escort her own children, the Smyth twins featured. *"Terribly plain,"* was the uncharitable com-ment, *"Just like Tee."* There were also adult social events, including Imogen Swain's own dinner-parties, and outings with other men who courted her. If Lady Imogen was a widow (there was the occa-sional reference to "poor Robin"), she was evidently a merry one. And the Diary ended, by chance, two days before the date on which Franklyn Faber vanished.

Otherwise Lady Imogen's absolute physical obsession with Burgo Smyth permeated the Diary. *"Cocoa with Bur"* (or the lack of it) meant that any day was either *"wonderful"* or *"miserable"* (sometimes even more strongly *"bloody day"*). Yet the sheer concentrated focus of her feelings appeared to have lulled Burgo into a sense of false security about his mistress's discretion. Because nothing mattered to her except *him*, Burgo had trusted Imogen not to betray him. On the evidence before Jemima, he had not been entirely wise to do so. He clearly did not know that Imogen kept a diary.

More than once Lady Imogen had made a note on the subject to herself: *"Remember LOCK UP DIARY"* and *"LOCK THIS UP. No one sees this. Not Bur, definitely not Bur. (And not creepy Nanny either.)"*

There had been *something* between Burgo Smyth and Franklyn Faber which had never come out, either in court or in the press after Faber's disappearance. It was something which could perhaps have ruined Burgo, condemned him, in his own words, to political death. Lady Imogen knew what this was, or at least the outlines of it. The references were fairly constant if elliptical, not deliberately so, but because Imogen Swain herself knew what she meant and saw no need to amplify it. The crucial Diary would of course be the one following and Jemima needed to consult that before she made up her mind about anything.

Rosenkavalier was turning away from post-coital sadness to the light-hearted mission of the young Oktavian, bearing a rose. The Chardonnay was not only seriously depleted, but getting warm. Time for a long, long bath, the greatest pleasure currently available to her. She would then play the video of her programme on the Faber Secrets Case, accompanied by the remnant of smoked salmon she had, thank heaven, spied at the back of the fridge.

In the event Jemima read the new Barbara Vine in her bath till even the fourth lot of hot water had grown cold. She ate the smoked salmon and finished off the Chardonnay, rechilled with lumps of ice, among the many lacy white pillows of her huge low bed. The rich foxy smell of the lilies was perhaps responsible for dreams in which someone called Ned Silver but looking like Franklyn Faber came calling on her in the middle of the night.

"Why have you changed?" asked Jemima.

"After thirty years, we've all changed," was the reply which even in her dreams struck Jemima as odd, although she could not precisely understand why. Then Ned-as-Franklyn leant towards her.

She was awakened by a terrible screaming sound, a cry, someone

was being killed outside her door . . . Moments later Jemima realised it was her new personal fax machine which Cherry had insisted
on having installed as a business necessity for JS Productions. ("So
we're always in touch".) But it was not Cherry who was keeping in
touch so early in the morning. Groggily, but very happily, Jemima
read an amorous message from Ned which must have scorched the
hotel paper when it was written. In the early sixties Burgo Smyth
had sent his love letters overnight by the late post from the House
of Commons. There were references to them in the Diary: *"Letter
from Bur: oh, bliss"*. In the nineties Ned Silver faxed his love letters on
the crested writing paper of a foreign hotel.

After a while, still keeping the fax like a talisman in her robe
pocket, Jemima made a mug of coffee. To bring herself to life, she
turned on breakfast TV but without the sound. She was still gazing
at the set unfocusedly when a picture of someone dressed as Titania
at a fancy dress ball filled the screen.

"My God, its *her*. Lady Imogen Swain. As she was. Beautiful—"
Jemima's reactions sharpened. Why on earth . . . By the time she
had enlarged the sound, she heard only the words "in Hippodrome
Square, West London". The image of Titania vanished.

Jemima switched channels. This time she got a picture of Hippodrome Square itself, an ambulance, and something body-shaped
being carried into it, which looked very dead indeed, under a black
cloth, no face visible. Jemima found she was shaking and her coffee
began to spill. In front of her, the small blue Diary with the initials
I.M.S. was spattered with drops.

CHAPTER 4

ANGER AND FEAR

ILLIE SWAIN WAS CRYING. SHE KNEW THEY WERE NOT PRETTY tears. Even now, in spite of what had happened, she was filled with rage and disgust at Madre, rage and disgust against herself. She was also frightened.

Millie had turned away to the window of her dressing-room in the Irving, although there was no view, just thick glass edged by thin flowered cotton curtains and nothing beyond. But Millie had to conceal from Randall Birley, standing awkwardly at the door, the truth about her emotions. The rage and disgust were too raw and could not be admitted at this point. As to the fear, that might be wrongly ascribed to first night nerves: pride forbade Millie to show more than a conventional apprehension.

Randall came and put an arm around her shoulder. Normally his slightest touch gave Millie a charge; now she felt nothing.

"I hate her," she was thinking, "Madre is dead and it makes no difference. I still hate her. I always thought I would be free . . ."

"Darling, she would be very proud of you—" It was not the right thing to say.

"*Madre?* So proud that she went and killed herself just before my first night?"

Randall Birley tightened the arm. "Darling Mill, you've had a horrible, horrible shock, and by the way fuck the first night. Audience, critics, the lot of them. You're going to be terrific. You *are* terrific—"

Millie turned to him and saw them together reflected in the long mirror. She noticed that Randall had composed himself into an elegant picture of masculine consolation. In her velvet suit and flared trousers, she herself had the air of a Renaissance boy being comforted by his patron, rather than a late-twentieth-century woman in the arms of her lover.

Suddenly an unbidden image from childhood came to her: her mother, so tiny and feminine, weeping in the arms of a man. It must have been Burgo Smyth; who else would have had Madre in his arms? What scene had she, Millie, interrupted? Had it been a farewell? Or just a common or garden scene? Even as a child, Millie had understood that her mother had a capacity for making scenes. Where on earth did that memory come from? It must have been jolted and stirred from the depths where it had lain for years, by the hideous events of the last twenty-four hours. She put the strange image away from her. Then for the first time it occurred to Millie that Randall, with his height and rugged dark looks resembled Burgo Smyth as she had once known him. Well, it was proverbial that actors and politicians had a lot in common.

"She jumped," said Millie abruptly. "Madre jumped. She went up to the top of the house some time after we left. And jumped from the old nursery balcony." She added: "Madre was *terrified* of heights. And the dark. She hated the nursery and she hated the cellar. She never went into the nursery and she had the cellar shut up."

Then Millie started to cry in earnest against the gloriously ruffled shirt which Randall wore with his black velvet dinner jacket. "They found her lying in the square. Madre's last night, my first night, in that order. A dramatic last exit, Olga called it. But then you know what Olga thinks about the theatre." The last was said half laughing, wholly crying. "Dramatic is *not* a term of praise with my sister Olga. Nor my brother-in-law Holy Harry."

Millie could see Olga's card on a modest bouquet of pink garnet roses among the first-night flowers on her dressing-table. It read (in a florist's handwriting): "Good luck tonight. Olga and Harry Carter-Fox". But Olga knew perfectly well the theatrical superstition by which you did not use the words "good luck" in advance, since Millie had often explained it to her. So maybe Olga had brought the bad luck . . . If so, Millie had to admit that it was bad luck on Olga too. And on Holy Harry.

"My poor Harry! On the eve of this very tricky election!" Olga's expressed reaction had been quite as unfilial as Millie's. She had even gone further and muttered something about having to cope as usual while Mille enjoyed the applause on stage. Both sisters understood (if Harry did not) that beneath such comments lay not only a deep shared anger at Madre's last exit, but a deep shared guilt. And then there was the fear, which they also shared, about what had happened the night before.

Images. Madre's hysterical weeping. Her screams turning to little animal-like cries as she staggered round the filthy decaying drawing-room on her high heels. At one point she trod on one of those monstrous creepy cats and the animal's protests had joined her own. Whenever Madre said any words that could be understood, they amounted to the same message: "No, no, I won't go. This is my house. Burgo's going to come here and fetch me. He knows where to find me. So I won't go. Burgo loves me. He's going to come back." And so on, as the sisters exchanged glances which were both furious and desperate.

It was Olga who got hold of the pile of Diaries and letter, half in and half out of a Safeways bag under her mother's chair.

"At least we're taking these away, Madre. Right now," she said firmly; it was the voice of a Tory MP's wife dealing with a constituent. "We've had quite enough of that." Curiously enough, Olga's dive towards the bag had the effect of calming Lady Imogen, or at least restoring her to some sense of the present.

"You can't take them. There's no point. I gave them to someone. I gave them away already. Didn't I?" Their mother now sounded more confused than hysterical.

"What on earth are you talking about, Madre?" rapped out Millie, too sharply.

Olga signed to her. "Millie, I know how to deal with this," she said quietly. Once again there was that sisterly sub-text, "Since I always *do* deal with it."

"Who came, Madre?" Olga went on. "Everything's here. We'll look after everything for you, won't we, Millie? These boring old letters and things are just a worry for you."

"That nice girl on television with the pretty-coloured hair. She took it all away and the letters."

Olga Carter-Fox raised her eyebrows over her mother's head. Millie responded with a grimace.

"Look, everything is *here*, Madre,"—Olga at her most reasonable and gentle—"all in this funny bag." Olga caught sight of a letter on House of Commons writing paper. For a moment she thought it must be from Harry . . . then she realised her mistake and frowned. At the same time Imogen Swain snatched at the bulging bag.

"You can't have that. Burgo's sending someone to pick it up. I think he's coming himself. Somebody came last night—who came?" She began to drift again.

Millie and Olga left the house a little later—together. Their mother was now sitting quite docilely in the drawing-room, her small figure almost extinguished by the two cats which had settled on top of her. Her last audible words, called after them in that little breathless voice, were: "You must find me somewhere where my girls can be happy." It never failed to irritate both Olga and Millie that their mother used the term "my girls" for the creatures they referred to as "those bloody cats". But at least Madre seemed to be reconciled to moving.

"And about time too," muttered Olga when Millie pointed this out. "You don't even know about the hair-dresser incident the other day! Madre turned up for an appointment at Luciano's in Curzon Street. Apparently he used to do everyone's hair in the fifties. Only the trouble is that everyone's dead, including Luciano. The salon is now a casino. Actually they were extremely sweet as Madre loudly demanded to have her hair washed for an important lunch date, amid the debris of late night gambling."

They were in the darkened hall. The lights of the chandelier above their heads had fused long ago and Madre, with her ridiculous persecution mania, "They're going to kill me", and so forth and so on, had persistently refused to have an electrician in the house unless Olga could find her a female one. This, Olga, with a deep sigh, had put on her list of Things to Do for Madre (T.D.M. as Harry called it). Olga was scrabbling for the key Madre generally kept in a broken Chinese bowl on the hall table. She could not find it. Olga opened the door to the dining-room and put on a light: it was a room unused for years and would, thought Olga, have conveniently done as a dining-room for Miss Havisham. The shaft of light revealed that the bowl, which seemed to have lost yet another piece, was actually empty.

"I thought I saw that key when I came in—"

"Well, we've still got one key; you take it," said Millie. "And listen to me, Olga, *it's not our fault.* Will you say that to yourself five times before you go to sleep? Take the Holy One's mind off the election with your mutterings."

"*Harry* says that to me five times a night already." Olga shuddered as she tried to rub some of the dust from the table off her fingers; something or other had also marked her beige skirt; how typically brilliant of Millie to have worn jeans! "What were we to do? He keeps saying that to me. Put her in a home by force, for Christ's sake? Well, I did once check up on the procedure, or rather Harry's secretary did, and frankly Millie, it's not that easy. If the patient doesn't agree it can be quite ugly. Look at tonight's little canter. Harry has to think about his image—our position. If only she'd agreed to have someone to live *with* her! Plenty of room, to put it mildly. She or they could have lived upstairs and just kept an eye . . . that sweet little Filipino, three months arranging for it all, and then she was sent packing in three minutes."

"Olga, listen to me," Millie turned fiercely to her sister on the doorstep, and spoke with great emphasis. *"We're* just *not* guilty. She's the guilty one, *not us.* And lingering on like a dotty, malevolent ghost in that great big house, not selling it, that's what's wrong. That's what's driven her off her rocker. She could have sold it and given us some money years ago—" The wind raised Millie's thick black hair as she glared at Olga.

"That's what Harry says," said Olga automatically. "Look out, don't let that cat out. It's just about to pour with rain."

"He is *not* right about his politics but Holy Harry *is* right about that. Damn her! Damn her to hell! And her cats!" But Millie gently guided the huge soft furry animal back inside the door. "Do you remember when this house was full of flowers?" she added irrelevantly. "What were those flowers that looked so drab and smelled delicious? Tuberoses. Whenever I smell that smell . . ."

"The drawing-room may have been stuffed with tuberoses once upon a time, I suppose *he* sent them, but I don't remember many flowers up in the nursery." Then Olga patted Millie's arm; the habit of peace-keeping was too strong in her to be resisted. "You take the dreaded bag, Millie. At least that stuff is waterproof. I don't want Harry to see it and be driven up the wall."

"I'll dash back and lock it up in the theatre. I don't want Randall to see it either."

"Millie," asked Olga slightly timidly, "is he—"

"Yes, absolutely gorgeous. Eat your heart out, sister." Millie Swain strode off into the shadows of Hippodrome Square as the wind began to toss the tops of the big trees. She was swinging the Safeways bag so energetically that Olga was left wondering fearfully if its contents might spill.

For Millie now, thinking back, none of this made for happy recollection (except perhaps her eventual return to Randall's Fulham Road flat). And the prospect of the police tomorrow morning was not a particularly cheerful prospect either. Since Millie had spent the night with Randall, she had not been contactable by the police. It was—so far—Olga who had dealt with them although Harry had nobly offered to identify the body officially, thus justifying his reputation for holiness.

But for now, thank God, it was time to work. And it was true that during the next two hours odd, Millie Swain hardly thought about her mother's death or her own guilt or her own fear; even moments of that troubling anger did not come to disturb her.

"Oblivion, perhaps that's why I became an actress . . ." The thought floated by, "Not just to show off as that horrible Nanny Forrester used to say." Her Viola was maybe just a little more intense than it had been at the Addison. "Swain's deliciously provocative air of relaxation," as the *Guardian* had put it, might have gone missing. ("I predict many swains for Swain"—*Daily Mail.*) But the first night notoriously did not produce the most relaxed performance.

No, Millie remained curiously and happily cut off in her capsule of Illyria, that is, until she went to Randall's dressing-room some twenty minutes after the curtain fell. They had exchanged a brief kiss on stage and some members of the audience had clapped. But why not? Randall also kissed his slightly elderly Olivia and his extremely juvenile Maria; he was after all the director as well as the star. But for obvious reasons, Millie had no family to visit her after the show; apart from Kevin Connelly, her agent, and Max Marmont, the producer, with his silent, smiling Japanese wife, there seemed to be a tacit conspiracy to leave her alone with what was presumed to be her grief. It was Randall who telephoned her from his dressing-room at his most expansive: "Darling, come and have a glass of champagne, meet everybody."

After Millie had pulled on her jeans—she seemed to have lived in them for the last twenty-four hours—she looked desperately for something appropriate to go with them to face the bright world of Randall's dressing-room. It pleased her sense of irony to find a black silk shirt, actually one of his. It could be said to provide a mourning touch . . . or even mourning chic if she decided, defiantly, to go to the first-night party.

This mood of detachment came to an end abruptly with the introductions in Randall's dressing-room. There was indeed a crowd, most of whom Millie recognised: Randall's agent Betsy Wright, for example, a tiny woman in her fifties who nevertheless managed to give Millie a hug which almost knocked her off her feet, "Ooh, darling, what they do to us. But you were of course magnificent, deeper, rounder, darker, not *too* dark of course, in a way also lighter . . ." Betsy Wright babbled on kindly.

But, "You don't recognise me, Millie," said the next person she encountered, a blonde young woman in a plain black velvet suit, high-necked white blouse and small pearl earrings. Unlike most of the people in the room, who were drinking champagne, she had a glass of Perrier in her hands. The face was vaguely familiar. Or perhaps the blonde woman's poise, the artfully plain perfect hair-style, simply reminded Millie of the sort of career woman who was photographed giving interviews to the newspapers.

"Then, why should you? We used to play together as children. And that's a long time ago." The stranger gave a smile showing teeth as perfect as her hairstyle. "Listen, I'm mad about those boots you wore. Are they yours or is that kind of thing specially made for the stage?"

It was Randall, putting his arm around Millie, who performed the introduction. "Darling, have you met my cousin Sarah Smyth?" He then put his other arm around the blonde woman's black-velvet-clad shoulders. "Sarah Smyth MP. The greatest ornament to the House of Commons, the *only* real ornament—"

"Don't be silly, Randall. There aren't any MPs at present. Parliament's been dissolved. There's a government and ministers but no MPs to bother them." It was said with a smile that made Millie think unpleasantly that Sarah Smyth must have attended the Virginia Bottomley school of charm. "I'm just a candidate at present, a candidate taking a night off to come and support the family on stage."

Millie felt sick. She was acutely aware that the Safeways bag containing Burgo Smyth's letters, to say nothing of those Diaries, was in this very theatre. Things got no better when Hattie Vickers poked her head around the door.

"Randall, Millie, see you six o'clock tomorrow." Then: "Great show. Fabulous reception. Come to think of it, see you all at the Café Royal."

"Come on Hattie, celebrate." Randall handed her a glass of champagne. Hattie blushed and shook her head. She had a mass of springy light brown curly hair and a skin almost exactly the same colour. Whatever the genetic mix which had produced Hattie, the effect to Millie's eyes was far more appealing than Sarah Smyth's cool Englishness. She hoped Randall agreed with her.

"Later," said Hattie, with a sidelong glance at Sarah Smyth which seemed to indicate that she shared Millie's feelings. "I've got work to do. And Millie, I locked all that stuff up—" She held up one of the keys on her large jangling key-filled ring.

Millie interrupted her. "Randall, I'm not coming to the Café Royal. You can explain." She could not resist adding, although it was not necessarily what she wanted just then, "See you later." As she went, she could hear Betsy Wright's voice explaining, "The most ghastly thing happened to her only last night, her mother went and . . ."

Not only had Sarah Smyth not congratulated her on her performance, reflected Millie, unless praise for her boots was intended to be symbolic, but she had not said anything about Madre's death. Didn't she know? Surely MPs, or rather candidates, watched the news obsessively? Was the fact that Sarah Smyth did not comment a good sign or a bad sign? All the anger and disgust—and fear—that Millie had experienced, came back.

About the same time as Millie Swain took a taxi back to her Islington flat—it was after all a first night and the weather was still terrible—Olga Carter-Fox was having a family conference. It was a conference of two (occasionally joined by her seven-year-old daughter Elfi, who loved to make appearances to impart tidings of her nightmares). The other person present was the man she too sometimes secretly thought of as Holy Harry, thanks to Millie's pernicious influence, but was otherwise her husband of ten years, Harry Carter-Fox, Member of Parliament for the West London constituency of Bedford Park in the last three parliaments and now its prospective candidate.

The conference had to be broken off from time to time not only to escort Elfi ("I dreamt I had no Mummy and Daddy") back to bed, but to watch the news programme *Latest.* Harry had done a pre-recorded interview on his favourite subject of social policies, on which he held, for his party, strongly liberal views. Every time the presenter showed signs of turning to a new item, the Carter-Foxes turned the sound up hopefully, before turning back to their increasingly agitated conversation.

"We've got to do something—wait, Olga, I think this really is it—no, well, dammit, this is getting seriously late, everyone will be going to bed—as I was saying, you should never have let Millie take the Diaries. I'm sorry, darling, but you know what Millie is like. Definitely not to be trusted, and I'm not just referring to her politics, or to the fact that she's an actress. There's something terribly unreliable about her quite apart from those two things. Like your mother."

Momentarily Olga was inclined to defend Millie against the charge of being like Madre but at that instant the unmistakable image of Harry Carter-Fox filled the screen.

"Pensions in a perfect world proliferate," he began; it was not an ideal sentence for a man who was visibly nervous and had a slight stammer on such occasions. As Harry leant forward gently and revealed the small bald patch in his hair, Olga's thoughts strayed and went down dark paths. She did after all know what her husband was going to say, having rehearsed it with him at some length. When Burgo Smyth came on the screen just after Harry, looking particularly suave (no perspiration for the Foreign Secretary) it was Olga who snapped the set off.

"Jolly good, darling," she said, "that showed them all right." But the sight of Burgo Smyth had soured Harry's mood once more; he had been unconsciously and rather touchingly smiling at his own face on the screen.

"Olga, we've got to do something," he repeated. "You know, this could be political death for me, absolute ruin to my career, if things get out. Whatever did or did not happen in the Faber Case, that's thirty years ago. It's monstrous that one's reputation should be put on the line now." Olga noticed that Harry was trembling.

"I've done something already and I'll do something more." Olga spoke in her calmest voice, the one she had developed to pacify her mother. "There's no question about it, Harry, you come first."

CHAPTER 5

LIFE-THREATENING

JEMIMA SHORE WRESTLED WITH HER CONSCIENCE AS SHE RE-READ the obituaries of Lady Imogen Swain, which she had cut out and collected. These were quite plentiful—ex-society beauties made for nice pictures in obituary columns—but short. "BEATON BEAUTY DIES" was a typical headline about a time in the late fifties when Lady Imogen had been chosen by Cecil Beaton as one of the ten most beautiful women in Britain. She had been the daughter of some obscure impoverished peer whose title died out when he was killed in the war leaving no son. One got the impression that being a beauty had been Lady Imogen's profession, and her professional success had greatly declined over recent years.

One question was answered: who was Swain? He had been a backbench MP, handsome but not rich, whom Lady Imogen had chosen for "romantic reasons" when as Debutante of the Year she could have married a wealthy duke—at least according to the obituary column of the *Daily Mail*. One of the papers reproduced that same photograph of Imogen as a bride which Jemima had seen in Hippodrome Square. In this version, Robin Swain, dark and slightly

saturnine, lowered over his tiny new wife. Even then, Imogen
Swain's heart had ruled her head. How sad that this "ideally happy"
marriage had been terminated so quickly by his "illness and prema-
ture death"—in those days, presumably cancer—when his daughters were mere babies.

There were no scandalous references even in the tabloids and no
hint whatsoever of Lady Imogen's connection to the Faber Mystery.
The truth was that Imogen Swain (unlike Margaret Duchess of
Argyll) had never featured in a divorce case, had never been publicly castigated by a judge so that the Press could salaciously print
his verdict on her character. So Imogen Swain was, in a sense,
unknown to history, marginalised like so many women in the past
whose moral and social worth had doubtless been far greater. When
the mainspring of her life—her love for Burgo Smyth—had been
broken, for reasons which were still obscure to Jemima, Imogen
Swain had somehow ceased to exist. "Love as a woman's whole
existence." Yes indeed.

Yet judging from Jemima's interview with her, and from the single Diary which she had read, Imogen Swain had known a lot about
one of the great recent British mysteries, the disappearance of
Franklyn Faber, at the moment the jury were considering their verdict. Thirty years later, due to a combination of circumstances—
age, senility and drink—she was preparing to reveal what she knew.
(Those references to "lots of naughty secrets" and "my side of the
story . . . my true confessions.") Then Imogen Swain had died.
Convenient? Yes, certainly. Suspicious? Jemima reviewed her
thoughts on the subject. She had to admit that, to the outward eye,
the death of Lady Imogen might be tragic but was hardly surprising.
On a stormy night an ageing woman, after a drink or two, for some
reason went up to the top of her ramshackle house (to fix one of
those windows?) and toppled from the balcony.

Jemima picked up another newspaper, one which contained a
report of the finding of the body in the area by a neighbour, one
Mrs. Humphreys, who had evidently lived alongside Lady Imogen
for some years and had a fair idea of her habits. ("She looked like a

baglady half the time but always so gracious, even if she was some-times a little, well, confused.") Mrs. Humphreys spoke graphically of her discovery: how the loud mewing of a cat had attracted her attention, how she had looked down, how she was horrified, abso-lutely horrified, etc., etc., poor old lady, poor cat or rather cats (for there were two of them, but only one outside the door mewing), what would become of the cats? For the time being, Mrs. Hum-phreys would of course oblige.

Jemima sat up suddenly. One cat was found outside the door in the early morning. It was mewing to get back in so it was not intended to be outside, there was no cat-flap for re-entry. How did it get there? She remembered the daughter's hostile voice on the telephone: "No, I won't let out the bloody cats." However sozzled or just plain gaga Lady Imogen had been when Jemima left, she still remembered to warn her against letting the wandering cat—Jas-mine, yes—out of the house. So it was presumably Jasmine who had succeeded in getting out.

Who was it who had let Jasmine out? Surely not the daughters. Regan and Goneril they might be, but one of them had been suffi-ciently aware of the problem to mention it in advance on the tele-phone. Lady Imogen had expected another quite separate visitor. Jemima had clearly understood that from the second telephone conversation, the one that had brought tears to Lady Imogen's eyes. Whoever that visitor had been, and to this Jemima had no clue, it was logical to suppose that he or she must have let Jasmine out of the house. In which case, was it equally logical to suppose that Imogen Swain had not given her usual warning on the subject? And if not, why not?

Jemima wrestled with her conscience: she knew she probably ought to do something about the single Diary in her possession, even though Imogen Swain had pressed it on her, "It's yours. I give it to you. It's yours." To this unease was now added a new unease about the remarkably convenient timing of Imogen Swain's death. But of course there was no proof that Lady Imogen had genuinely been in fear of her life, beyond her ramblings towards the end of

their conversation, when she had drunk a great deal. All that para-
noid talk about people who wanted to kill her; lonely old people
did succumb to these notions. Then Jemima remembered the existence of Lady Imogen's original letter of application for the "Memories" programme. Hadn't that made some rather odd reference?
Cherry must have it in the office and here she was in her flat.
Jemima Shore blessed the inventor of the fax machine, and Cherry,
who had made her install one at home.

The letter, when it arrived by fax, came together with a drawing
of some "wicked" shoes which Cherry had just bought. "Life-
threatening," Cherry had added. It was not clear whose life Cherry
was referring to; Jemima hoped it was not her own. Most of Imogen
Swain's letter was innocuous, although Jemima did note how the
bold black handwriting had deteriorated: it had become larger yet
much less legible since Imogen Swain wrote the earlier Diary. One
phrase however was remarkable under the circumstances: "Since I
don't know how much time I have left," wrote Lady Imogen, "for
safety's sake I hope you will respond quickly." The first part of the
sentence might refer to fragile health, not uncommon in people
who responded to a request for "Memories," but the phrase "for
safety's sake" was surely a little strange.

Jemima sighed. Perhaps she ought to speak to the police. What
she wanted to do was to read the rest of the Diaries. She promised
herself that before long she would contact her old friend Detective
Chief Superintendent John Portsmouth, a.k.a. Pompey, of the Yard,
and a senior member of the Royal and Diplomatic Protection Unit.
In the meantime she looked up the number of the Henry Irving
Theatre, where she knew that Millie Swain was playing to rave
reviews ("A young Vanessa and we're not referring to her politics"—
Evening Standard.)

Jemima read again the account of the inquest where Millie Swain
had given evidence. There was a photograph of her, so tall and
straight that Jemima could see the Redgrave reference, but Millie
Swain was quite dark, beetle-browed in fact, in Shakespeare's
phrase, where her mother had been fair. She was photographed

with the supporting arm of that rising star Randall Birley around her. Millie had spoken calmly but sadly of her mother's increasing confusion. Since the postmortem provided evidence of a deal of alcohol in the blood, the coroner was not disposed to question that. But one thing did give Jemima Shore a special pang, as no doubt it did to Millie Swain. When asked by the coroner to suggest what might have drawn her mother up to the nursery floor—so long disused—Millie had replied, "Recently my mother had begun to have a rather dislocated sense of time. Sometimes she thought we were still up there, my sister and I, still children up there." She added, "She probably went up to see if we were all right. My mother was frightened of storms: the odd thing is that we weren't—"

The coroner, a kindly man, passed on to his next question. In any case, the level of alcohol in Lady Imogen's blood was sufficient to convince him that she would scarcely have been in a competent condition when she ascended to the top floor of the house. Since the window was open to the balcony from which she fell—and still banging a little when the police examined it—it was possible that Lady Imogen had gone upstairs to fix it in the exceptionally windy conditions of that night. In general, the coroner went out of his way to deal tenderly with Millie Swain and her sister Olga Carter-Fox.

Millie Swain spoke of the need to sell the house and move their mother to what she called "sheltered housing." How her mother had seemed to accept this, which was made inevitable by Lady Imogen's deteriorating condition. "Not exactly life-threatening" (that phrase again, thought Jemima) "but not far off it." Harry Carter-Fox, past and presumably future MP for Bedford Park, provided identification of his mother-in-law.

Lady Imogen's doctor was perhaps the only unsatisfactory wit-ness (although the coroner treated him, too, kindly) since he admit-ted that he had not attended his patient recently. Lady Imogen had apparently been reluctant to admit what she called "strange men" to the house, even in the hours of daylight.

"Latterly she lived very much in the past," said the doctor, without expanding further. Jemima wondered whether Lady Imogen had also talked to her doctor about one not-so-strange man from the past: Burgo Smyth. However the other daughter, Mrs. Olga Carter-Fox had smoothed that one over. She had been on the verge of providing her mother with a woman doctor when the tragic accident occurred.

Jemima Shore left a message for Millie Swain at the Irving to call her and on reflection, another for Olga Carter-Fox, whose MP husband was democratic enough to be in the London telephone book. Jemima felt restless. Having her curiosity frustrated was not an experience she enjoyed; she liked to be able to take action. Besides, the rainy weather had finally given way to something more like spring. How pleasant for the politicians! Recent pictures of them on television, members of all parties in wellies and macs, had made them look more like a series of judges at an agricultural show than candidates at an election. It occurred to her that a discreet pseudo-jog in the direction of Hippodrome Square might produce some interesting results, especially if Mrs. Humphreys was around.

As a matter of fact, Jemima Shore detested jogging, which made her feel quite unfeminine—talk about life-threatening! She much preferred the solitary sport of swimming, otherwise playing tennis with (or against) her current boyfriend. But she kept this unfashionable view strictly to herself, with the exception of Cherry, whose splendid anatomy made her too a natural enemy of the jog. Nevertheless, Jemima found that a "jogging" track suit and trainers often provided a reassuring camouflage for an investigation. Of the people she interviewed, no one had so far asked why, alone of all joggers, Jemima Shore still had a cool, pearly complexion, and hair untouched by sweat.

Hippodrome Square had changed its aspect since her last visit. It looked quite romantic in the spring night; under the street lamps, Jemima could see some early daffodils. One could imagine that the shadows and trees of the square gardens concealed young lovers (although a locked gate and bars actually made that unlikely). Several of the houses were brightly illuminated since it was not particularly late; smart lights at the well-painted front doors, lighting up those chained-down bay trees she had noted on her original visit. Then there were the houses ripe-for-development, dark, with perhaps one light on in the basement and a big white For Sale notice wired up somewhere. And lastly the houses in the process of joining the bay-tree club with their scaffoldings, on which flapped dark cloths and scruffier builders' boards.

Number Nine would of course be in darkness unless the daughters had left on the odd precautionary light. What would happen to it now, she wondered. A sale, a profitable sale, and then perhaps another private hotel like the trendy Hippodrome, especially if various houses could be run together. Jemima stopped short. There was indeed a light on in Number Nine, more than one. She had not realised there were so many light bulbs left in the house.

Had she got the wrong house? No, there was the number, and Number Seven, Mrs. Humphrey's house (she lived in the ground floor flat) beside it. How strange! Jemima hesitated. Was it really so strange? Houses lived on, even if their owners died, or rather in the case of Number Nine mouldered on. For the house looked no more appetising now than when Lady Imogen's arm had emerged from a window brandishing the key.

Jemima continued to stare, mesmerised, at the yellow windows. It was noticeable that not one curtain was drawn, supposing the curtains upstairs were still viable: she doubted whether the tattered drawing-room curtains would have covered very much. She began to count them and calculate: the first floor and its balcony, where she had last seen Lady Imogen gazing forlornly into the gathering storm. The row above, from which the key had been flung, must be the bedroom floor. Above that was the so-called nursery floor with its own little balcony. She remembered Millie Swain at the inquest: "When we were children, there was netting over the balcony to stop us falling over. But over the years it rotted away and my mother, not using the top floor, never had it replaced."

As Jemima's mind's eye was busy seeing the small, hopeless figure tumbling down, something surprising happened. The light in the

top window went out. A few minutes later, the lights went out on
the next floor. And so on down. Jemima felt she was tracking the
progress of the unseen hand as it descended; sometimes the delay
was greater, sometimes shorter, but the downward darkening progress was remorseless. There was an eerie moment when a flicker of
light—a torch?—could be seen through the fanlight of the hall.
Jemima remembered the missing bulb in the hall. That too was
extinguished.

Jemima was still standing there when the door of Number Nine
opened and a woman came out of the house. The street light was
not close and there were of course no chic carriage lights outside
Number Nine (or Number Seven for that matter) but the woman
looked to be youngish. Jemima's heart leapt. What luck! One of the
daughters! It had to be. Millie Swain was presumably at this moment striding about the stage of the Irving Theatre in her trousers
or exchanging loving kisses at the final curtain with the charismatic
Randall Birley (Jemima had just seen his remake of *Rebecca* and fallen
mildly in love). In any case, from her photographs Millie was tall
and dark. So it had to be the other one, married to the MP.

Jemima took a deep breath. Nothing ventured . . . MPs' wives
had to be on the look-out to please the public at this juncture in the
election. The polls, which had been making the two parties neck
and neck for so long, were now allowing Labour to inch ahead.

She had begun, "Mrs. Carter-Fox, I'm Jemima Shore, please forgive me for bothering you—" before Jemima realised that the
woman was not alone. And the fair young man behind her was
definitely not that worthy but inarticulate do-gooder Harry Carter-
Fox, the terror of the political talk-shows since he was always available, always eager, yet never able to get his admirable sentiments
into a communicable form.

The woman, equally fair, but with the air of being slightly older,
stared back at her. "I'm afraid I'm not Olga Carter-Fox," she said.
She spoke calmly and pleasantly, as though she had been trained to
put people at their ease, despite a natural instinct to suppose they

were somehow in the wrong. "I'm Sarah Smyth. Do you remember? We met on that pilot programme for 'Women: Why Ever Not?' "

Jemima groaned inwardly. Sarah Smyth had mentioned one of her few conspicuous failures, and Jemima decided, unfairly, that it was typical of this archetypal polished career-girl Tory, still in her eighties shoulder-padded suit, to bring the subject up. It was true that the title of the programme had been a hostage to fortune: the New Cherry had criticised it from the start as being too negative. But the memory of those headlines above the hostile reviews still haunted her (they ran the gamut from JEMIMA: WHATEVER NEXT? in the *Daily Mirror* to WOMEN: WHATEVER FOR? in the *Spectator*).

"I'm so sorry. Idiotic of me. It's just that, I assumed, coming out of this house—I visited Lady Imogen just before her death—I assumed, that as it now belongs to her daughters and I'm trying to get hold of them—"

It was Sarah Smyth who brought this uneasy rush of explanation to an end. She raised her eyebrows. Even in the half-light Jemima had to admire the fine arch which nature (presumably) had given her; they were dark eyebrows too so that either Sarah Smyth had darkened them skilfully or she was one of those infuriating blondes who had been granted dark eyebrows and eyelashes as well as flaxen fair hair. Probably the latter, thought Jemima gloomily. Then Sarah Smyth gave a smile, which was clearly intended to be comforting but did not comfort since it revealed maddeningly perfect white teeth.

"Oh by the way, this is my brother Archie. Jemima Shore." Sarah Smyth paused. "Jemima Shore *Investigator*." She gave an unmistakable emphasis to the third word. "Is that right? Do you like being called that? And by the way, may I say too what a smashing track suit! Is it your own or do you have it made specially for work?"

The two of them, so neat, blonde and handsome—if you liked the type—gazed at Jemima. She was irresistibly reminded of Wagner—Gunther and Gutrune perhaps in *Gotterdämmerung*, the brother and sister who had brought poor dumb old Siegfried to perdition.

Archie Smyth smiled. He had exactly the same smile as his sister; otherwise their main likeness was in their colouring. Neither bore any resemblance to their father, and Jemima felt that she must be looking one way or another at the image of Burgo Smyth's wife, the despised "Tee" of Lady Imogen's Diary.

"Oh, but the house doesn't belong to Lady Imogen's daughters. At least technically it doesn't." Sarah Smyth revealed her level white teeth again. "It belongs to my father. Lady Imogen left it to him in her will. Didn't you know? No, after all, why should you?" Another intensely reassuring smile, and Archie Smyth, his arm by now around his sister's shoulders, smiled too.

CHAPTER 6

"I COULD HAVE KILLED HER"

YOU HAVE TO UNDERSTAND THAT THIS WHOLE THING COULD RUIN him—my father, *our* father. I could kill her. Or rather I could have killed her. It's lucky she's done it herself." In spite of the angry words, Sarah Smyth's poise was unruffled even when she took a swig (no other word would do) of whisky. They were in the bar of the Hippodrome Hotel. They had all three, Jemima and the Smyth twins, adjourned there after that odd, uncomfortable encounter outside the house at Number Nine. There had been a brief conclave between the twins. After that the adjournment had been at the suggestion of the Smyths, or rather at the suggestion of Sarah Smyth. For the time being, Archie's role seemed to be limited to smiling, or rather grinning, and agreeing with whatever his sister said.

After a short while, Jemima decided that on the one hand Archie was abominably lacking in all the attributes important to her; on the other hand he had a kind of native cunning which would—in her totally unprejudiced opinion—make him an excellent Conservative MP. Sarah Smyth was another kind of animal altogether; it was fascinating that she gave the impression of being several years older than her twin: a question of seriousness perhaps. "As a matter of fact I am four minutes older, but I've decided it was a long four minutes." Sarah Smyth's comment was one that Jemima was certain she had made before.

Jemima's judgment on the Smyths' respective characters, was formed when the earnest face of Harry Carter-Fox filled the small television screen in the corner of the Hippodrome bar. (In Jemima's opinion, its presence was an unwelcome concession to the election, now a week away, in a place where normally you swam in glass and unreality and fashion.) Harry Carter-Fox, the stereotype of an honest man who happened to be fighting a marginal seat, had been allowed on to the party political broadcast in order to take part in the current Tory conjuring trick—whereby it was going to be convincingly demonstrated that higher taxes and lower benefits meant that everyone, especially the poor, would be much better off. Although the sound on the set was low, it was not low enough. Harry Carter-Fox could still be heard holding forth on "the philosophy of pensions" and some figures followed.

Sarah Smyth listened intently as though the broadcast were directly given with her approval in mind. Occasionally she gave a telling little nod; once or twice her lips (surprisingly full, even voluptuous in such a blandly perfect visage) tightened as if the pupil had made a mistake. Archie began by groaning aloud.

"The Carthorse! Christ, no, we can't listen to the plonking Carthorse, we'll all go to sleep." After a minute he muttered: "Pensions, schmensions," and lastly: "The philosophy of *what*? Is he serious?" Then something in his sister's attitude got through to Archie and his expression changed to one not unlike that of Harry Carter-Fox himself, in which decency, righteousness (and a touch of self-righteousness) could all be traced.

"Good old Carthorse," pronounced Archie Smyth as though speaking for the first time. "Party needs people like him. People who *care*!" He made caring sound an esoteric activity, like archery. "Big heart and all that. Voters like it. *I* like it," he added generously.

"Big heart and *impeccable* private life." Sarah Smyth's tone had something slightly acid about it which could have been aimed at her brother. "Olga Carter-Fox is one of the *nicest* wives, so totally unlike her unspeakable mother. It often happens that way, doesn't it? And there's an adorable little boy, or is it a girl? A very happy marriage. Voters like that too. No scandals about Harry Carter-Fox." She sighed. "What a relief."

"So far my sister has a constituency for private life," said Archie Smyth. "So that takes care of that."

Sarah ignored him. "And that brings me to my point, Jemima," she went on. "Look, turn that TV off, will you, Archie? I've had enough of Harry Carter-Fox. He got all those figures wrong by the way; those were the *Labour Party* figures. Still I don't expect anyone will notice, least of all in the Labour Party itself, let alone the Liberals! That idiotic woman they've selected to combine the two never even took her A-Levels."

Sarah Smyth took an even bigger swig of her whisky. "Scandal, yes, plenty of it. And a close-run election. The polls are becoming torture for both sides as they seesaw up and down twice daily. Personally, I'd ban them. Anyway, we don't want it to touch Dad. This whole thing, the will, that ghastly old woman and her stories could ruin him. And lose us the election. He's Mister Clean, isn't he? And he *is* Mister Clean, it's all true. The past is the past. The one member of the government everyone trusts, apart from Harry Carter-Fox, that is." Jemima wasn't sure whether this was intended to be a joke. "You have to understand that this whole thing could ruin him—my father, *our* father," she ended.

Jemima had not expected her to be quite so direct, nor was she prepared for what Sarah said next. "He did give evidence at the Faber trial and yes, as far as we know he did have an affair with Lady Imogen. But that's thirty years ago," said Sarah fiercely. "Why should it all be dragged up now? What is it all to do with politics, let alone government now, the problems which we all have to face in this country *and* abroad, which are—"

Archie interrupted her. He had gone slightly pink. "Just because

that dreadful old bat lost her marbles and started making threatening calls, telling the newspapers about it, or trying to, Dad's paid
the price. He was young then but he's paid the price and he doesn't
have to pay it twice. Or rather Mum paid the price. For him. You
say you could have killed her, Sarah, but I could have cheerfully
strangled her. I wish I had."

"Our mother found the situation very difficult to cope with."
Sarah spoke with extreme care. "She doesn't go out much these
days. As you know, she never travels with Dad, doesn't act as his
hostess, never has done, just lives quietly in the country."

"Oh come on, Sarah, don't be so mealy-mouthed. We're asking
Jemima to be open with us, to tell us what the old girl said to her.
So don't let's try to be tactful. Jemima had better know the truth.
Mum drinks. People do. She does. She probably drank a bit even
when she was young—look at Uncle Pel, permanently blotto, and I
believe our grandfather died of drink. But she certainly drank a hell
of a lot more after the Faber Case. All those whispers about Faber
visiting her in Dorset, she helping him to disappear, all nonsense of
course, just inventions, rumours. But not helpful.

"She's still a great person on a good day. And she doesn't need
any of this. This shit—the Press and all that all over again. I put
that above Dad's fucking career, election or no election. So, are you
going to tell all about it on television, Jemima?" The pinkness of his
smooth skin was quite intense.

To her surprise, Jemima was moved, but why should she be surprised? Part of the idiocy of an election was the way people became
demonised. Until now the Smyths, to say nothing of their secluded
mother, had been lay figures to her, and not particularly sympathetic ones. Now she saw them all as potential victims of this mis-
chief from the past. But she also made careful note of the reference
to Teresa Smyth, the "clever, clever Tee" of Imogen Swain's Diary,
and now apparently drunken, drunken Tee. Another victim, like
Imogen Swain herself. How ironic—if you like—was the fact that
both the women in Burgo Smyth's life had ended up destroyed,
whereas he had prospered. This had to be considered later.

The laws of libel had prevented even the most scurrilous accounts of the Faber Mystery from dwelling a great deal on the
character of Teresa Smyth. It was apparent from her son's attitude
that in certain circles the rumours had been far stronger in that
direction than Jemima had realised. In a way Teresa Smyth too had
been marginalised, written out of the story much as her rival Imogen Swain had been: two invisible women. But Teresa Smyth at
least must have been happy to be invisible. Jemima wanted to get
back to her flat and rethink one or two things. . . .

"Of course I'm not going to put it on TV!" she exclaimed, "Whatever that means. I'm an investigative reporter, not a muck-raker.
Lady Imogen wrote to me in answer to an advertisement about
memories, I went to see her. That was it." But that wasn't quite it,
whispered the voice of conscience. You've got that Diary still,
haven't you? Lady Imogen gave it to you. And you know about the
other Diaries, you know about their father's letters, don't you?

Jemima decided to go for honesty, or at any rate limited honesty.
"Look," she said, "I did see Diaries and I saw letters though I didn't
read them. I assume they were from your father because they were
on House of Commons paper."

"Not necessarily so," Sarah pointed out in her gently reasonable
voice. "There is her own son-in-law."

"The Carthorse!" chimed in Archie eagerly.

"This letter began 'My beloved'—"

"That settles it," said Archie cheerfully. "Definitely the Carthorse.
What a devil. He was bonking his mother-in-law."

"Shut up, Archie. OK, Jemima," went on Sarah, "I grant you: they
were Dad's letters. I do know there were letters." She hesitated. Why
did Jemima have the impression that Sarah was about to lie, or at
any rate not tell the whole truth. It was that compassionate politician's face, yes, that was it, the expression which said sadly, "I so
much regret that I am about to deceive you." Archie too looked
uneasy, making Jemima wonder how much of his buffoonery was
deliberate, another form of political deception, on a level with his
sister's.

"She spoke about the letters on the telephone to Mum," said Sarah firmly. "She rang up our mother too, did you know that? Oh God, I could have killed her all over again for that." Somehow this time the outrage was just a touch affected. "She talked about the Diaries and I guess, from one or two things Mum said, she also talked about Faber. Then there's the Press. She somehow got in contact with the Mack McGees and talked about her True Confessions. Nothing . . . very specific, I gather. And Mack McGee is a decent enough fellow for a Press tycoon and Mrs. McGee is a real sweetie. Between ourselves Mack McGee tipped off Dad. All the same—"

"A word at a City banquet," interrupted Archie. "Both of them in their white ties. 'Fly, Foreign Secretary, all is known.' Except I suppose it was in a Scottish accent. 'Och aye, Foreign Secretary.' " Sarah frowned. "The Establishment at work, right," finished Archie triumphantly.

"We need those letters, and we need the Diaries too," said Sarah. "Or rather we need to know where they are."

"Search and destroy," muttered Archie.

"As far as we know, they're not in the house any longer." Sarah stopped. She showed her first real sign of discomposure since they had met.

"You looked," said Jemima neutrally.

"A purely casual inspection. Why not?" It was the polished Sarah again. "After all it's technically Dad's house—not that he will keep it of course. And we wondered, Archie and I, whether you might speak to them, the daughters . . ."

"We thought we'd *hire* you, Jemima Shore Investigator and all that." Archie produced his boyish grin again. "What are your rates? You could get someone to fax them to us."

I could unleash the New Cherry on Archie, thought Jemima grimly, but I won't. Instead she spoke in a tone of gentle reasonableness to equal that of Sarah Smyth.

"Olga Carter-Fox is a friend of yours. Surely—"

"Not exactly a friend. I didn't quite say that. More of a colleague's wife. And that's the problem. It could seem that one was leaning on her, on him, on Harry. Particularly with Dad's position. Arm's length is better I think. The other sister, the actress, Millie Swain, I've met her briefly. Somehow she's not a very sympathetic person. One of those left-wing actresses always handing in unnecessary envelopes at Number Ten for the benefit of television—"

"Millie Swain, is that the one our famous cousin Randall is having an affair with?"

"That's not the point, Archie," Sarah sounded irritable. "Although I must say I think affair is perhaps too strong a word." Jemima had a feeling that Sarah Smyth, married to her constituency as she might be, still had time for her famous cousin. And who could blame her? Jemima, who had no cousins or close relations of any sort, would make do with Randall Birley for a cousin if she were able to choose one.

Archie, whether to tease or not, pursued the matter.

"I mean, he could speak to her. No, not on stage, exactly. In the interval or something. When they're in the wings. Always lots of hanging about in Shakespeare, I remember from school. Good preparation for the House of Commons!" This time Sarah glared at her brother.

Finally, Jemima did agree to try to find out what had happened to the Diaries (and letters) from one of the Swain sisters. She did not see fit to mention that finding out where *one* of them was would be remarkably easy.

"You mean on a professional basis, just man to man?" queried Archie.

"In a manner of speaking," said Jemima sweetly. On second thoughts, she really must bring Archie and the New Cherry together one day. The results could be interesting.

Sarah Smyth's farewell was characteristic: "And now are you going to jog home in that wonderful suit?"

"In a manner of speaking," repeated Jemima with even greater sweetness. In fact she could hardly wait to get into a taxi. She needed to rush back to her flat, perhaps to find messages from

Swain women, but also to go through the Burgo Smyth saga—the
Faber Case—yet again. And she needed to sort out, away from the
dominant Sarah Smyth and the joker Archie, just what had struck
her as false about the recent conversation.

Once in the flat, she established that there were four messages
for her, but they were all from Cy Fredericks at Megalith, who had
"a most exciting proposition, which only you can handle" to put to
her. On the second and third messages he sounded extremely put
out that she had not rung him back although, according to the
timer on her machine, a mere five minutes had elapsed between
each call. On the fourth message he sounded quite heartbroken,
"Jem, oh my gem . . ." The message clicked off.

Jemima put her telephone firmly back on answer (by now Cy
would have put the exciting proposition which only she could handle to someone else) and reached for the video of her programme
on the Faber Mystery once more. By her side, she also put the Faber
Mystery file, clippings and all, which Cherry had managed to ac-
quire surreptitiously from Megalith TV, to whom it technically belonged (with the aid of some admirer who, like Jemima, was too
much in awe of the New Cherry to resist her).

What on earth *had* happened to Franklyn Faber? People, even
dead people, didn't just vanish off the face of the earth. True, Lord
Lucan had, but the comparison was apt: in the case of Franklyn
Faber, as in that of Lucan, many wild theories had been put forward
to explain the absence of the corpse. For example, Faber had been a
passionate gardener and naturalist at his Dorset cottage, not far
from Powerstock Manor, the Queen Anne house belonging to the
Smyths, for which Imogen Swain had felt such passionate jealousy
(or at least of the connubial life lived in the house). Dorset was an
ancient and mysterious county, as Jemima knew, and Ned Silver
would discover if he ever managed to get there. One theory—
unconfirmed by any evidence but popular for all that—was that
Franklyn Faber had chosen to go literally to ground in Dorset,
killing himself in a remote cave which he knew would never give up

its secrets. She realised now that some people had linked Teresa Smyth to all this. Maybe even Imogen Swain had?

Why on earth should Faber do that? asked the voice of reason. The note he left in his London flat—not far from where Jemima now lived—did not point to Dorset. It pointed to no particular place. It was true that Faber was reported by "a friend" to have reflected more than once on the possibility of disappearing in an unspecified Dorset cavern or pothole. "It was an obsession with him," said this friend (such intriguing situations always produced such anonymous friends). But another "friend" was equally convinced that Faber's real heart (or rather his body) lay in the Highlands since he had been on a walking tour of the north-west at some point and at the time he had talked about disappearing there. Nobody explained how Faber had got to Dorset, let alone the north of Scotland, without a single plausible witness sighting him. (There had been some implausible ones, to say nothing of the voluntary contributions of a seer and a medium who backed Lake Windermere and Epping Forest, respectively.)

One had the impression that both friends had been male. Had Faber been gay? Jemima rather thought so and her friend Pompey of the Yard had tipped her off that there had been at least one incident of a dropped prosecution, to do with a young man (or men) in a public lavatory. The dropping, it seemed, had been due to the influence of the Press lord who then owned the paper on which Faber worked, the *Sunday Opinion*. This Press lord had long ago gone to his rest or wherever media tycoons went, leaving the *Op* in the hands of Mack McGee.

Faber's sexuality was of course difficult to tell from the Press reports. The coded words of the Sixties were very different from those of the Nineties, and needed to be, given that homosexuality between consenting adults was only legalised in 1967, three years after Faber's disappearance. Nowadays the old euphemism of "a confirmed bachelor" was hardly necessary. An interest in nature, in gardens, in long-distance walking; none of these were indications of special sexual proclivities. Long-distance walking was after all a hobby that Faber had had in common with Burgo Smyth at Oxford; they had gone on expeditions to Scotland together. And no one had ever suggested that Burgo was anything but heterosexual.

Back to the suicide note itself: did it in fact point to suicide? There had been a fierce argument about that at the time, but as the months passed and Faber did not reappear, the likelihood of suicide naturally increased. It was true that accounts of Franklyn Faber being spotted abroad also proliferated. The United States, his country of origin, provided a large field; but since the offence with which he had been charged was probably not—so far as she could now recall—extraditable, it was difficult to see why Faber should not have emerged there after a while (perhaps under another name, and perhaps in another profession). Faber was after all still an American citizen, and his Irish Catholic Boston family, which had known a black sheep or two in its time and understood how to deal with them, could have gathered him discreetly to its bosom.

Then there were classic haunts of fugitives, Brazil and so forth. Once again, there had never been any plausible stories of encounters. One surely had to discount the piece about Franklyn Faber marrying and bringing up a family in a remote corner of the South African veld, since his views on the South African state in those days would have kept him well away, even supposing he could have gained entry.

As for the note, it was found by the man who was temporarily sharing Faber's flat following the break-up of his marriage: John Barrymoor, a fellow journalist on the *Sunday Opinion*. Barrymoor had handed the note to Faber's solicitor the next morning when that solicitor, a woman named Laurel Cameron, came around to collect Faber to go to court (when Franklyn disappeared he was technically jumping bail). Finally the note reached the police, having been read first by the judge; it could not under these circumstances be kept from the Press.

"I've gone out," the note read. "I'm keeping a rendez-vous, a strange rendez-vous. And as Captain Oates said in a very different kind of storm, I may be some time." The note was signed "F.F." (At the *Opinion* Faber was generally known as F.F., the initials by which he signed his weekly column of radical denunciation.) The mention of Captain Oates was surely a reference to suicide, given that Oates had deliberately abandoned Scott and his companions towards the end of that ill-fated Antarctic expedition, when he believed his frostbite was hampering them all. And Oates *had* perished: unquestionably that had been a form of suicide.

Jemima Shore, in her account of the mystery, had come down on the side of suicide, while hedging her bets at the very end with the words "The Question Remains Open," the convenient title of that particular series. After all no one at Megalith, not Jemima Shore and certainly not Cy Fredericks, wanted to be confronted by the sight of Franklyn Faber, emerging from obscurity alive and well, and flanked by libel lawyers.

That left the real puzzle; why Faber should have killed himself at that precise juncture in the trial. He had not yet been found guilty (the jury was still undecided on the morning that Laurel Cameron had to report her client's absence). Even if he were to be found guilty, it was not clear that Faber would go to prison. It might be a case of a heavy fine, in which case the *Opinion* would presumably pay. There was however an unpleasant element in the whole case, of course, the hub of the prosecution's argument: the fact that Faber had copied a Top Secret document taken from his friend's briefcase in the country, and then sold it to his own newspaper through an alleged intermediary (actually himself operating under a false name and from an accommodation address). The money—£10,000, a handsome sum in 1964—might well stick in the jury's throat. The judge had not let the point be overlooked.

Jemima riffled her way to the crucial place in the transcript. She found Mr. Justice Lionnel in full flow in his summing-up. "Ladies and gentleman of the jury, Mr. Faber has been painted to you as an idealist or at the very least as a campaigning journalist, whatever that may mean." (Sycophantic laughter from all those in court who wished to keep on the right side of the judge.) "This is the primary defence which is offered for his action, which he does not deny, in abstracting the Special Armaments Supply Briefing from Mr. Smyth's briefcase, copying it, and causing it to be published in a national newspaper.

"You must ask yourself whether an idealist or even a campaigning journalist" (another mild titter) "would be interested in acquiring £10,000 in the course of the deal. You will remember Mr. Faber's own explanation for this: that he wanted the newspaper to take the Briefing seriously and you may well wonder why a newspaper should not take any suggestion from one of its leading journalists seriously. You may wonder what it was about the money, an enormous sum, which was supposed to validate the document, a document Mr. Faber might otherwise have validated personally. And you will recall that Mr. Faber on his own admission put the money into his personal account, where it allowed him to clear off his overdraft."

Mr. Justice Lionnel continued, "We have of course heard a great deal of evidence in this court of the high reputation of Mr. Faber, from people of the greatest probity, including the proprietor of the *Opinion*, who spoke of his campaigning zeal. And to this evidence too you must pay most serious attention. It is your duty, ladies and gentlemen of the jury, to weigh all this in your own minds." No, Mr. Justice Lionnel had definitely not summed up in favour of Faber, although he had been careful to be fair-minded, no doubt with the aim of avoiding an appeal against his judgment. The money was awkward, Faber's overdraft even more so. The suicide—for one had to accept the explanation—must have been caused by the prospect of a ruined reputation.

Laurel Cameron's take on all this was interesting. Jemima went back to the video, flashed forward to her interview with the solicitor, whose wild iron-grey hair and full figure in a denim jacket and long denim skirt contrasted with the photographs of her in the sixties, back-combed black hair, piquant flicks of which framed her pixie-like face with its pink lipstick and black-ringed eyes. Whatever had happened to her appearance, Laurel Cameron remained a radical campaigner. In her interview with Jemima, Laurel Cameron spoke, as she generally did these days, of injustice. But for once it was injustice past, not injustice present or (a favourite theme) injustice to come.

"Yes, I believe Franklyn Faber committed suicide," she said to the camera. "All that about the money broke his heart. He was a real person who cared for others. Just because he got his finances in a muddle—we all do that. But we don't all get pilloried for it. That rotten government pilloried him just to draw attention away from their own cover-up. The Special Armaments Briefing was so politically embarrassing, wasn't it? Imagine selling to *Cuba*—however indirectly—in 1964! Our American masters must have had a fit! They did everything to blackguard poor F.F. to draw attention from what they were doing."

Laurel Cameron had gone on, with a certain grim humour, to issue some frank comments on the character of the current Foreign Secretary, well aware that they would not survive into the programme. "As for that slimy creep, Burgo Smyth, with his big soulful eyes, talking about 'his friend' and 'the years of friendship,' and his 'great trust, unfortunately not justified,' he got away lightly, didn't he? What was he up to, do you suppose, with that document in an unlocked briefcase? Or are they suggesting that poor F.F. picked the lock? There were a lot of questions that were never put about Burgo Smyth's part in all this, and I know why. The government, in order to cover up, *needed* to keep Burgo Smyth loyal and pour all the dirt on Faber . . . It stank, Jemima, it stank then and it stinks now. . . ." But as Laurel Cameron had known, all that fell on the cutting-room floor.

Jemima flashed forward over her next question and picked up Laurel again: "Yes, he did telephone me that night, the night of his disappearance. Briefly. He had some appointment, or I got the impression he had some appointment. Afterwards I racked my brains of course but he really didn't say more than that. He was in an odd mood, and F.F. was an unpredictable person in some ways, moody, yes, which doesn't mean he wasn't an idealist." Laurel Cameron's voice was rising at this point, and there had to be another cut (this was not one Laurel had anticipated) since she held forth for some time on the idealist in society. (Laurel Cameron wrote Jemima a cross note afterwards: "I'm sorry I bored you so much—or perhaps your boss—on the subject of idealism.") The crucial passage was her account of Franklyn Faber's conversation on the telephone.

"What he said to me was, 'They're trying to make me the fall guy. You've been great, no question about it. A rock. But I can't go through with it. Not prison, if it's a question of prison. I've been betrayed. I never thought it would end with a betrayal.'" Laurel's huge dark eyes, so vibrant under the wild grey curls, dilated as she emphasised the word "betrayed." "And so he had," she added, "betrayed like so many others by the Establishment. He died because of that."

The Establishment! That word again. According to Archie Smyth, it was the workings of the Establishment which had caused the upright Mack McGee (in a white tie at a City dinner) to tip off the Foreign Secretary about his mistress's inconvenient revelations. Now Laurel Cameron, from the opposite angle, blamed the Establishment for Franklyn Faber's death. And Lady Imogen's death? As convenient as her revelations were inconvenient. Jemima sighed. She pondered television's role in the Establishment. Where would one place Cy Fredericks, for example?

It was at this moment that the telephone rang. No doubt Cy himself . . . she did not move to answer it. But it was a very different voice she heard—a woman's voice, quite deep, rather beautiful and well-modulated. "Jemima Shore? This is Millie Swain returning your call. I too very much want to meet. I'm hoping you'll be able to help us. I'm just leaving the theatre . . ." Jemima grabbed the receiver but it was too late. She cursed Cy Fredericks for the missed opportunity and cursed him even more when the telephone rang again. This time she answered it and it was Cy Fredericks. "My gem . . ." he began tenderly.

CHAPTER 7

AGES AGO

THE NEXT NIGHT FOUND SARAH SMYTH, ARCHIE SMYTH AND HARRY Carter-Fox in their respective constituencies (two in or near London and one in Surrey, the latter being Archie's, and a safe seat, unlike either of the others). It found Burgo Smyth on television leaning forward in that paternal way he had, as though he might at any time stretch out his hand from the screen and pat the grateful viewers on the head. But Jemima Shore did not watch him. Instead she went to the Irving Theatre to see *Twelfth Night* and visit Millie Swain afterwards.

The theatre gave the impression of being completely full. But Jemima had known that the production was A Hit long before she entered the dark crimson auditorium, with its wild gold cherubs flying from the boxes. On second thoughts it was not so much A Hit, as A Happening. It was the people in the foyer bar—and above all their conversation—which informed her that she was present at A Happening. These were the people who always just happened to be there, where everyone who was anyone needed to be. They didn't need to consult one another, let alone read the newspapers

(since they formed the fashion rather than followed it). Some in-
born herd instinct guided them to the right play, the right film, the
right music festival, and of course the right restaurant afterwards.

A favourite phrase of the naturally fashionable, Jemima had discovered, was "ages ago." Indeed she heard a woman with a tanned
face and long streaky expensive looking hair, use it even as she
entered the foyer.

"We first saw it ages ago," the woman was saying. She was wearing tight faded jeans with a black velvet jacket and antique diamond
earrings. And it turned out that a number of the foyer fans (as
Jemima mentally termed them) had already seen *Twelfth Night* on the
fringe at the Addison Theatre. Her companion, also a woman, small
and neat, in a very pretty pink Chanel suit which was probably the
real thing, replied, "Oh, but I spotted Randall Birley and really fell
for him ages ago, in fact ages before the Addison, though I did see
it of course there, but ages before that—"

"I love being with Randall," one confident beauty in black suede
platform soles exclaimed. Then the beauty trod on Jemima's foot.
Her companion—male, in what looked like an Armani suit—was
holding himself in that particular crouchant position, somewhat re-
sembling a discus-thrower in Greek statues, which indicated that he
was talking on his mobile phone.

In a rage as she rubbed her foot Jemima wanted to point out,
"Well, you're not going to be with him tonight, are you? Unless you
plan to clamber on stage with those massive hooves of yours." She
began to wonder whether it was necessary for the foyer fans to go
to the performance at all (since they had all seen it ages ago). The
foyer itself being sufficient for The Happening to take place, special
tickets might be sold for it which did not necessitate sitting through
the performance.

The one thing that no one in the foyer talked about was politics.
Perhaps they were crowding into the theatre to get away from the
eternal ding-dong battles of the politicians on television. With under a week to go, the pollsters were becoming increasingly breath-

less—like racecourse commentators—as the race remained so
thrillingly open. Everyone agreed (night after night the same
cliché) that "it could go either way." No wonder the Smyth twins
were worried about their father: a nice juicy scandal might indeed
tip the balance. And in that case, the foyer fans probably *would* be
overheard talking politics, or at least their version of it. Jemima
could just imagine the phrases: "Oh, I knew Imogen Swain ages
ago . . ." and "I've known Burgo Smyth for ages, you see . . ."

People did of course recognise Jemima Shore and several talked
to her as if they knew her (they didn't) but she was used to that; the
people who thought you were a friend from seeing you so often on
the box. It was indeed her image as Jemima Shore Investigator
which inspired people to turn to her for help. Even people like
Sarah and Archie Smyth—and perhaps Millie Swain.

In the interval, yet another would-be client for her help emerged.
Jemima was sitting in a seat procured by Millie Swain (but paid for
by Jemima at her insistence). A still, dark-haired woman sat beside
her. Her face was vaguely familiar but Jemima did not get the
feeling that she had seen her on television or in the Press. The
woman on the other hand gave Jemima a nervous half-smile as
though she had recognised her but did not intend to trespass on her
privacy.

It was noticeable that throughout the first half of the play (Randall Birley had divided it into two acts only), the woman neither
laughed nor stirred. The intensity with which she watched the action made Jemima wonder whether her neighbour was perhaps a
true and passionate lover of the theatre, rather than a foyer fan. The
woman's stillness gave way only as the curtain dropped. She ex-
haled her breath sharply, gave a rather perfunctory clap and then
turned to Jemima Shore.

Jemima, having adequately enjoyed herself, was still clapping
politely. Actually, she rather disliked *Twelfth Night* for its cruel humiliation of Malvolio-in-love. However, like her dislike of jogging,
she intended to keep this view to herself. What Jemima had really

enjoyed, to be frank, was the sex appeal of Randall Birley—why wasn't Orsino a bigger part? His Byronic appearance was even better on stage, she decided, than on television as Max de Winter.

Then there was Millie Swain's performance. Jemima was thankful to find that she genuinely admired it: no embarrassments in the dressing-room, no need for insincere cries of "Darling, you were wonderful!" or even the final insincerity of a prolonged "Oooh." Actually, Millie Swain was probably the better actor of the pair; there was a purity about her performance, hinting at fire beneath, which moved Jemima. The trouble was that Randall Birley was a star.

"Jemima Shore?" Her neighbour spoke rapidly; she had a remarkably low, even harsh, voice for a woman. "I'm Millie's sister, Olga Carter-Fox. Listen, Millie told me you were coming. You've got to help us, Harry and me. Yes, I know you rang me. So I want to make an appointment. Could you come for a drink tomorrow? Harry will be there—Saturday, no politics." She grimaced.

Olga Carter-Fox handed her a card. In facsimile handwriting, it read: "Sorry you were out when I called. Olga." Beneath the signature was printed (in small letters) "Olga Carter-Fox, wife of your Conservative candidate," then (in big letters) the name Harry Carter-Fox and an address in Shepherd's Bush.

"Forgive the calling card, but it gives you the address. I push it through the letter box, sometimes without even ringing the bell. It shows that I care." Olga said this, so far as Jemima could make out, without irony. She added, "What do you think of the production? Or rather, isn't he gorgeous?"

"Definitely," said Jemima. "And so is your sister—a brilliant actress, I mean."

"Ah, Millie the actress. I wouldn't know about that." There was an undisguised bitterness in her voice. "I'm just a humble politician's wife or an even humbler Mum, very square in Millie's eyes. But I suppose I know something about *her*; I should do after so many years of being her younger sister."

Jemima realised that Olga Carter-Fox's puzzling resemblance was to her sister, whose photographs Jemima had been studying. But Millie had an attractive vivid gypsy look; Olga looked merely dour, her olive skin sallow. Their voices too were similar, although nature or training had made Millie's quite thrilling, a Lauren Bacall of a voice, whereas Olga's was merely deep. She could have been mistaken for a man on the telephone (now was that a useful asset for an MP's wife?).

After the play finished, Olga showed signs of leaving fast, muttering something about her daughter and babysitters even as tumultuous shrieks of delight and cheers were greeting the cast, especially Randall Birley. At the last moment, she turned back to Jemima: it was the moment when Randall gave his ritual-but-romantic kiss to Millie; whether by design or not, Olga distracted Jemima from this appealing sight.

"This is what I know about my sister," Olga said, the timbre of her voice enabling her to be heard quite clearly despite the audience. "She has no interest in family values. Maybe all actresses are like that, although some of them do wonderful things for charity. Susan Hampshire, people like that. But with Millie—family, decent things mean nothing to her. Unlike me; I'd do anything for my family." Then, looking rather darkly witch-like, Olga Carter-Fox stalked out.

Decent things mean nothing to her? Just because she didn't believe in "family values?" Jemima looked at Millie Swain with a speculative eye when she arrived in her dressing-room. There was no one else there. Some flowers—not particularly fresh—and some cards decorated the room but it had a melancholy feel, like Millie Swain herself now that she was no longer the ardent love-stricken tomboyish Viola.

Jemima shivered. To her there was something desolate as well as dingy about theatres when you went backstage: the face of the theatre behind the mask of paint was sagging and full of lines. You went from the splendidly gilded auditorium to shabby areas which looked as if they had received a rough renovation after housing the homeless. You got a glimpse of a rather squalid-looking shower, door open. It was as though whoever ran the theatre was determined to rub your nose in the fact that all the splendour you had seen on the stage, the glitter and the velvet, had been a sham— slapped-on olive green paint, uneven corridors without carpets, this was reality. There was no Happening here.

Even the roar of football from a small television screen in the little cubicle by the Stage Door had a tacky sound. As for that Stage Door cubicle itself, with its rows of keys, it had a poky, claustrophobic look. The oldish man in charge, nursing a mug of something, who was not actually watching the ranting football on his television screen, did not add to the impression of luxury.

"What do you want?" he asked abruptly, as though Jemima Shore might want a number of things, but he could not imagine approving of any of them. It appeared to be an unpleasant surprise that any stranger (Jemima's programmes definitely did not feature among his viewing) should come to the Stage Door in the first place. He telephoned down to Millie Swain with the same surly air and seemed genuinely disappointed that she was expecting Jemima. Did he dislike all visitors (it had to be admitted that he made an efficient watchdog), or was it the crush of people, mainly women, demanding to see Randall Birley which got on his nerves? Jemima had noted a little crowd of autograph-hunters on the side street outside, quite apart from the "friends" demanding admittance.

More agreeable but also more agitated was the young woman who guided her to Millie Swain's dressing-room, talking all the time. She was short, not much more than five feet, and quite plump, at least she looked plump and heavy-bosomed, in her black T-shirt with its *Twelfth Night* logo (a pair of crossed legs in tights—Viola's? or maybe Malvolio's?). Her guide chatted compulsively as they spun around one corner then another, descended some stairs, trailed down further corridors which should have brought them back to their starting-point, and finally reached Millie Swain's dressingroom.

"I'm Hattie, Hattie Vickers. I'll take you. Oh God, I've had such an awful day. Don't mind Mike and his grumpiness by the way. We think it's because he bet Randall the show wouldn't last, saying he's never wrong after a hundred years in his job, and now he looks like he's losing his bet. Oh heavens, everything's gone wrong today.

"Actually Mike has quite a responsibility," Hattie went on. "I do his job on Thursdays, no, not just fielding the fans but all the checking and locking up. My God, you should see the keys! I feel like Mrs. Danvers. In more ways than one. It's quite spooky some-times, seriously spooky."

"Phantom of the theatre? Sir Henry Irving goes walkabout?"

Hattie paused. They were, Jemima noticed, outside Randall Birley's dressing-room: "Number One: Mr. Birley." Jemima had to admit to a sneaking desire to barge in unannounced and congratu-late the star . . . just for a minute. She was persuaded otherwise by the sound of a girl's voice, confident and clear as a bell.

"I always said you were a wonderful actor, Randall. Ages ago, when we were all staying with Desmond in Ireland and we did charades. You were this brilliant *rat*—"

"Still is," said another voice, equally confident, male. There was the noise of loud, distinctly upper-class laughter and the popping of a champagne cork.

"Randall always has lots of visitors," said Hattie. There was some-thing wistful about the way she said it and the sense of inane or at least agitated chatter faded. Then Hattie gave a shake of her springy brown curls and returned to the subject in hand.

"No, not Sir Henry Irving. Not that kind of ghost. I could live with that. I'm really into the paranormal. I find it really interesting, don't you? I mean, you probably come across a lot of it in televi-sion." Now what on earth did she mean by that? "It's the feeling of humans in an empty theatre," went on Hattie, "humans who shouldn't be there—that's what spooks me on Thursday nights. I sometimes think I'm seriously psychic. It's getting to me now really. Perhaps it's the awful day I've had. Something weird happened, there was a sort of burglary, I still can't work it out. Could *that* be a ghost? A phantom burglar? That would be rather amusing—never mind. Here we are. Sorry for the trek." Hattie knocked on the door, ushered in Jemima and scurried away.

Jemima accepted a glass of wine from Millie Swain (no champagne, but why should there have been?). She complimented Millie sincerely on her performance and quite unexpectedly moved into discussing unrequited love via Viola's undeclared passion for Orsino.

"You took me back to a very painful time in my life," Jemima found herself saying. "A married man, and the worst of it was that when he was with his wife, I had the impression that he was betraying *me*. Did Viola feel that about Orsino's obsessive love for Olivia when he sent her off to do his wooing?"

Millie Swain looked at her. "It all ended happily for Viola, didn't it? That's what matters."

Jemima did not tell Millie that the man concerned, Tom Amyas, had been an MP, like Burgo Smyth, that he had written to her on House of Commons paper, as Burgo Smyth had written to Imogen Swain. Nor did she think it necessary to tell her that these painful memories, including the mistress's jealousy of the wife, had been stirred by Imogen Swain's Diary and those references to "Tee."

The Diary! That single-volume still locked up in a file in her flat, the police in the shape of Pompey of the Yard still not contacted. It was now or never. Jemima took a deep breath.

"Look, Millie, whatever you're going to say about your mother—and I'm very sorry about her death, by the way—whatever you're going to say, I must tell you something. I took away one Diary. Your mother gave it to me. She was insistent about it. Kept saying, 'It's yours.'" She saw a startled look on Millie's face. How should she proceed? Jemima settled for the convenient word "confusion," not knowing how often in the past, with dread, Millie and Olga had heard the word applied to their mother.

"There was a good deal of confusion on the subject that night. At one point your mother seemed to think that someone had either fetched them already or was going to fetch them later. A visitor she somehow identified with Burgo Smyth but clearly wasn't." Even as she spoke, an image sprang into Jemima's mind: Sarah Smyth and her compassionate politician's face, the one that meant, "I do so much regret that I'm about to deceive you."

Could it have been Sarah Smyth, discreet emissary of her father, without the attention of the world upon her, whom Lady Imogen had expected? What was it Lady Imogen had said? "Someone's going to come round tonight to see me but it won't be Burgo." Something like that. Jemima would certainly bet on Sarah rather than Archie being chosen for this task: in Jemima's opinion, Archie Smyth was the kind of son sent to plague successful fathers. And if her hunch was right, Sarah Smyth must also have come around on some previous occasion. Imogen Swain had breathed something about that too. But the actual collection must have been planned for that fateful night; it had not taken place before because Jemima had seen the bulging plastic bag, with her own eyes.

That led to the crucial question: where were all the letters and all the Diaries (save one) at the present time? Jemima decided to ask Millie Swain straight out before she had recovered from what was evidently—and understandably—a shock about the single missing Diary.

"Naturally I'm quite prepared to hand it over as soon as possible, to join the others. When your mother gave it to me to take away, as a gift, she said I should take the lot, but I didn't." Jemima realised she had injected a righteous note here: she must make it more casual. "Where are they, by the way? Where are the rest of them?"

Millie Swain continued to stare at her.

"A good question," she said finally, in a level voice from which the usual deep thrill was conspicuously missing. "The frank answer is that I haven't the faintest idea. You could try asking Hattie, I suppose." It was Jemima's turn to stare back. Millie added: "Hattie, the ASM, the young woman with the great hair, she showed you in here. Look, have another glass of wine. Randall wants us to go and have a glass of champagne with him, by the way. He says he's a terrific fan of yours, and then we might have supper in the Italian place opposite and talk. But first I'd better fill you in about Hattie."

"Hattie, she who had an awful day?"

"*She* had an awful day!" Millie exclaimed. "I'm the one who's had the awful day or rather evening." Jemima's wine was by now rather warm. She had a craven desire for Randall Birley's champagne which she instinctively felt would be ice-cool. However . . . *Hattie.* What on earth had curly-haired Hattie to do with Imogen Swain's letters?

"Hattie's really let me down," said Millie angrily. "You see, we, Olga and I, we took the whole works—or rather we thought we took the whole works—away from Hippodrome Square. Naturally Olga didn't want to take that ghastly bundle into her precious temple of a family home, high priest Holy Harry Carter-Fox. So I brought it back to the theatre. But I didn't want it here in my dressing-room either. So I gave the bag to Hattie Vickers. She was still here at the time, even though it was quite late because it was her night for locking up. Not her usual night but old Mike at the door had flu, or a hangover from the weekend or whatever. In fact when I got there, Hattie was chatting up rather than locking up. She was chatting up Randall. Everyone knows she's got a crush on Randall, not a secret."

"Not a crime either. Like a good many of us."

"Oh quite. And shortly you shall have that champagne. Fan shall meet fan. But first of all the story, or rather the Hattie version. Our Hattie had access to some kind of safe or secure locked cupboard somewhere in this rabbit warren backstage and she said she'd put the whole thing in that. By this time, I should say, I'd incarcerated everything in yet another bag, an airline travel bag I had here, Air India. *Not* very appropriate for poor Madre, she never went anywhere near India. Hattie said she'd lock everything away safely and what with the first night, that seemed the ideal solution. The one thing I *didn't* do was read them myself. Couldn't face it. I wonder if I will ever face it."

Millie gave a kind of groan. "That all seems ages ago now, doesn't it? Madre still alive. We were so worried about her. I remember Randall making some joke: 'Your ma's love letters, anything red-hot there? Maybe they are worth a packet.' It seemed like a joke at the time. He even said: 'Come on, let's read them.' "

"And did he? Did he read them?" The whole conversation, with Imogen Swain dead, had a tasteless ring: the three of them in Randall Birley's dressing-room late at night, joking about that poor woman's long-gone love affair. One had to remember, as Millie Swain had pointed out, that Millie had believed her mother to be alive at that point. And that it was late. And the tension of the last preview . . .

Wait a moment, thought Jemima as her investigative mind took over. "How did Randall Birley *know* the packet contained your mother's love letters? You told him? And Hattie, too, I suppose."

"No, of course he didn't read them. And yes, I did tell him, lightheartedly if you like. As for Hattie, no, I didn't tell her, though it's possible she might have heard. Hattie is always hanging about, she's like that. After all, I had to explain where I had been, why I'd come back. All of that. I didn't mention the Diaries. Everything I said was *light*. But no, of course we didn't read them. Hattie just took the bag away and locked it up. She always seemed so reliable.

"Cut to this afternoon," Millie went on. "I wanted it back, the whole caboodle. We had to decide what to do, Olga and I. The whole thing about the Hippodrome Square house had made it very complicated. Do you know that Madre actually *left* it to him, our noble Foreign Secretary, Burgo Smyth? Can you imagine? No more welcome to him than to us."

"Yes, I can imagine," said Jemima carefully. She did not think it necessary—just yet—to mention her encounter with the Smyths outside Number Nine Hippodrome Square, at which Sarah Smyth had broken the news of the embarrassing legacy.

"No doubt it will all be fixed with great discretion. One of the good things about the Establishment, you could say, if you're on the receiving end. Burgo Smyth will resign his rights, waive the bequest

or whatever it is you do. No big deal for him! He hardly needs it
financially, and politically he doesn't need it at all. As a matter of
fact, Madre only left it to him quite recently, when she started to
live in the past, as it were, so I suppose we could have fought it,
unsound mind and all that. Thank God we didn't have to. All this
will be fixed, presumably when the election is over." Millie Swain
gave a rather sweet smile, a relief from the fierceness with which
she had been speaking.

"Let's hope he's out of office," she said. "Unlike Olga and Holy
Harry, I am *not* a Conservative, Jemima." It did not seem the right
moment to point out that since Jemima had seen Millie demonstrating here there and everywhere against the government, she'd had
some inkling that this was the case.

"After that, Olga and I will get what we always thought we were
going to get, half each. We'll sell that house, sell the past with it as
far as I'm concerned, just as we'd always planned. Quite welcome in
my case: I don't own my own flat. Even more welcome to Olga.
Says something about wanting more children before it's too late,
but Holy Harry is the sort of person who thinks it's socially irresponsible to have more children than you can afford to bring up
properly. She's always telling me they're absolutely desperate, what
with Elfi's private school—naturally—and Holy Harry not being
the kind of MP who gathers directorships like nuts in May."

"Why not? Everyone else seems to."

"Well, would *you* want Holy Harry on your board to enhance the
image of your company? He'd spend his entire time worrying his
pretty head about the pensions of the workers, a sort of Robert
Maxwell in reverse, and I don't somehow think that's what Tory
directors are for."

Jemima laughed. "I've not met him. I'm going round there tomorrow."

"Ah. You may find yourself breaking the news to Olga: we'll see.
The thing is that it would be really helpful if those letters at least
could be quietly handed back. And now they've vanished. Poor
Hattie was in floods of tears, and yes, I do feel sorry for her, very

sorry. I'm sorry if I was mean about her just now. I shouldn't have flown at her. Hattie is great. I shouldn't have involved her in the whole mess. Why is it that everything about my mother is and always has been such a mess?" For a moment Millie sounded hysterical. She went on more calmly. "Hattie just can't think how it happened. But the cupboard is bare."

"A burglary? Here, backstage?"

"Some sort of deliberate theft, that's for sure. Randall keeps telling me to relax. It'll all be for the best. How on earth can it be for the best? Unless those bloody Diaries vanish forever and are never seen again." Millie sighed. "I can't decide whether I'm glad or sorry I never read them. Actually, I've hardly digested it yet, Illyria and all that intervening. So now that you know all, shall we go and join the ladies? In the shape of the ladies thronging Randall's dressing-room."

But when they got to the dressing-room, the door was locked. A note was stuck to the door. "Millie darling, some of us have gone on to Gino's. Do come, please come." The writing was rather beautiful: an italic hand slightly loosened up. There was a PS: "Do bring Jemima Shore Investigator." Jemima fancied that Millie Swain looked upset, but she did not think it was in reference to herself. Maybe it was just that the atmosphere of the empty corridor was indeed, as Hattie had suggested earlier, creepy. As the two women trailed back up to the stage this feeling of unease did not go away. They drew level with the cubicle by the Stage Door. Millie handed in her dressing-room key.

"Good night, Mike. See you." But the bent back of the man watching television did not stir nor did he answer. There was no sign of the distressed Hattie Vickers.

CHAPTER 8

FAMILY VALUES

"ELFI, DARLING, DON'T BE SHY. GIVE IT TO JEMIMA." JEMIMA SHORE understood "it" to be a piece of criticism which Elfrida Carter-Fox aged seven had written about a recent television programme. The programme had not featured Jemima, nor had Jemima seen it; having no children of her own, her interest in children's television was at best peripheral—limited to those programmes enthusiastically endorsed by her goddaughter Becky Robertson. (Since Becky was the child of Jemima's best friend from Cambridge, a former social worker, now a therapist, who had married a dedicated teacher of under-privileged children, Becky had plenty of leisure to develop a truly appalling taste in television.) None of this seemed to deter Elfi and her mother.

"I'll read it, I think." Elfi began with great self-possession to read in her high confident little voice: "My favourite programme, by Elfrida Mary Carter-Fox. My favourite programme is when the little monkeys are so naughty, but the little children tell them to be good—" Jemima recalled Olga's reported desire to have more children "before it was too late" and wondered privately whether it was not too late already . . .

There was no sign of Harry Carter-Fox. The house in Shepherd's Bush, cramped and not particularly pretty (surely Olga must have resented her mother all alone in cavernous Hippodrome Square), was inundated with election literature. Piles of pamphlets stood on the table in the hall. There was a large blue and white poster in the front window and two more upstairs. As Jemima parked her car and walked down Shepherd's Avenue, she had noticed that the Tory posters in the windows just about equalled the posters of their opponents. A perfect representation of the state of the country, at least according to the polls. There were, however, rumours that the polls in the Sunday papers the next day would show a slight tilt away from Labour and the Liberals. The latest civil conflict on the fringes of Europe had resulted in bombs in major cities, including Istanbul and Athens. Here Burgo Smyth's reputation as an experienced handler of such situations was standing the Tories in good stead. Helen Macdonald, leader of the Labour-Liberal coalition, had no such experience. Perversely, a country which had warmed to Mrs. Thatcher as a war leader, cartoons of Boadicea and so forth, now shrank from the younger woman's potential military leadership. Or so the polls were beginning to record. Sarah Smyth had been right about one thing: torture by poll was a painful state of affairs. And there were still five days to go.

There was another rumour, unconnected to the polls, which had been reported to Jemima that morning by Cherry, who had called up from her mobile phone on her way to the airport: she was setting off to Nice with her latest boyfriend, a meek but wealthy computer studies expert. (Sometimes Jemima envisaged a future in which she was *entirely* jealous of Cherry, instead of just most of the time.)

"Jemima, they seem to have got hold of it. Burgo Smyth, your Lady who jumped, the old scandal and all that. They know it but they probably can't use it. Just hints for the time being."

"Who?" Jemima shouted. Since Cherry was shouting, she felt she ought to join in.

"The *Op*, who else? The *Sunday Opinion* is our remaining campaigning newspaper, whatever you think of its methods."

"John Barrymoor?"

"Who else?" screamed Cherry amid a blur of hisses.

"Who told you?"

"John Barrymoor's researcher, Margaret Rose. You remember her. Afro-Caribbean. She worked on our second birth control programme." Jemima thought, not for the first time, that at some levels there were female networks and very strong networks too.

The line on the mobile phone crackled loudly. Cherry's next words included the name "Franklyn Faber." Then the line cut off.

Jemima could easily imagine that John Barrymoor of all people would make the connection. He had been living in Faber's flat at the time of his disappearance, had read his note, had given evidence. In those days Barrymoor had been the epitome of the campaigning journalist with his violent red hair and blazing blue eyes. Thirty years later his hair had gone white (like Burgo Smyth's) but his eyes had not lost their glare. His elder statesman stance on television, to say nothing of his Sunday column, gave him the power of a prophet, one who in a changing age had never deserted his radical principles.

Jemima's line rang. It was Cherry, back with her.

"Did you hear that? She got on to him! Your Lady Imogen rang him. Incredibly, she still had some kind of number for him, his ex-wife's ex-son-in-law answered and put her on to the *Op*. Told him she knew the real truth about Franklyn Faber. Twenty-four hours later, before they can meet, she's dead. How's that for bad timing?"

Alternatively, how's that for good timing, thought Jemima when the line had gone dead once more. It was a cliché that in politics, timing was of the essence—which did not mean that it was untrue. Were the hounds of the media closing in on Burgo Smyth and, if so, was that really justice? Once again, Jemima found herself in agree-

ment with Sarah Smyth in her fierce question: what was it all to do
with government *now*, the problems everyone had to face in the
country and abroad?

Of course, while that was manifestly true about an ancient sexual
scandal, it was not true about every kind of scandal. In the meantime, Jemima had to test her hunch about Sarah Smyth and Imogen
Swain. She had an appointment with Sarah at her house in Fulham
immediately after her meeting with the Carter-Fox family or, as it
turned out, the female members of it. For Harry Carter-Fox was
represented only by his earnest face on the pamphlets and posters,
the eyes wide apart behind their rimless glasses, the hair vanishing,
the expression intended to be magisterial perhaps, but actually
rather pleading. As she listened to Elfi, Jemima wondered when, if
ever, she would have Olga to herself. The answer turned out to be,
when the candidate himself arrived.

Harry Carter-Fox bustled in, his briefcase half open and bulging
with papers. It fell open completely and the papers torrented on to
the floor. Olga Carter-Fox, with an expression of tenderness Jemima
had not seen on her face before, bent to pick everything up. Elfi
flung herself at her father.

"I'm afraid poor Mrs. Lowe was very confused about her new
water tax," he threw at Olga. "And frankly it's not too easy to
explain. I think the PM missed a trick there when he turned down
my offer to help—or Central Office anyway. I could have helped
them to phrase all this new stuff."

"If you can't explain it, darling, no one can." Olga was not only
tender but she was also admirably loyal. Shortly after that, Harry
Carter-Fox took Elfi off for some paternal ritual. Whatever it was, it
kept her mercifully away from the living-room. Jemima found herself facing a very different Olga. All tenderness had fled.

"Vanished! What on earth does Millie mean by that? This is
catastrophic. Doesn't she see that? Here we are, trying to get the
whole thing about the house arranged with the greatest discretion.
It's all so embarrassing for my poor Harry, quite apart from anything else. *My* mother—our mother, if you like, though Millie

hardly took that line when she was alive—and Burgo Smyth, the man who may well be leader of the party if we lose this election. I can't think that Horace Granville will want to soldier on, for him it will be back to those wonderful estates, those forests of his, which make such good television. Then Harry's chances may improve. HG has never really rated him, such a cynical man, frankly, but Burgo Smyth has always understood Harry is a *good* man—"

Olga Carter-Fox recalled herself from her political dreams for Holy Harry Carter-Fox. All the while she had been methodically tidying the contents of her husband's briefcase. Such a man, thought Jemima, both serious-minded and untidy, could have few secrets from his wife.

"And now this has happened! How on earth are we to tell him? Burgo Smyth, the Foreign Secretary!" Even in her distress Olga savoured the title. "Oh what a mess." Unconsciously Olga echoed exactly the word her sister had used, and added another virtually identical phrase: "It seems that the mess my mother—our mother— always created, lives after her. But I blame her, Millie, not Madre. How could she have let this happen? Or are you going to tell me that everyone in the theatrical world just helps themselves to private property as and when they feel like it? People just walking in and out. Just because they're artists."

Before Jemima could answer—she was prepared to make some allowances for Olga's exasperation but this was going a little too far—Harry Carter-Fox returned.

"Darling, Elfi was really so lovely, she prayed for everyone in the government of course, and she prayed for us to win. I *think* that's all right, don't you?" He sounded anxious. "It was her idea. But after that, wait, she prayed for the Labs and Libs as well. She says that Jesus wants us to be kind to everyone, everyone we see on television. Wasn't that adorable?"

"How sweet," said Olga absently. Then in a voice from which she had carefully eliminated all traces of her previous anger, she told her husband what had happened. There was an instant of silence. Then Harry Carter-Fox's broad face turned alarmingly red.

The struggle within this professionally patient and kindly man not to burst out in expletive-filled rage was almost palpable. When he finally spoke, it sounded as if he were choking.

"Olga, you must get them back." He ignored Jemima. "You must. This dreadful development must be kept secret. It's a disaster, a political disaster. They must be destroyed, no, handed back. But the Diaries must be destroyed. You must do it."

"I will, darling, I will. Trust me." Olga Carter-Fox was still patting her husband's hand when Elfi appeared, framed in the doorway. Maddening as Elfi might be, she was, Jemima had to admit, an exceptionally pretty child, with her enormous eyes and small heart-shaped face. It occurred to Jemima that Elfi was more like her grandmother Imogen Swain than either of her parents. Was Olga to spend the second half of her life coping with the histrionics of her daughter, having spent the first half enduring the vagaries of her mother?

"Mummy!" cried Elfi, choking back her sobs with about as much success as her father had choked back his anger. "Daddy! There was this dinosaur—"

Jemima thought she would leave this post–Jurassic Park child to her parents. Besides, she had her appointment with Sarah Smyth to keep. There was just one more potentially embarrassing point to be covered: the single Diary in her possession. She broke the news to Olga and Harry in between Elfi's sobs.

Harry's reaction was instantaneous. "I want it burnt immediately, totally burnt, in your biggest fire." My biggest fire! thought Jemima, he seems to envisage me living in some mediaeval castle with a Great Hall; I can hardly burn the wretched Diary on my gas-fired coals. "I'll shred it in the office" was what she said out loud.

"And you will help us to get the rest of these unfortunate—*things* back?" put in Olga anxiously. "You'll talk to Millie again. I just don't feel like talking to her myself at this point, she's so chippy about everything and this, which is *all her fault*," she emphasised the words, "will just make it worse. And you're going to talk to the Smyths. I'm sure we all of us agree that this needs *very discreet handling*." Olga emphasised these words even more vehemently.

Whatever Harry was about to say to this was interrupted by a more coherent wail from Elfi, "Mummy, don't go out tonight, don't leave me."

"Darling, you know I don't leave you."

"You do, you do, you go out at night and leave me. When I come downstairs after my nasty dreams, you're not there. It *did* happen," Elfi persisted as Olga put her arms comfortingly round her.

"Hush, Elfi," said Olga. "No stories please."

"It did happen. It's not a story. It happened. The night when you met Aunt Millie, then the babysitter went home, then you went out."

"Elfi, darling, stop this." Olga's tone remained gentle but Jemima was suddenly and acutely aware of something steely beneath the gentleness. The hand which was round Elfi's small shoulders was, she noticed, clenched, not necessarily to restrain her child, perhaps to restrain herself. This quickened Jemima's interest in a conversation which might otherwise have drifted past her as conversations of this sort between parents and children tended to do. She glanced at Harry Carter-Fox; he was staring at his wife with an expression which hovered between fear and respect.

Not long after this Burgo Smyth was to be found addressing a meeting which consisted of his daughter Sarah and his son. He stood in Sarah's pretty but diminutive drawing-room, dwarfing the two small armchairs in their pale blue linen covers and the tiny sofa in its perfectly chosen complementary print. When he raised his voice the collection of Dresden-type china ornaments on their glass shelves beside the mantelpiece rattled slightly, which the Foreign Secretary found extraordinarily irritating. He had disliked these ornaments when they were part of the decoration of his own home, as arranged by his wife, and he disliked them even more now that they had been passed to his daughter. They were somehow so excruciatingly feminine and demanding . . . Burgo Smyth withdrew his irritated glance from the offending shepherdess (it would be a shepherdess). He had more urgent problems to consider.

As Harry Carter-Fox had lost his philanthropic look, so Burgo Smyth with his children had entirely put aside the paternal manner he always produced for the media. (As a result of this celebrated manner, his approval rate with the electorate was nearly 20 per cent higher than that of Horace Granville, the languid aristocratic Prime Minister.) The mouth, so full and sensuous when he was a young man, was set in a line which was quite thin, and the famous dark eyes with their long eyelashes which had given rise to the nickname of the Tory Elvis were certainly not gazing at his children softly. Confronted with his real-life son and daughter, Burgo Smyth looked not so much fatherly as grimly angry.

"I forbid it," he said. "I absolutely forbid it." Even his voice had lost its habitual mellow tone: that wonderful natural bass which had thrilled generations of women voters down the years. "Sarah, Archie, do you hear me? Archie, you are to listen to me and for once you are to do *exactly* what I say." Archie's expression, at once embarrassed and defiant, indicated that he knew what his father was referring to—unwise dallying with some *very* far-right forces in his constituency which the Press had picked up.

"This is not, I repeat not, the route we must take. I *abhor*—" Burgo began with vehemence, then hesitated as the politician took over—"I do not care for things like that," he concluded lamely.

The doorbell rang. Sarah Smyth, who had not spoken for some time, looked at her father. "That's her," she said, "Jemima Shore. I hear you, Dad. Whatever happens, *you* won't be involved. Trust me. Trust us."

"It's too bloody dangerous. I forbid either of you to do that." Burgo Smyth was briefly ferocious once more; but by the time Jemima Shore was admitted no trace of anger or fierceness was visible.

"Now this really *is* a treat for me," said the Foreign Secretary tenderly, grasping Jemima Shore's hand as if she and she alone were responsible for voting in the next government. "In the midst of this horrible election, to meet my heroine—or should one say hero nowadays?"

Without committing herself, Jemima flashed him one of her television smiles, the sort that made television viewers think she really was a sweet person. She just had time to wonder which if any of her programmes he'd watched, when Burgo Smyth pressed on: "That series about Asian women and their varying legal rights in different countries opened my eyes to so much, things I should have known about long before . . ."

Out of sight, behind louvred doors in her plant-filled kitchen, Sarah Smyth was opening a bottle of champagne.

"Doctor's orders," she called out cheerfully. "For Dad. They made him give up whisky, too many late at night in the corridors of foreign powers, definitely not good for you." Sarah turned to Archie, who was lounging beside her; out of family habit he did not offer to help his sister since long experience told him that Sarah did everything, including opening a bottle of champagne, more competently than he did.

"We go ahead. Right?" said Sarah in a low voice. "Dad's just covering his tracks. No one knows except Randall of course and I've sworn him to secrecy. He can be ruthless in a good cause. A Jacobean conspiracy, he called it."

Archie looked blank.

"Forget it. He's all for solidarity. Family values if you like. Thank God for Randall."

"Bloody dangerous indeed!" snorted Archie. His fair face was flushed, something that most unfairly never happened to Sarah. "The whole situation is bloody dangerous. And it's all going to get worse. Someone on the *Sunday Times* has seen the *Sunday Op* story—"

"I know," said Sarah curtly. "I've heard what it's going to say." The pop of the cork meant that she made another cheerful call to the drawing-room where Jemima Shore, with Burgo Smyth's eyes bent upon her, was finding herself, at once reluctantly and enjoyably, succumbing to *something* about him. The seduction was not, she hoped, entirely his deep knowledge of her work . . .

"Sorry to be such ages!" Sarah cried. Then to Archie again in a lower voice, "I rang Mrs. Dibdin in the country. Told her to cancel the papers, pretend there's a strike. It doesn't matter."

"Mum never reads them," said Archie morosely.

"She may not but others do. *Someone* always tells you. Haven't you noticed that? Someone told her about you and your little Neo-Nazi friends." Then before Archie could comment, Sarah triumphantly bore bottle and glasses away.

In the living-room of the Carter-Foxes, in Shepherd's Bush, not far away in mileage from Sarah Smyth's bijou house but far away in the sense that its decoration showed no signs of money at all, the Carter-Fox parents were at long last alone. Elfi, visited twice by Harry and once by Olga, had fallen into that deep untroubled sleep of the victorious, since she was installed in her parents' bed. Olga poured Harry a whisky without asking, and a glass of rather sour red wine for herself, which for some reason or other had got parked in the fridge. Harry stretched out his legs and, after sipping the whisky, closed his eyes. Olga saw with love and anxiety that his normally florid face was quite grey with exhaustion.

"I think I'm going to lose the seat," he said after a moment, without opening his eyes.

"Darling, you're tired. Anyway there's another life, other than politics, I mean, especially for someone like you with all your interests. I've always said that. I believe that."

"I don't want another life. Don't you understand? I want this life. I have things to say, things I must say, about this country—" He stopped. Olga thought her husband had fallen asleep and delicately picked up her book, a new biography of Marie Antoinette which she was finding strangely consoling whenever she got the time to read it. But Harry was not asleep.

"Olga, did you go out? Did you go out again that night after the babysitter went?" he asked after a while, still without opening his

eyes. Olga, her head bent industriously over details of the Diamond
Necklace affair, did not answer.

"You'd never leave Elfi alone," said Harry after a further pause. It
was a statement rather than a question.

Olga looked up. "Has it occurred to you that our *au pair* often
comes back early? When her lovelife doesn't work out?"

Olga bent her eyes back to the book. "I'd do anything for you,
Harry, you know that. Poor Marie Antoinette, what a price she
paid . . ." Olga read on.

"Like tonight," she said, some time later. "Tessa is back early
tonight because her lovelife has gone wrong. So I could go out even
though it's Saturday night and we have no babysitter. Or we could
go out. In theory, that is." Olga turned once more to her book.

CHAPTER 9

IN A DARK PLACE

T WAS SURPRISINGLY EASY, THOUGHT THE STALKER, TO FOLLOW someone in an empty theatre late at night: the semi-darkness was full of noises. It was easy and even in a way—if the matter had not been so urgent—rather fun. Unexpected creaks, the shifting of swinging doors, distant sounds which might or might not come from the street. All these masked the progress of the stalker.

There were occasions when the stalker and Hattie Vickers were both standing still; and yet somewhere far below them in the stalls of the Irving there was a distant sound. The second time this happened the stalker wondered if there was actually a third person in the theatre joining in the chase. Since the stalker had Hattie in full view as she stood motionless at the back of the Upper Circle, the extra sound below was quite menacing. Being a stalker did not free you from fear.

Another alarming experience had been their shared passage through the front of the house to the foyer; the stalker did not know that Hattie herself was by no means as confident as she appeared. First the pass door had to be negotiated. As Hattie unlocked it by punching in the code and pushed it open, the faint ripple of air caused other doors far away to swing in reaction. Whenever this happened, Hattie tried to tell herself that she was well used to this knock-on effect. Although when she had first locked up for Mike, she had found it the spookiest moment of all. There was the stage, invisible and sealed off behind its substantial Safety Curtain. In the half-light it had been only too easy for Hattie to imagine that someone was down there below her in the stalls.

"What would I do if someone was there, sitting there?" Hattie had thought the first time she took Mike's keys. "Reason with them? Talk to them? Or rush out of the theatre screaming?" Hattie had upwards of forty keys on the metal key-ring and she tried to tell herself that the whole bunch would make a lethal weapon. She repeated to herself the words of Hermia in *A Midsummer Night's Dream:* "How low am I? I am not yet so low But that my nails can reach unto thine eyes." For nails, read keys, decided Hattie. It was her performance as Hermia in a student performance given a prize by Randall Birley which had brought her within his orbit; her job at the fringe Addison Theatre and now the Irving had followed.

Given Hattie's undeniable lack of inches, everyone agreed that Hermia was absolutely her part. Her motto, she determined, should be Helena's dismayed description of Hermia, "And though she be but little, she is fierce." But Hattie was not really fierce. Inside her bravado was a frightened creature who secretly found the Irving Theatre as daunting tonight as she had ever done. Only she did not want to admit it to herself. For example, she still did not close the pass door behind her because once, in an excess of fright, she had forgotten the extremely simple three-figure code.

The stalker now began to experience something else besides dread. There was also—let's face it—a growing horrible excitement at the idea of what was to come. It was like playing a sinister game of Grandmother's Footsteps. The stalker followed Hattie along the side of the Dress Circle, willing her not to turn around. Then the stalker let Hattie push aside the heavy dark red curtains which divided the Dress Circle (on street level) from the foyer. Hattie passed quickly through them. It was easy to watch her from the shadow of the half-drawn curtain, really an ideal observation post.

It was late Saturday night, after the sell-out second performance of *Twelfth Night*, even the five o'clock matinée had been heavily booked. The heavy glass doors beyond the Box Office looked directly on to the street, but they were padlocked. Two passers-by on the opposite pavement were like people in another world. If you screamed, they would hardly have heard. If you rattled the door, you could not get out (Hattie did rattle the door conscientiously to check that the lock was in place). Despite its being Saturday night, there was little noise of any sort audible in the foyer. Gino's, the Italian café, was around the corner and out of sight. The sound of the Haymarket traffic did not penetrate.

Hattie dreaded the mirrors most of all. The stalker did not know about this phenomenon of the darkened staircase; it was not something you would notice in the ordinary course of events. In theory Hattie was prepared. She had once involuntarily jumped backwards, losing her footing badly, on seeing a black figure looming at her on the corner of the first flight to the Upper Circle. It took her some time to realise that she had leapt away from her own reflection. In spite of being prepared, even tonight her heart began to pound in anticipation as she began the ascent. Fortunately for the stalker— unfortunately for Hattie Vickers—the stalker had decided to let her get well ahead on the staircase, not fancying the idea of a confrontation there, with Hattie for once having the advantage of height. So the telltale mirror did not trap the image of the stalker in pursuit as it might have done, whatever that might have meant for Hattie's future, for better or for worse.

As it was, Hattie wondered briefly whether her general fear of mirrors (she had nothing but a pocket mirror in her Earl's Court bed-sitting-room) meant quite simply a dislike of her own appearance. Or was it something more interesting: a primitive apprehension that her soul would be stolen away? And that would reach into the circumstances of her childhood . . . Making a mental note to talk through this newest manifestation of her insecurity some time soon, and rather cheered by the discovery, Hattie bounded up the second flight of stairs. She did not even gaze in the second large mirror as she reached the Upper Circle of the Irving Theatre. The stalker waited patiently in the shadows at the bottom of this last staircase and watched her.

Standing at the back of the Upper Circle itself, at the top of the steep rake which led down to the balcony, Hattie conscientiously surveyed the entire auditorium spread out before her. She never had any idea what she was supposed to be looking for—Mike had gazed at her testily when she asked the question—but it had occurred to her that the boxes would be the ideal place for an intruder to hide. And Hattie, frankly, found these pools of blackness, like the mirrors, quite disquieting from above. Of course, when you were actually *in* a box, the little red room could be utterly private, your own paradise. That brought her thoughts around to Randall: that magic secret night he had made love to her in the so-called Royal Box.

Secret, yes. Hattie was confident that no one knew about what had happened. But in retrospect, was it magic, truly magic? To be honest, Hattie was no longer quite sure about the whole thing. At first she had been filled with such rapture . . . It had after all come about quite naturally; she, unlike Hermia, had not needed to make fierce pursuit of her lover. One evening in Randall's dressing-room—somewhere she had a perfect right to be, and anyway he had invited her to have a drink—she had found herself telling him about her late-night vigils. And then she told him about the bet. One of the other actors, Charley Baines, an old friend of hers from Bristol playing a rather young Sir Toby Belch in a ridiculous white suit, had bet Hattie she would not dare to spend a night in the Irving Theatre. She remembered Randall looking at her speculatively, and she had not even realised that he fancied her.

Then he said, "Does it have to be a night alone?"

Those were the words that had led to—what had it been? An episode was how she put it to herself. Strangely enough, afterwards she had felt robbed of something precious to her: not her virginity, hardly that, Hattie was a thoroughly modern girl in that respect.

Nor did she complain that Randall readily produced a condom without asking her. That was good, not only modern but necessary, with no questions about who was protecting whom and from what.

No, something about the whole *episode* had made little Hattie Vickers feel like a trophy of war, a maiden being enjoyed by a hero as of right. She remembered the old theatrical chestnut about the famous classical actor who on being asked, "Did Hamlet have Ophelia?" answered, "I don't know about Hamlet, but I always did on tour." For Randall, was she the local Ophelia? Her unease was nothing to do with the sex itself. Randall had made love to her, not only with passion but with care for her pleasure just as, in her fantasies, she had always known he would.

Randall Birley had been her hero, but paradoxically the whole episode had robbed her of hero-worship. Be honest, Hattie, was it because you knew Randall had finally left you to go to join Millie Swain? Hattie Vickers prided herself on modernity in this respect too: sex to her did not necessarily mean immediate commitment. Nevertheless no one could be *quite* that modern, to think of a lover going straight back . . . she recalled the plot of *Fatal Attraction*. She did not intend Randall to pay the penalty for a one-night stand not likely to be repeated (was it?) but she admitted that for the first time she saw the point of view of the Glenn Close character.

Of course, Randall did not tell her that this—returning to Millie —was going to happen. But in her capacity as ASM Hattie knew many things which she should not perhaps have known. She certainly knew things about Randall that she was sure Millie Swain, for example, did not know. A locked dressing-room door, a message to be given to Millie which did not square with the facts. Why not face it? There was a compulsion in Randall Birley: with all his talent, his looks, his charm, his popularity, he seemed unable to rest happily in the company of any woman over the age of consent and not yet in her dotage unless he had established some kind of sexual supremacy over her. Hattie recognised the type: her adoptive father, with a good deal less charm (or talent), had been just the same, and rather wearily she recognised her attraction to the type.

In her mood of disillusionment Hattie was not even sure that Randall felt love for anyone, let alone Millie Swain, for all their public togetherness. They made a fine, a fascinating couple, playing in *Twelfth Night*, but Hattie did not give much for Millie's chances once the run was over. (Of course there was talk of a film; that might prolong things a bit.) Randall certainly did not love her, Hattie Vickers; she had no illusions about that. Millie Swain did have illusions, that was the difference between them.

Millie Swain: now that was a worrying situation, a really rather horrible situation in its own right. Those wretched letters and Diaries: if only she had not agreed to take them, not told Randall something about them. If only she had not *read* them . . . everything, everything terrible had started from that. Millie Swain had trusted her, thought she was a nice, trustworthy person (well, in most ways she *was*). Or to put it another way, Millie Swain had thought she was a dumb idiot. But in some respects Hattie was not at all dumb . . .

Hattie hovered between blaming herself for what had happened next and blaming Millie Swain. Her last therapist had emphasised over and over again, "Don't blame yourself for everything, Hattie." All the same it was difficult not to blame herself just a *little*. Something about the circumstances of her upbringing, an unhappily adopted single child, had made Hattie insatiably curious about other people's family relationships, that was the truth. She was a natural snooper. But it could be dangerous being a snooper. You could get more than you bargained for. How was she to know who that smart-arsed cousin of his was?

Hattie hated all politicians and would not dream of voting in the election even if she had a vote (she didn't, due to frequent changes of room and, it had to be said, to a dislike—a principled dislike, naturally—of paying Poll Tax in the past). But Tories were worse than Labour and women Tories the worst of all because as women they should have known better. Thus Sarah Smyth, so sure of herself, so cool in her expensive clothes, represented something Hattie

Vickers would have found distasteful even without her possessive behaviour towards Randall. (Here Hattie Vickers was in total agreement with Millie Swain.) Back to the situation and the burglary: suspicions, the most surprising suspicions were beginning to form in Hattie's mind. She might be insecure but she was not stupid.

Hattie gazed down the steepness into the pool of blackness. With these thoughts, none of them pleasant, not even the erotic memories of Randall's possessive touch on her body, she lingered longer than she generally did at the top of the Dress Circle. The stalker watched and waited for the moment when she would go down the steps and peer over the balcony. The stalker would then act extremely fast to terminate the danger Hattie Vickers had become. Hattie began to descend. She went quite fast and with determination. The edge of the balcony loomed in front of her. The stalker, no longer careful, ran down lightly after her. Hattie turned her head. Her last sight was of the stalker silhouetted against the single light behind them both. Her eyes opened in horror and disbelief as the stalker stretched out gloved hands.

The deed itself was easy, as the stalker had expected. Surprise was the best weapon of attack. Even so, after the deed was done, just as easily as the stalker had worked out, Hattie's final scream came as an unpleasant shock. Somehow the stalker had imagined that Hattie could just be extinguished, snuffed out; instead she had gone screaming to her death, a blood-curdling scream which would have been heard by anyone in the theatre, or even backstage, had they two not been utterly alone there. Even the feel of Hattie's soft springy hair as the stalker gathered her into a last lethal embrace was shocking. The thump of her body, a surprisingly loud thump for such a small person, was also quite horrifying.

Altogether the stalker felt sick once the deed was done, sick with revulsion at what had happened, sick with anger at what Hattie had made necessary. All sounds died away. Only far away, somewhere far below, something caused a door to swing. It was time for the stalker, mission accomplished, to depart.

In another dark place, there was another intrusion, not long after Hattie Vickers fell to her protracted fate (she was still breathing but lay unconscious, huddled between two seats in the stalls). The searcher in Number Nine Hippodrome Square, unlike the stalker in the Irving Theatre, had plenty of time to work carefully and methodically. The main problem the searcher had to face was dust.

The searcher, like the stalker, was wearing gloves. This was a treasure-hunt, wasn't it? The searcher decided to begin on the bedroom floor, which was the most likely place for the search to succeed. The nursery floor would come later. Determination and proper method would prevent any flinching from *that* room, the room from which Imogen Swain had fallen to her death that windy night. In any case it was not necessary, even rather dangerous, to open the balcony doors. Method, *thoroughness*, these were the aims to pursue. The searcher had a torch cased in black rubber with a single strong focused beam which should be sufficient to carry out most of the task.

The dirt was no less on the second floor and in the large front room which had once been Imogen Swain's bedroom. Oddly enough, this was the only room which contained some element that caused the searcher to hesitate on its threshold. The door was apparently shut. After a moment, the searcher grasped the door-knob firmly in a gloved hand. The knob came off. This gave the searcher a certain grim amusement: how typical! *Now* how to proceed? In fact, the door had not been properly closed, so the searcher had merely to push it open.

The beam illuminated the faded and tattered hangings of an enormous bed, an impression of peach-coloured taffeta, or what had once been peach-coloured taffeta. There were no bedclothes; just a vast heap of folded pink blankets and a pinkish satin eiderdown. Pink was, or had been, the predominant theme of the room. Even the walls had pinkish material on them and on the organdie covering of the wide dressing-table, now distinctly grey, some bedraggled pink bows could still be seen.

There were no photographs on the dressing-table, no trinkets, nothing except a set of glass boxes with silver tops (IMS engraved there and everywhere) and silver brushes. The torch raked on. It stopped abruptly on a little clock, so small as to be hardly visible in the beam. The searcher took a step forward, then stopped. This was no time for sentiment. The cupboards must be systematically searched and whatever lay behind them, if anything did, examined.

What did lie behind the cupboard doors with their painted fragments of ribbon and roses was a complete woman's wardrobe. The searcher felt rather than saw the jackets and little skirts (how tiny she had been!) and recoiled suddenly from the jab of a hat pin in a straw hat tangled in veiling. Something else soft and hairy was also repugnant: the searcher realised it was an ancient hank of false hair. Ugh! The smell of scent, stale and rather sweet, haunted the searcher: every now and then an empty scent bottle was disturbed lying among the underclothes so silky to the touch. One rattled to the floor. The searcher shone the torch on the glass bottle and saw the words: Joy and Jean Patou. The sight checked the searcher much as the glimpse of the little clock had done.

There was another faint smell, pungent, not so sweet, beneath the aroma of perfume. The searcher identified it: cat. The contrast of the two smells, one expensive and cloying, the other rank and feral, summed up the unpleasant double aspect of this deserted house. But the search had to go forward. Too much was at stake for it to be abandoned now.

At that moment a loud noise, more like a shout perhaps than the scream which poor Hattie Vickers had uttered, came from below, somewhere in the bowels of the house. The searcher stiffened and put out the torch. The thump of footsteps followed—heavy, vast, coming up the stairs. Sooner or later they would reach the bedroom on the second floor. The searcher's grip on the torch tightened. The searcher illuminated the doorway as the second searcher stood there, panting.

"Oh Christ, it's so ghastly. I've found something, something horrible." The second searcher sounded hysterical. "Listen. I've found a lot of bones there, down in the cellar, the inner cellar beyond. There's a skull. I think it's a skeleton. Oh God, help me. God help us."

It was at about this moment that Hattie Vickers, in another dark place, slipped quietly into death.

CHAPTER 10

SLEEPING SKELETON

W|E SHOULD CALL THE POLICE. SCOTLAND YARD, TOP PEOPLE ANY-
way." Sarah Smyth flicked distastefully at the rubber gloves she
had used to search Number Nine Hippodrome Square. She
added in her coolest voice, "I suppose that's the right thing to
do."

"I need a drink," said Archie Smyth. His fair hair was tousled, his
face smudged with dirt. He was wearing jeans with a black polo
neck sweater; in the torchlight he looked very young indeed. Sarah,
her combination of an immaculate coiffure, two rows of pearls and a
designer track suit giving her a curiously middle-aged look, might
almost have been his mother. "Jesus, what a nightmare. It was like
being in the Ghost Train at the fun fair when the skeleton rushes
out at you and you scream."

"You certainly screamed. What a ghastly treasure-hunt! Not a
good idea, as it turned out." Sarah touched Archie's arm. "Come on,
Boy, brace up, where is our gallant paratrooper now?" She was
referring to her brother's stint in the army after Sarah had sailed
effortlessly into Oxford, from a girls' school not renowned for its

educational possibilities. Archie Smyth, from Eton, was declared "not university material." "I'll find something for you to drink. There's bound to be something to drink in this house of all places. Although for obvious reasons, I wouldn't fancy anything in this cellar. Must all have lain here for years, including *that*. Quite ghastly, isn't it? The rest of the house, I mean. The way it's all so untouched makes it worse. And the most terrible cracks everywhere. Subsidence.

"And do you know, Archie," Sarah hesitated, "*she* had a little clock just like Mum's. I noticed it before when we went into the house the first time, after her death. Before that, I was never upstairs. And she used the same scent."

"Mum? She's not exactly into scent, is she?"

"Joy. I remember how delicious she smelt if you don't. Dad used to give her huge guilty bottles for Christmas, and now we know he was giving it to his girlfriend at the same time."

"What a bastard!" Archie was pleased to find he sounded quite flippant. He stretched out his hand. It had stopped shaking.

"A practical bastard," said Sarah dryly. The Smyths were standing close together in the first big cellar at the bottom of the steep staircase from the ground floor of Number Nine Hippodrome Square. There were various old trunks there. One of them, which looked like an ancient school trunk, had the words IMOGEN CORY 113 painted on it, and the lid was open. There were also some packing cases stuffed with crumbled yellow newspaper, and more paper on the floor.

There was no window in the cellar; it was blocked up entirely from the basement area outside. Sarah propped her torch next to Archie's on a suitcase (once pale or even white leather, initials I.M.S.). She shone her torch on a fragment of the newspaper which looked to her to date from the thirties, but the date was 1958. Otherwise the main contents of the cellar were tins of paint with the lids lying beside them, and a good deal of white paint was sloshed in random fashion in solid pools on the floor and on the walls.

"We've got to think about all this, Girl." Archie, like Sarah, was using the private, half-mocking nickname of their youth when the grown-ups had endlessly introduced them with the words, "Archie-is-the-Boy and Sarah-is-the-Girl." Generally speaking, the names had fallen into disuse and Archie, in particular, disliked being called Boy by Sarah; at this moment, however, their use indicated not so much mockery as sibling loyalty. "After all, we're hardly responsible."

"No, of course we're not responsible. That doesn't mean we can just walk away."

"For God's sake, why not? We didn't put it—him—there. We can just shut the door up again and quit. Those bloody letters certainly aren't down here, that's for sure."

"Him, why do you say him?" asked Sarah sharply. "Do you *know* it's a man?"

"Of course I don't know whether it's a man or not, do you think I did a quick forensic examination? I let out a fucking scream, didn't I? It may be the skeleton of a she-bear, one of the last she-bears in London, for all I know."

"I wish I knew what to do—" Archie found Sarah's admission touching because it was so rare. He gave her a hug.

"Come on, Girl, where is our gallant Amazon now?" This was a return dig about a recent Jak cartoon showing a bunch of Tory Amazons, including Sarah Smyth, with flowered hats instead of helmets.

"We've got to protect Dad. That's the first thing and the last thing. That's why we were here in the first place, to get rid of all the embarrassing traces. Secretly and silently. No questions asked. Those daughters, Millie Swain, with her ridiculous oh-so-trendy, left-wing views, I simply don't trust her. Extremely evasive about all that. Dreadfully keen to get the house back, but 'we'll be back to you about the letters.' We had to take independent action. As for Olga Carter-Fox, so meek in public, there's something sly about her, I always think; one of those maddening wives who secretly thinks she'd be a much better MP than her husband."

"In the case of Mrs. Carthorse, who's to say she is wrong? But Girl, Sarah, since it was Randall tipped you the wink about all that, weren't you going to see him tonight? Before you came here?"

"Oh that didn't work out," said Sarah quickly.

"Was he off with the trendy left-wing girlfriend?"

"No he was *not!*" Then Sarah carefully lowered her tone. "Let's leave Randall out of it, shall we? I'm one woman he doesn't manipulate."

Archie looked at her and said nothing.

"It's true. He respects my strength. We're a partnership. Always have been, since we were little, you remember that."

"I remember that you were going to get married to him when you grew up. What happened to that?"

"Who says anything happened to it? I'd be a damn sight better wife for Randall than—" Sarah stopped. "Shall we drop the subject? This is hardly the time and place. Let's concentrate on the papers.

"Yes, Randall did tell me that Millie Swain had deposited some family things in the theatre, but for some reason he knows that they were moved back." Sarah took a deep breath. "Archie, I'd better have a look for myself. At it. At him. Your bear's skeleton. And—we can hardly walk away, since you broke down the door or what remained of it. Fingerprints and all that. Besides, there is something called responsibility. I am a Member of Parliament, don't forget."

"You were a Member of Parliament. Currently, we're both candidates." But Archie only muttered the words as Sarah was making her way purposefully towards the concealed entrance to the inmost cellar. With her torch in her hand, she reminded Archie irresistibly of the Jak cartoon; it was not a thought he could share with her. He followed his sister.

They looked, with their two torches, Sarah's slightly shaky, into an extremely dark and low recess. It might be low, it was also extremely deep. Once upon a time it must have been virtually impossible to detect the existence of this inner space. There were already two outer cellars leading off each other. The second of these contained numerous pieces of collapsed wood and some more stable metal stands: old wine racks which were now virtually empty. Two Coca-Cola bottles did incongruously adorn the lowest rack, one with its top still on, the other broken and on its side. There were other bottles, a few, black and very dusty and something else broken which looked as if it had once been a bottle of Gordons gin. Apart from the incongruous Coca-Cola bottles, the cellar might not have been used for generations.

It was the decay of time rather than Archie Smyth's detective instinct which had led him to the discovery of the inner aperture. (Sarah was secretly infuriated by Archie's boyish curiosity, the curiosity which had led him to penetrate the inner depths of the cellar. How typical of Archie! There was no question of the vital things being down here. Always such a Boy's Own Adventurer, and now look what he had got them into—and Dad. She did not however share this thought with her brother any more than he had revealed his secret amusement at her Amazonian posture.) When the racks were full, and pulled against the inner door, it must have been invisible even to people looking for something. Outsiders would never have noticed it.

The weird thing to Sarah was that the skeleton was so markedly visible for what it was. It could have been something that medical students studied. How long would it take to reduce a human being to bones? She had no idea. She shuddered. Her anger with Archie faded and was replaced by an even greater worry.

"Oh Archie," thought Sarah as she looked into the aperture, "why couldn't you have let sleeping skeletons lie?" What she said aloud was: "The Home Office. The Home *Secretary*. That's who we should call. She'll direct us to the right person, the right person in the police that is, if we need to call the police."

"That woman! HG's stupidest appointment. She'd faint if she saw a skeleton: I'd almost rather talk to Helen Macdonald."

"You may yet find yourself doing just that," replied Sarah coldly. "If we lose the election. Sandra Makin is a fine person, and even if she weren't, the appointment is extremely popular in the country, calling for stiffer penalties while she wipes a tear from the corner of

her eye with a delicate lace hanky. Furthermore, she's crazy about
Dad."

But it was Archie, gazing now quite coldly at the mass of bones,
including a skull, in front of him, who came up with the interim
solution.

"Why don't we call her? No, not *her*, old Mother Makin. Call
Jemima Shore. Get her advice." Archie bent forward.

"Don't touch anything, Archie, for God's sake don't touch anything more."

Archie shone the torch deeply into the hole. "There's something
there, Girl, glinting. Gold coins, hidden treasure! I'm going to get
it."

"You are *not*." Sarah put her hand firmly on her twin's arm. "Yes, I
do see the glint, something glinting. It may simply be an old can.
All the more reason for us not to touch it. We need a witness. O.K.,
let's call Jemima Shore Investigator. She's supposed to be helping
us. The telephone still works upstairs. I lifted the receiver in that
morgue of a drawing-room."

"What do television people *do* on Saturday night?" murmured
Archie dubiously.

"Watch television, I suppose. What else have they got to do?
Other than criticise politicians for what they can't do themselves.
She'll be watching television." It was fortunate for the future of the
Smyths' relationship with Jemima Shore Investigator that she could
not overhear this snatch of dialogue: fortunate because it happened
to be true. Jemima Shore was indeed in Holland Park Mansions
watching television (CNN, the end of an enjoyable black-and-
white thirties film on television which she switched on too late, and
after that a good deal of disconsolate channel-hopping as, contrary
to Sarah's supposition, she tried to avoid all mention of politics).
But it had not been how she had expected her evening to turn out.

Tea with the Carter-Fox family, drinks with the Smyths, had
been in the line of duty. That is, her duty to the investigation which
continued to confuse and fascinate her had led her to both places.
In one sense all this had begun with the single Diary which had

ended up in her possession. But in another, truer sense Jemima recognised that it was her original unease concerning Imogen Swain's death which was driving her on. She felt instinctively—had felt instinctively from the beginning—that there was something wrong about it. So finally her habitual curiosity, fuelled by this special unease, was responsible.

Duty was one thing and Jemima Shore had a strong sense of duty. Pleasure was another thing altogether, and Jemima had a strong sense of pleasure. She did not see that the two things contradicted each other. Which is where Randall Birley came in. Correction, which is where Randall Birley should have come in. That supper at Gino's after her Friday night at the theatre: she'd known that Randall had been attracted to her. But then he'd made such an open flowery declaration of his passion that she could hardly have been unaware of it.

"Oh yes, he's really mad about you. He always watches you on the box," confirmed that little girl, the distressed, curly-haired ASM, sitting like an adoring groupie at the end of the table. (Jemima did notice that in the general reckoning up of the bill, always an interesting occasion on which to observe social nuance, Randall paid for Hattie Vickers with a genial wave, "No, Hat, I'll treat you.") His attention to Jemima was flattering and light-hearted, but what made Jemima suspect that the attraction was real (however temporary) was the behaviour of Millie Swain. She was too charming by half. While at Cambridge, Jemima had been involved with a professional heartbreaker and she remembered all too clearly her desperate use of the same technique. But this was not the point. The point was that Jemima in her turn, if she were honest, was fiercely attracted to Randall Birley.

"Oh Ned," she thought, "this is your fault. You should have come back. We should have gone to Dorset." But Ned had not come back; he had become a man linked to her only by a number of passionate faxes. Marilyn Monroe was supposed to have said that you couldn't curl up with a career on a cold winter's night and the same might be said of faxes. Thus Randall Birley's call on Saturday

morning was not unwelcome. Nor was it a total surprise. Nor was
his casual suggestion all that surprising either: that they might have
supper again after the second house.

"Somewhere a bit quieter than Gino's. The West End is hateful
on Saturday night. More in your direction perhaps. I'd love to continue our conversation about Marlowe. I could hardly hear anything
last night, could you? At one point I was talking about *Doctor Faustus*
and I suddenly realised you were talking about *Edward II*." There was
of course no mention of Millie Swain (who had been rather interesting on the subject of Marlowe and his female characters). And
Jemima Shore, naturally, agreed to the date.

The surprise lay in the fact that Randall had telephoned her quite
late—seven o'clock—and with deep apologies postponed the date.
The apologies sounded genuine ("an unexpected professional obli-
gation") but then Randall Birley was of course an actor. Thus it was
that Jemima Shore Investigator happened to be at 27 Holland Park
Mansions when Sarah Smyth telephoned her from Number Nine
Hippodrome Square.

When Jemima Shore arrived, she found Sarah Smyth's first remark curiously bathetic. "Oh dear," murmured Sarah, "that lovely
outfit. That pink is so gorgeous with your hair. I'm afraid everything
here is absolutely filthy. There's also a lot of whitish paint about in
the outer cellar, but that's been dry for generations." Jemima wondered if Tory training meant that you always commented graciously
on people's dress no matter what the occasion. It seemed to be
Sarah's chosen way of relieving tension.

Jemima's frank question (hardly surprising under the circumstances), "What on earth are you both doing here?" was met with an
elliptical reply from Sarah. "You could call it a treasure-hunt. Which
went wrong," she said smoothly.

Archie, on the other hand, chose to be slightly belligerent: "We
were having a bit of fun," he replied. Jemima thought he scarcely
looked as though the word fun was appropriate. Altogether, Archie
Smyth was much less gracious on the subject of his discovery and a
good deal more forthright. "This thing. This skeleton. What the

hell can we do about it? Sarah says we can't just wall it up and of course she's right as usual. But Christ, it's nothing to do with us, Jemima. We just don't want to be involved."

None of this—neither Sarah's social manner nor Archie's aggression—prepared Jemima for the grisly sight in the inner cellar. The three of them gathered around the hole. Then Jemima, granted Sarah's torch, crouched by it and the twins stood behind her. The whole experience was extremely unpleasant; even the Smyths' standing so closely behind her was not exactly reassuring. Supposing this were all a plot . . . Come on, Jemima, she told herself, these are Tories, not trained assassins, and even for a Labour voter there has to be some difference.

Like Sarah Smyth, Jemima was disconcerted by the perfect shape of the skeleton. But unlike Sarah, she'd had some experience of forensics (one particular previous investigation) and knew that the corpse in question had been dead for a long, long time.

Her torch caught the glint of something bright beside the bones. Jemima thought there were fragments of clothing there as well, dark pieces of something. "What's that? Did you see that? It could be a clasp of a belt or even a watch."

Archie said, "I think I should fetch it out, whatever it is. It may be a clue."

Sarah Smyth issued a protest, "Archie, let's *discuss* it." But by this time her brother had half crawled, half walked into the hole, his fair hair illuminated in the beam. He picked up the object without much difficulty; it seemed to be lying to the side of the bones, which Jemima noticed he managed, delicately, to avoid touching. Archie made his way, still crouched, out of the hole. He rubbed some of the dirt off the object in his hand and held it in the direction of the torch which Sarah held. Jemima watched while Sarah shone the torch downwards. Not hidden treasure as Archie had suggested, not an old can as Sarah had thought, not a belt buckle, not a watch—but a medal.

Jemima Shore, the former convent girl, suddenly recognised it for what it was: St. Aloysius, the patron saint of youth. The good little girls of Blessed Eleanor's Convent belonged to the Order of St. Aloysius around the time of their First Communion, and wore medals like this on green ribbons. Whatever, if anything, had once dangled this medal was no longer attached to it. From the fact that the medal retained some brightness it was probably made of gold.

Archie turned the medal over and Sarah shone the torch even closer. "There's something on it, a date I think," said Archie. He rubbed again.

"Here Archie, let me do it. You hold the torch." Sarah was taking charge again.

Jemima experienced a pang of dread. Why? she wondered later. Nevertheless, dread and even a kind of fear—not for herself but for others—was what she felt at that moment. The fear was for other people, circle upon circle, circles which might reach ever further away like the rings of water in a pool when a stone is dropped in. In this case, the stone was an engraved medal.

Perhaps it was that premonitory dread which enabled her to see, in advance of the Smyths, what the initials said.

"F.F.," said Jemima Shore slowly. "I can't make out all the figures. The last two look like a three and a nine: thirty-nine. But those are definitely two Fs." Again Jemima Shore realised far more quickly than the Smyths what those letters must inevitably mean.

F.F.: Franklyn Faber. Easy to remember because "F.F." was what Faber had been called by most of his friends on Jemima's television programme about the Faber Mystery, including Laurel Cameron, the lawyer. And Faber himself had used them. Including on that last note—the suicide note?—which he had signed. F.F. for Franklyn Faber, the journalist-on-trial, missing for thirty years and now presumably found. Burgo Smyth's friend; the man who had betrayed his trust, sold his government's papers for publication, found in the cellar of Smyth's ex-mistress. Jemima had a horrible feeling that they had stumbled on the solution to the Faber Mystery, and it was not going to be good news for anyone once involved and still living.

The Smyths did not make the connection. Even Sarah seemed bemused. Archie was frankly baffled.

Archie spoke first, "Well, that's good, isn't it? I mean the police will be able to trace him."

"Or her," put in Sarah automatically.

Archie ignored her. "Poor bugger. F.F., whoever he is. Stuck in that hole. I wonder where he died and how he died. My God, I hope he wasn't just shoved in there and left to suffocate. F.F., who on earth could he be? Do you suppose he was murdered?"

"Archie, enough." Sarah's sharp voice indicated to Jemima that she was beginning to be aware of the implications of the medal. Sarah steadied herself. "We must now all consider quite calmly and rationally how and what and above all when we tell the police."

"Listen, both of you." Once more, Jemima Shore could not explain to herself afterwards why she felt this protective instinct, but she did. "The man—and I think it is a man—has been dead for a very long time. In fact he's a skeleton, not a man. Call the police whenever you like. We'll all make statements about what we found."

How to put the next bit?

"But first of all," she went on carefully, "first of all, I think you should tell your father."

CHAPTER 11

THE TWIST

DIDN'T KILL HIM." BURGO SMYTH SOUNDED INFINITELY WEARY. HE had taken off his spectacles; his eyes could be seen to be red with exhaustion. Curiously enough, the effect of their removal was to make him look younger and more vulnerable. He rubbed his eyes and blinked several times as though unaccustomed to the light, a nocturnal animal. The dark eyes unconcealed and the lashes still much too long for a man, gave Jemima Shore a glimpse of the young man he had once been, the appealing younger man generally hidden in the carapace of the fatherly politician. It was that same appealing young man of course who had been the lover of Imogen Swain.

Nobody spoke. Finally Burgo Smyth said, "I assume you will believe me when I say that." He now sounded not so much exhausted as very sad.

Jemima Shore did believe him and she was sure his children believed him. On the other hand, some niggling voice in her ear insisted on adding, "Just as you believed Randall Birley. Successful politicians are actors too."

It was by now extremely late at night, or, to be accurate, it was very early on Sunday morning. The point was made by the presence of the Sunday papers—some of them, the early editions available late Saturday—lying on the Foreign Secretary's broad desk beside his armchair. The *Sunday Opinion* was on the top of the pile and some of its numerous sections had been pulled out. (Since the *Op* had been bought by Mack McGee, it had spawned a new joke: "What's the difference between the *Op* and a grapefruit? Answer: The *Op* has more segments.") The section called OPTOP which contained John Barrymoor's notorious campaigning column (notorious to politicians, that is) was clearly visible.

On the back of OPTOP was the equally notorious Mousehole column signed Catwatchman. The Mousehole was supposed to be social comment, whatever that might mean. It actually contained a lot of peculiarly vicious gossip, vicious because it was generally true. The Mousehole was an ancient institution in column terms; Franklyn Faber had started life on it before graduating to his own column. It was fashionable to say that the Mousehole had gone downhill (or wherever a hole went). Jemima privately wondered whether it had ever been quite the force for good that people nostalgically remembered.

Jemima thought Burgo Smyth must have been reading OPTOP when they arrived. She remembered Cherry's hint on Friday over the mobile phone and wondered what the Mousehole and/or John Barrymoor were discussing. This was hardly likely to have been Burgo Smyth's night: Sunday was not likely to be his day either.

A bizarre event as the Smyths and Jemima left Number Nine Hippodrome Square had reminded her all over again of the tangled mystery of Imogen Swain's death. Jemima had looked with a shudder into the basement area where Lady Imogen had fallen. Sarah Smyth, whether because she was still so shaken by recent events or out of genuine indifference, followed the direction of her gaze without visible emotion.

"That's where she died," she said, quite casually. At that moment two enormous fat black and white cats emerged out of the area where they had been lurking. One started to mew, the other purred raucously as it rubbed itself against Jemima's legs. The purring cat then transferred its attentions to Sarah Smyth, who immediately lost her air of indifference and delivered what looked like a very sharp kick.

"Get away. I *hate* cats," she added, slightly unnecessarily in Jemima's opinion. Joy or Jasmine? Which one had been unwise enough to desert cat-lover Jemima Shore for fastidious Sarah Smyth? Jemima recognised Imogen Swain's "girls"—those wandering cats named, as she recalled, for Lady Imogen's favourite scents, and disliked by her daughters with the same virulence as Sarah Smyth had shown. Jemima thought that she would at least establish one thing about the situation if only to satisfy her own curiosity.

"You came here, didn't you, Sarah, that night?"

"Naturally. We met *you* that night—"

"No, the night of her death. It was you who let out the cat, one of the cats."

Jemima was interrupted by another plaintive cry, this time it was human.

"Girlies, girlies, where are you, girlies? Joysie and Jassie, Joysee . . ." Mrs. Humphreys, the next-door neighbour, had somehow got saddled with Joy and Jasmine, probably for life. Better with her than with either Swain, let alone with either Smyth; the latter pair, she was convinced, never looked at any animal smaller than a labrador. Jemima was relieved that the vague notion she'd had of taking on "the girls"—the cat-lovers' equivalent of adopting orphan children featured in the newspapers—had proved unnecessary; it would have horrified the existing animal incumbent of Holland Park Mansions, the princely Midnight.

Shock had made Sarah much less guarded: for once she did not give Jemima the benefit of her frank I-am-about-to-deceive-you politician's smile.

"It's true. I was supposed to collect the letters. Dad's letters. It was all set up. We had to do something. All those calls she was making. Including to our mother who went on the binge. If only . . . no point in saying that now. But when I came around exactly as arranged, they were gone. She was drunk and dotty and kept telling me that I'd already taken them. Then she cried, howled really, told me things about my father that I really did *not* want to know, intimate things which, true or untrue, no daughter should know about her father." Remembering Lady Imogen's style of revelation, Jemima believed Sarah.

Sarah Smyth went on, "Then she talked about her ghastly daughters and how they were so cruel to her and how they were going to throw her out of the house. Take her house away from her, then put her in a home. And so on. All most unedifying. At least drink makes our poor mother paralytic. She never speaks at all."

Not one but two drunken women in the life of Burgo Smyth; did he deserve that? Her original question returned to her: how much of it was his responsibility? In the sense that he left a trail of destruction behind him, while he, Burgo Smyth, went on to have a brilliant career. On the other hand, it was more than possible that the women themselves chose the path of self-destruction. Women did, people did.

Jemima said: "Did Lady Imogen tell you she was going to leave the house to your father?" They were walking towards Archie's car, a Porsche. Well, it would be.

"Of course she didn't," Archie broke in. "Otherwise Sarah would have damn well put a stop to it. At source."

That was another curious phrase, thought Jemima. What exactly did "at source" mean? She now knew for certain what she had for some time suspected, that Sarah Smyth had been the last person to see Lady Imogen alive before she went to her death over the nursery balcony: unless, that is, there had been some further person present in the house, still later that night, who had assisted Imogen Swain to her lethal fall. There was, let's face it, a third grisly possibility: that Sarah Smyth had done the assisting, in order to "put a stop to it," in Archie's phrase. She may well have wished to put a stop to the tide of political gossip which was beginning to swell around her father's name, thanks to Imogen Swain's periodic dam-

aging telephone calls. Sarah Smyth was a determined, strongly mo-
tivated woman. But a killer?

Then there was Archie Smyth. It was no doubt reversely sexist to
regard the man of a couple as a more likely killer than the woman.
Jemima in her investigations had had experience of female as well as
male murderers. Nevertheless, it was a primitive response to cast
suspicion on Archie as the perpetrator of the deed (if there had
been a perpetrator; if there had been a deed). Of course she had no
proof that Archie had been present. Sarah's admission of her presence had come about as a result of Jemima's guesswork. The most
damning aspect of the whole affair (from Sarah Smyth's point of
view) was that Sarah had not reported her late-night visit to the
house to anyone. But you could argue that meant genuine inno-
cence, plus a natural wish for non-involvement in something potentially scandalous.

Non-involvement! Every politician's dream—to be untouched by
scandal and present an immaculate family-man (or woman) face to
the electorate. The theory was that this unspotted personal reputation was essential, otherwise the electors would rise up in indignation and cast whoever it was into the outer darkness. As a result,
again and again politicians marched to their doom with personal
behaviour in striking contrast to their pious public sentiments.
Looked at from another angle, of course, such behaviour simply
proved that they were human like everyone else.

Currently, Burgo Smyth bid fair to be in that long line of politicians marching to their doom. Originally Jemima had felt sympathetic to him on the subject of the ancient sexual scandal being
resurrected. Now she wondered. Old scandals were one thing, old
murders were quite another: for peccadillo read crime. Her mind
leaping ahead, Jemima wondered why on earth Burgo Smyth would
have wanted to kill Franklyn Faber. Surely the damage—considerable—had been done by the trial before Faber died?

"We're there," said Sarah Smyth. "Archie, park the car discreetly,
will you?"

The Foreign Secretary's residence in Carlton House Terrace was curiously impersonal, although Burgo Smyth must have occupied it for long enough. Perhaps it was the lack of a woman's touch, pondered Jemima. She gazed at the Foreign Secretary, admiring quite dispassionately the image he projected of dignity based on integrity. Presumably this image was about to be shattered.

"I didn't kill him," repeated Burgo Smyth, rubbing his naked eyes once more. "But, yes, that is Franklyn Faber. What remains of him— and just at present, please don't tell me. I'll save you the bother of wondering, is it? is it not? Too late for that, or it will be shortly. Yes, it is Franklyn Faber. You have there the solution to the Faber Mystery." Smyth managed an ironic smile in the direction of Jemima Shore: "You must wish that this grisly discovery had taken place before you did your programme."

The smile faded. "I didn't kill him, but yes, I did know he was dead. That's my crime. And it *was* a crime, of course, concealment of a death, a body. I knew quite enough about the law to know that. Even then. And since then," the faint, ironic smile returned, "I've even had a stint, a short stint, as Home Secretary."

"Dad, I can't believe I'm hearing this!" exclaimed Sarah. She looked white with shock; her strong hands, whose large size was at variance with her general trimness, were clenched together. "You mean you *knew* what had happened to him, you knew all along." Jemima, who had recently looked up Sarah's biographical details, remembered that she had studied law, and had been an aspiring barrister before she got into Parliament. Even though company law was her special interest, as Jemima recalled it, Sarah would still appreciate all too keenly the legal consequences of what her father had done.

"It was an accident, and an accident at which I wasn't present." Burgo Smyth was now speaking with his habitual authority. "This is not the moment for further details, although they will certainly come, have to come. All you need to know for the present is that it was an accident. Frank came secretly to her house—*the* house, the house you have just left. There was an accident; he fell; he tripped, fell down that staircase to the cellar on his way to fetch some drink.

She called me. I did it, she and I did it, together we hid the body. That's all you need to know."

"But Dad, for Christ's sake." Archie looked if possible even more devastated than his sister. "We've bloody well got to know a lot more than that. For example, who else knew about this? Were there witnesses? We need to help you, protect you, cover this up—" His voice died away.

"I don't think so, Boy," said Burgo gently. "I made a terrible decision thirty years ago. I've got to pay for it now. I think you'll find that's the case."

Nobody looked at Jemima Shore. There was no need. Jemima knew that Sarah Smyth, for all her maddening values (just because of these maddening values), was not the kind of character to cover up anything like this, even to protect her beloved father. About Archie, their could be more doubt, fairly or unfairly, but then it was not up to Archie Smyth.

"So you did it, that terrible thing, which is going to ruin you, to protect *her?*" asked Sarah fiercely. Her eyes glistened as though she was about to shed tears of anger or frustration.

"Oh Sarah, I did it to protect us all, even you and Archie, certainly Mum and of course myself. Think of the scandal. Dead man, centre of a controversial case, found in my mistress's house. My precious political career. Worth saving or not? History will judge. In the meantime *you* can judge. I had such belief in myself, my destiny, in those days. Saviour of the country and all that. I saved myself, if you like, in order to save the country. How long ago it all seems!"

Burgo Smyth had not offered any of them a drink. Perhaps he thought it was too late—or too early. She knew he did not drink spirits—doctor's orders—and his favourite champagne would have been inappropriate. A cup of coffee might have been nice. She thought Burgo Smyth himself could do with some stimulant.

Saviour of the country! He hadn't exactly been that, supposing that such a person could exist in these modern, allegedly peaceful times. He had been a thoroughly decent and responsible Foreign

Secretary, and a short-lived Home Secretary, too liberal for most
members of his party. Could you balance that against the deliberate
concealment of a dead man, the hoodwinking of his country's justice? Of course, in human terms, you could say that the issue turned
on the grief experienced by Franklyn Faber's family or friends.
There had been no wife, that was certain, but what if there had
been a girl friend or, as seemed more probable, a boy friend, what
about his or her feelings? Suspense could be even more damaging
than certainty.

"It was madness," said Burgo Smyth. He spoke as if considering
some knotty point of international diplomacy. "Of course I regret it
passionately now. In fact I regretted it quite soon. But we'll talk
about it, you—Sarah and Archie—and I, another time. Tomorrow
and tomorrow and tomorrow, I've no doubt."

He pointed at the Sunday newspapers. "They're on my trail of
course. You knew that. She took to ringing up the papers, names
she remembered I suppose. Let's face it, it's never all that difficult to
get through to the Press. She even paid a call on the McGees. But
of course the Press don't know about this—what shall we call it—
this twist."

Archie turned to Jemima. He found relief in belligerence. "You're
one of them. So what are you going to say about all this?"

"I'm going to make my statement to the police, not the Press,"
replied Jemima sharply, "and please remember that I came to Hippodrome Square at your express invitation."

"Cut it out, Archie." Sarah turned back to her father. "What
happened after that? I must know. Did you go on seeing her? All
the time, all our childhood, when poor Mum was so dreadfully
unhappy? All the time you were making love to this woman, this
murderess—well, maybe she was a murderess, you say you weren't
there, Dad, not in the house at the time—"

"She wasn't a murderess. And no, I never saw her again," he
replied sombrely. "Not after that night. It was part of the bargain,
you see. We could never meet again. Too dangerous for us both.
There had never been any connection between them: Imogen and

Frank. No public connection at least. We had to take advantage of that."

"So you left her to it?" In spite of herself and her genuine desire to be neutral, Jemima knew there was criticism in her voice.

"If you want to put it like that, yes. For both our sakes, we never met again, never in private. And we avoided the sort of occasions where we might have met in public. But sometimes, of course, I did catch a glimpse of her at parties, big parties given by your relations,"—he gestured towards his children—"on the rare occasions Mum wanted to come up from the country. At first it was agony to see her. Then I steeled myself. I was busy. Threw myself into my career, as they say. No more affairs, ever. All that was over. If I neglected Mum, it was for politics, nothing else. The pain dulled. It went away."

"Did it go away for her?"

Burgo Smyth looked at Jemima. He put on the spectacles which he had been turning in his hands and contemplated her as if she had been some random questioner at a foreign affairs conference. He was wearing his celebrated paternal expression. "Probably not. Women are different, aren't they? More romantic. More steadfast. Don't you agree?" It was almost as though Burgo Smyth was about to give vent to that traditional smooth answer of the politician, "I'm so glad you asked me that question."

Jemima wanted to say, "They used to be. When they had nothing else to think about. Have you ever considered that? Your wife was driven to drink, first by your infidelity, then by your coldness and separateness; and still I understand she loved you. Lady Imogen had a broken heart at the end of your affair and so did you. But she also had a broken life. And you didn't." In short, it was back to Byron and love, which for a man was a thing apart, and woman's whole existence. Things were different for Jemima Shore. Ned Silver, watch out . . .

But these were the small hours of the night. This was no moment for Burgo Smyth to be instructed in the different emotional responses of the liberated career woman. Instead, Jemima asked—this

she could not help, this was the ineradicable interviewer in her—
"How did you feel when the calls started coming? From Lady Imogen. All those years later. You had once been in love." It was imper-
tinent. It was irresistible.

Burgo Smyth stared at her from behind his reinstalled defences,
his spectacles. What he said surprised her. It was a quotation she
herself knew well.

" 'But that was in another country,' " said the Foreign Secretary,
" 'And besides, the wench is dead.' Those lines have always haunted
me. That's what I felt when Imogen started all the crazy calls. The
woman I had loved was dead long ago. Webster, I fancy."

It was in fact Marlowe. Was it only just over twenty-four hours
since she had been happily quoting those lines to Randall Birley at
Gino's? She knew it was time to go away and leave the stricken
Smyth family to work out their plan of action . . .

Ye Gods! the election! The full enormity of what was going to
happen to Burgo Smyth struck Jemima as she walked away from the
Foreign Secretary's residence, down the empty Mall. It was also,
presumably, going to happen to the Tory party. Could something
like this, revealed about the nation's favourite father figure, persuade
the dithering electorate to make a definite choice, in the opposite
direction? Jemima passed a police car. Its two occupants looked at
her with impersonal attention. In spite of that, she felt she must
continue to have some fresh air. Another police car went past her at
a slow pace. There were one or two lights on on a high floor of
Buckingham Palace. This was one scandal-at-the-top which would
leave its inhabitants unscathed.

Jemima felt utterly chilled by what had happened, but she was
well into Knightsbridge before she hailed a taxi to take her to
Holland Park Mansions. She had time to ponder on the coincidence
of the Foreign Secretary quoting Marlowe. She also had time to
reflect that the wench in question—Lady Imogen—was well and
truly dead now, not just in the romantic imagination of Burgo
Smyth. The Faber Mystery was at least partially solved; the Swain
Mystery had deepened. What a strong motive Burgo Smyth would

have had for killing Imogen Swain! Jemima knew him to be a ruth-less man, not so much because all politicians were ruthless (her general conviction), but because he had already carried out one colossal deception, and lied and lied and lied, and shown a bland uncaring face to the public. Had he carried out a second and even more daring crime to rid himself of this unhappy incubus from his past? Jemima shivered.

When she opened the door of Holland Park Mansions, Midnight was crouching on the carpet in front of her, imitating a sphinx. And the telephone was ringing. Jemima looked at her watch. At this hour even Cy Fredericks would not dare, unless he was in Los Angeles, eight hours behind, in which case he would dare all right with that indifference to other people's sleep (and time zones) that was, in Jemima's opinion, one of his least lovable characteristics. But Cy Fredericks was not in Los Angeles. He was in London, getting ready to play a prominent part in the annual David Garrick Awards ceremony on Sunday night.

Which is actually tonight, thought Jemima.

It could only be Ned. She picked up the telephone just as the answering machine got there too. That meant that all Ned's sweet nothings would now be recorded. She decided not to point that out to him. She would have a passionate cassette to add to her collec-tion of passionate faxes.

But it was not Ned.

"Jemima, thank God you're there!" said a man's voice. "I thought it would be the dread machine."

Jemima wanted to say, "Actually it's both of us," but she had no chance.

The voice swept on, "I feel so awful about tonight, awful for *me* that I missed your company." It was only at this point that Jemima recognised the voice of Randall Birley, since he had never bothered to announce his identity. "I couldn't explain properly because it's all a little delicate about this film. And I just had to meet the great Helen, and I couldn't say so with—people around."

"Helen Macdonald?" Jemima had not figured Randall Birley as at

all political, unlike Millie Swain, but perhaps he had been persuaded by Millie to do a commercial for the Labour-Liberal coalition. (In which case what about his devoted cousin Sarah Smyth?)

"Who?" demanded Randall.

"Helen Macdonald. Leader of the Labour Party—the alliance.
Possibly our next Prime Minister." Jemima was right about Randall
Birley not being political.

"No, no, of course not. This is show business. Helen Troy. Absurd name but she can get away with it, and anyway it's her real
name. The biggest female box-office draw in the US ever since that
film, I can't remember its name. *Chased?* No, *Chaste.* She's interested
in playing Viola in my film. She was trained as a classical actress,
you know. It's fantastic!"

"Fantastic for whom?" thought Jemima crossly. "Why is he telling
me all this?"

But Randall had rattled on, "Now listen, what about tomorrow?"

Before Jemima could reply, Randall Birley had run on yet again.
"Oh shit," he said. "No, tomorrow is the Garrick Awards. What a
bore these things are. Boring if you win, even more boring if you
don't."

So far Jemima's contribution to this late-night conversation had
consisted of one piece of fairly obvious political information about
Helen Macdonald. Jemima knew that she absolutely had to go to
bed, be purred over by Midnight. Anything to stop the world and
get off, however momentarily.

"What a happy coincidence! I myself am presenting one of the
boring Garrick Awards. So I'll see you there." And Jemima rang off.

But she could not sleep. After a while she got out of bed and put
on the tape of her Faber Mystery programme, falling asleep as the
final credits rolled. The handsome saturnine face of the young
Burgo Smyth haunted her dreams. In her dream—one of those odd
upside-down dreams which plagued her, especially when Ned was
away—Burgo Smyth was an actor, and he was receiving some kind
of award. Jemima wanted to protest about it, but in her dream could
not remember why.

CHAPTER 12

WHAT PRICE PRIZES?

CAN'T THINK WHAT'S HAPPENED TO HATTIE, YOU KNOW, OUR HAT-
tie, ASM at the Irving, Hattie Vickers—" Charley Baines was
peering crossly into the gathering crowds around the vast Trumpet Cinema. Most of them stared back blankly, their eyes shifting
onwards when they realised that Charley Baines was not famous.
Or rather Charley Baines was not famous enough: his Toby Belch in
Randall Birley's *Twelfth Night* had been nominated for a David Garrick Award in the category of Best Character Actor in a Comic
Performance in a Fringe Production (by no means the most obscure
category in the long list of awards).

"She was so desperate to come," Charley Baines confided to no
one in particular since everyone on the edge of the Trumpet foyer
was desperate to move on, either wanting to get out of the limelight
or more likely to get into it. Certainly nobody had time to worry
about Hattie Vickers. You could not exactly call the Garrick Awards
ceremony at the Trumpet Cinema A Hit, since it was for one night
only once a year, but it was certainly A Happening.

Up to this point nobody had missed Hattie throughout the

whole of Sunday. She was not that kind of person. Arrangements were pretty casual for the inhabitants of the large, shabby house in Earl's Court where she lived, even on weekdays. Not everyone was in work and those that had work did not necessarily work regular hours. After all, Hattie's own hours, including the nights when she stayed late to lock up the theatre, were irregular enough. Hattie was friendly with a couple of middle-aged actors who came and went; one of them was currently working in a theatre in Wales and the other was thought to be in Edinburgh.

As for Sunday, that was when the whole house was sometimes completely silent, as though all the lodgers were under some kind of dusty spell. Hattie regarded Sunday as a day she had to herself. Her adoptive parents—her mother, whom she had loved, and her father, whom she had both loved and loathed—were both dead. The small cousinage into which she had been introduced by her adoption had by degrees politely distanced themselves from Hattie after her parents' death. In any case, Hattie felt no particular need to impose herself on their Sunday lunches, at best in the country near Guildford, at worst on the outskirts of Woking.

Hattie had always told herself, "the theatre is my life." (She had not foreseen that it was also to be her death.) The friends she had chosen to keep up with after university were entirely those who shared this passion. One of these was Charley Baines. Charley felt a genuine affection for Hattie which included playing the role, in so far as she would let him, of brotherly protector. It helped that Charley did not particularly fancy Hattie, and she certainly did not fancy him. Hattie, as Charley had kindly told her on more than one occasion, was a star-fucker; Hattie herself would have preferred to say that she had a capacity for hero-worship. In other words, Randall Birley was by no means the first hero in her particular world to receive the gift of Hattie's devotion. He was, however, Charley thought, the one who presented the most danger to Hattie. He simply did not trust Randall where the vulnerable were concerned. He was a user—he would certainly use Hattie if it suited him.

Although it was getting late, one or two major stars were still arriving at the Trumpet, a progress indicated by the flash bulbs of the paparazzi. Was that or was it not Joan Collins? A little bunch of protesters, all women, all holding placards, took a chance that it *was* Joan Collins. They started their chant again, the chant with which they had been periodically enlivening the proceedings. The words that Charley could hear most clearly were, "Garrick Pigs! Garrick Pigs!" So far as Charley Baines was concerned, the organisers of the David Garrick Awards would certainly turn out to be pigs if his *bête noir* Su Waggoner, also on the short-list in his own category, won a Garrick for her atrocious Mistress Touchstone in the all-woman *As You Like It*. Otherwise he could not quite see the connection.

"Where on earth *is* Hattie? She's generally so reliable." The crowd shifted and Charley found himself standing beside Millie Swain, who was also waiting for someone. Like Charley, Millie had been nominated for a Garrick Award (as had Randall Birley, but he, unlike his colleagues, had been nominated in no fewer than seven categories, including his role as a director and his appearances on television in the latest remakes of *Rebecca* and *Wuthering Heights*.)

Millie Swain looked magnificent, more Cleopatra than Viola, with her glossy hair cascading down in snake-like ringlets worthy of the Egyptian queen. She was wearing an extremely short white beaded dress in twenties style, suspended—becomingly low over the bosom—by thin silver straps. In spite of the cold spring, Millie Swain had no wrap. Charley Baines realised that he had never before seen Millie in such a revealing dress, showing not only her décolletage but her legs. Everyone knew that Millie Swain had wonderful long legs in trousers or tights; she now made it clear to the world that she had wonderful shapely legs and ankles in pale stockings and satin shoes.

Charley Baines admired Millie's talent enormously. "I hope she wins and he doesn't," was roughly his point of view about the Garrick Awards, Randall Birley and Millie Swain. "But I bet it'll be exactly the other way round. He'll win everything, including an award for *Twelfth Night*, and she'll miss out."

Talented as Millie might be, Charley had never before thought of her as sexy. There was something daunting about her, he found. It could be a question of her height (Charley himself being short and stocky, not to say short and tubby), but Charley thought that was not the point since he much enjoyed wrapping himself around willowy beauties in so far as they permitted it. No, there was an odd air of austerity about Millie Swain which had put Charley off. Tonight was different: she looked adventurous, appealing.

"Have *you* seen Hattie?"

"Have *you* seen Randall?" Millie countered. Her large heavy-lidded eyes, unusually adorned with shimmering eyeshadow and eyeliner, roved over the crowds. Charley stared at her appreciatively. Millie Swain caught the direction of his gaze and grinned.

"You like it? I borrowed it. A leftover from some ghastly parody of a Coward production. As for the make-up"—she mentioned the name of a celebrated make-up artist—"we did that ghastly television series about Malta together, friends for life."

The David Garrick Awards were sponsored by the *Sunday Opinion;* you could not be in much doubt of that if you gazed up at the huge banners which decorated the auditorium of the Trumpet. On the other hand, for Cy Fredericks, whose company, Megalith, was televising the Awards, giving the *Sunday Op* due credit for its sponsorship came low on his list of priorities.

"Lose the banners!" he cried imperiously to a young woman passing, whom he imagined by some flight of fancy was a member of the Megalith staff. She was in fact that Su Waggoner whose success in the category of Best Comic Character Actor was dreaded by Charley Baines. Despite being a modern young woman, Su Waggoner gave Cy Fredericks an extremely old-fashioned look, in which astonishment and indignation were mixed in roughly equal parts.

"Of course we've absolutely no intention of giving them the oxygen of publicity, as it's now known." Guthrie Carlyle, the Megalith producer responsible for the programme, moved smoothly to his chairman's elbow.

Cy Fredericks gazed at him respectfully. He was prepared to deal with the *Sunday Op*'s claims in the most Machiavellian manner, which would leave Megalith triumphant but deny Mack McGee the opportunity for a legitimate grievance. But even Cy had not contemplated denying the *Op* any publicity whatsoever. He felt a new admiration for Guthrie Carlyle, whom he had always privately held to be something of a liberal wimp.

"This whole thing about the Garrick is more than usually ridiculous," went on Guthrie. Immediately Cy Fredericks's expression changed from that of new-found respect to one of deep habitual unease. His membership in the Garrick Club was of long standing but it continued to be something that he treasured—which was not always true where Cy was concerned, the oxygen of novelty being his particular fix. Every now and then he had an anxiety dream about finding himself in the Garrick Club dressed only in one half of his pyjamas, not the sort of dream that he would ever have about other places allegedly more crucial to him, say the boardroom of Megalith. Cy Fredericks did not like the conjunction of the words "Garrick" and "ridiculous." Who or what was ridiculous? Since it could hardly be the club (that was unthinkable) it must inevitably be him, Cy Fredericks . . .

It took Guthrie Carlyle some time to explain that he was referring to the protesters' placards rather than the banners of the *Sunday Op*. Nor could Guthrie altogether blame his chairman for not being able to grasp the point at issue. The protesters were demonstrating about the failure of the Garrick, an all-male club having absolutely no connection with the ceremony, to admit women members as a result of a recent vote. The coincidental use of the name of the great actor by the organisers of the Awards, had, in the protesters' opinion, given them their chance.

"It's a photo-opportunity, that's what," said one of the protesters cheerfully to Guthrie as he entered. Guthrie knew her: Cynnie, a pretty red-headed young woman who worked for another TV company. Beside her stood Margaret Rose, that marvellously beautiful black woman who had worked at Megalith for Jemima Shore; Guthrie nourished an unrequited passion for her.

"Isn't that what Award ceremonies are all about?" shouted Cynnie. "Seeing and being seen."

"It seems not quite fair to the David Garrick Awards, which are totally separate—"

"Since when were prizes fair? We're just part of the general unfairness, we're drawing attention to it, that's all." Cynnie looked even more cheerful as she threw in a special "Garrick Pigs!" more or less in Guthrie's face.

"Garrick Pigs!" drawled Margaret Rose. Guthrie looked yearningly in her direction. Unlike Groucho Marx, he wished to join any club of which she was a member, even if it were as alien to his needs as the Garrick.

Outside, Charley Baines had decided that something must have happened to Hattie Vickers (there were still some hours left before he would discover just how right he was: the Irving Theatre, locked after the second Saturday performance, normally remained unvisited until the cleaners arrived early on the Monday morning). But before he could move inside, the rush and glitter of the photographers intensified into an exploding galaxy of light and sound. Millie Swain, still beside him, looked stunned and disbelieving. Charley Baines witnessed the phenomenon of her new radiance being extinguished as if some plug had been pulled. A moment later she had vanished into the auditorium.

Framed in the halo of lights—including Megalith's television lights—stood a tiny figure in a black felt hat and a man's check suit much too big for it. Who on earth? Some Charlie Chaplin lookalike? Charley looked again. The figure revealed itself as female, and the features under the hat resolved themselves into that combination of features so beloved of the camera—the high slavic cheek bones, small neat nose, pouting mouth and huge slightly protuberant eyes which photographed flat. In short, this was the famous Hollywood star, Helen Troy. Her escort, however, Charley had no difficulty in recognising: for he was Randall Birley.

It was Jemima Shore, not Charley Baines, who was the unwilling witness to the subsequent colloquy between Randall Birley and Millie Swain. Like Helen Troy, but with a good deal less ballyhoo, Jemima was expected to present a Garrick Award. Cy Fredericks had taken a personal interest in this aspect of the Awards, although it was not, strictly speaking, any part of Megalith's remit to do so. Such arrangements were theoretically handled by the organisers; Megalith's responsibility was simply to televise what took place. But Cy Fredericks had announced that Jemima would present an award, and she had found herself seated close to the various short-listed actors.

It was true that this year there was an additional responsibility for Megalith. Parts of the ceremony—the actual presentations— were to be shown live, after recorded scenes of the arriving celebrities, and a panel of luminaries—also live—discussing the general theme, "What Price Prizes?".

The live ceremony meant, for example, that the Carter-Fox family, all three of them, were able to settle in front of the television on Sunday night, to watch, as Olga told Elfi, "your aunt Millie win one of her lovely prizes."

Elfrida Carter-Fox was a child who fully understood the concept of awards. Some basic instinct enabled her to shine at precisely those activities most likely to be rewarded publicly with prizes. "Will it be a silver cup like I won with my running? Or a book of fairy tales like I got for my Progress? Or—"

Harry Carter-Fox had his eyes closed with exhaustion, although he was not asleep: he found it increasingly difficult to sleep even during the short hours he was able to spend in bed. His depression about the possible outcome of the election in his constituency had not lifted. The Sunday polls might be showing a small shift to the Tories nationwide but it was not reflected in the soundings taken by his workers in Bedford Park. Harry Carter-Fox knew he was being squeezed between the excellent centrist Liberal-Labour candidate— an Asian lawyer who had been to Harrow—and a rogue Tory Independent so far to the right that he would make Archie Smyth's views seem positively moderate.

Harry was meditating on his mistakes: "Should I have made that

fighting speech about pensions at the party conference?" he wondered. "Olga was worried at the time." For a moment he had a
gratifying image of the Prime Minister calling him "the conscience
of the party" as he congratulated him at the end of it. But did the
conscience of the party necessarily get re-elected? Certainly HG
had skipped away from his side pretty swiftly after that, before a
single camera had a chance to record them together.

Elfi's piping voice caught his attention, and Harry frowned. He
wanted to say to Olga above Elfi's head (in French) that this concentration on prizes was surely unwise, but unfortunately he could
not remember the French word for prizes. Furthermore, he had a
gloomy feeling that his daughter would already know it, since at
the age of seven she had already won two of them for French.

"You would never think that all television used to be live!"
groaned Guthrie Carlyle to Jemima. They were old friends from
Megalith days. "I don't trust my panel one inch. The live camera is
bound to bring out the worst in them."

"Who have you got? Melvyn? Germaine? David Mellor? That
sort of person?"

"For God's sake, Jemima, we're talking elections here. No one
who has ever expressed even the teensiest weensiest opinion of any
sort is allowed even to peep round the door of this programme.
Given that Germaine has expressed more or less every opinion, it's
terribly unfair, and of course Mellor and David Melvyn, whoops,
correction, are out of the question. I can't even get Jamie Grand as
chairman—and he'll chair anything that moves—because he's already chairing the panel of the Garrick judges, given that he's
moonlighting these days as dramatic critic for the *Sunday Opinion*. I
suppose, Jemima, that you—" "I am a very political person," said
Jemima firmly. She had so far done nothing for the Labour Party
during the election, but disliked having to admit it.

It was due to the election that the Garrick Awards ceremony was
being shown more or less live on Sunday night; normally an edited
version would have been put out on the Monday. The remaining
evenings before the election were occupied by a series of lavish

political commercials in which it could be said that the various parties presented themselves with awards.

Where Randall Birley and Millie Swain were concerned, Jemima was still at this point unaware that they had not arrived together. But she was transfixed by Randall's voice. He did not bother to moderate it. "Betsy, yes Betsy Wright. My agent, just to remind you. Have you any objection if I have supper with my agent from time to time?"

Millie on the other hand was trying to whisper, except that emotion made her voice difficult to control and thus audible. "But you were so late! I was there for ages before I just pushed off. Why did you give me your key if you don't expect me to turn up? I think I'll give it back to you, by the way, then if you want to stay out half the night with someone else—including your agent of course—you won't have any problems, will you?"

Jemima, uneasily aware that Randall must be lying if he had told Millie that he had spent his evening with his agent, wished that she had not overheard this conversation. In an attempt to stop it, she turned around and smiled as charmingly as possible at Millie. Fortunately the angle of her head enabled her to ignore Randall. Jemima was on the point of making some anodyne remark about hoping Millie would win (perfectly sincere: like Charley Baines, Jemima really did hope that Millie would win) when the lights dimmed. Cy Fredericks came on to the stage.

Much later there would be those who described Cy Fredericks's speech as deliberately provocative. Mack McGee, as publisher of the *Sunday Opinion*, would have been far more suitable, expert as he was on long home-spun speeches which left everyone secretly grateful they had not had an Aberdeen upbringing. No, Cy was a disaster. After all, someone had to be responsible for what happened next: a noisy disruption of the ceremony by the "Garrick" protesters. Not cheerful Cynnie and glamorous Margaret Rose but others in the media world who had genuine invitations to the occasion, discreetly distributed round the auditorium. Even Jemima, Cy's devoted friend in spite of everything (which encompassed a good deal) wondered why he had chosen this particular function to make a courageous stand. Generally speaking, courageous stands were no part of Cy's pattern of behaviour. However this particular controversy had evidently touched a nerve.

"Proud to associate myself with the manly name of Garrick," he began. The words aroused a torrent of cries, "Garrick Pigs! Garrick Pigs!" from all corners of the auditorium and his next remarks were drowned.

Of course there were also those who said that Cy was innocent of provocation since he had not for one moment understood the issue at stake. The kind of woman Cy Fredericks so passionately admired—Lady Manfred, for example, the elegant chairman of the Arts Council—had no wish to belong to any club since they were already ruling the Establishment effortlessly.

As for the unfortunate choice of the word "manly," Jemima for one was quite prepared to believe that it was a coincidence. She had noticed before how Cy homed in on words he associated with Britain's chivalrous past. This was especially true when he was making speeches; "Arthurian" had been a previous favourite. It was a pity, in a way, that it had been superseded. "The Arthurian name of Garrick" might have led more to puzzlement than protest.

Order was not restored for some time. It was certainly not restored before poor Jamie Grand had waded through his long chairman's speech, full of careful allusions to winners and losers in dramatic literature. The babble of protest and counter-protest made it difficult to follow, even supposing it had been easy to follow in the first place.

"Humour and loss: let Beckett lead us by the hand," Jemima heard him say during a temporary lull. However, viewers at home, in contrast to those at the Trumpet, had the full text delivered to them. This was because Guthrie's cameras, resolutely denying the oxygen of publicity to the anti-Garrick protesters, had perforce to close in on Jamie Grand with no possibility of cutaways.

"What on earth's happening to that fucking panel? This is their chance to pull their weight," Guthrie Carlyle exploded, driven beyond endurance by Jamie Grand's lecture and definitely not prepared to let Beckett lead him by the hand. For one ghastly moment Guthrie, who tried not to swear, feared he was close to a live mike. But he was spared that particular trauma.

At home, Elfi Carter-Fox, who believed in airing her knowledge where possible when watching TV, was busy relating the sad story of Thomas à Becket to her parents. "You see, you have to be very careful about wishing bad things to people, in case bad people hear you, like four bad knights—" But her father had at last been granted the gift of sleep by Jamie Grand's lecture and Olga was too preoccupied with her own agonised, unvoiceable thoughts to listen to either Jamie Grand or her daughter.

At the Trumpet it turned out that Guthrie's so-called anodyne panel was also nothing but trouble. Really, it would have been far, far better to have the professionals, however allegedly political— Germaine, Melvyn, David Mellor and company. A glass box had been built within the Trumpet auditorium, so the panel could be seen (but not heard) by those in the audience, as they made their illuminating comments on the awards. The idea was that these comments would be cut, at relevant moments, into the programme. In the event, the audience at the Trumpet found themselves treated to a fascinating dumbshow which made it clear the panel itself contained at least one anti-Garrick protester. When the first (male) fist was raised and the first hank of hair (also male) was demonstrably pulled, Guthrie thought it wise to plunge the whole panel into darkness so that the Trumpet audience should not watch further events.

This, as it turned out, was an unwise decision. For at that very moment, for some reason no one ever discovered, the panel—now shrouded in blackness—found itself live on television. Among the confused sounds, "You bitch!" was the first audible cry and things went downhill from there.

"Mummy, Daddy, the television's broken," said Elfi Carter-Fox.

But she did not regain her parents' attention until she asked brightly, "What does 'sod off' mean? I know what a sod is, we have sods in our garden—"

Jemima Shore began to think that she would have to present her own award—for the Best Actress in a TV Serial in Period Costume—amid a hail of barracking. For the individual protesters had staggered their interventions to prolong them as much as possible. This meant that the chucking-out process was also prolonged.

John Barrymoor got up to receive the prestigious Doctor Johnson Independent Voice Award, for the third time in a row. His awesome presence, that shock of hair which still trailed wisps of glory of its former fiery red, and his undimmed blue eyes bent fiercely upon the audience, had the effect of calming everybody. It was either that, or the last protester had been evicted. Barrymoor's speech was comparatively short (for him). To Jemima, it bore a particular significance. He spoke of corruption, the need to root it out, to expose scandals and treacheries "however ancient." He concluded menacingly, "There is no statute of limitations where evil in high places is concerned," and stalked from the platform amid a tempest of applause.

This time it was Elfi, of the Carter-Fox family, who had fallen asleep. Her long eyelashes were fanned out on her petal-pink cheeks. Olga's heart churned with love for her daughter, whose prattling voice was for once silent. Olga pulled Elfi to her; over the child's head, her eyes met those of Harry.

"What is that dreadful communist snooper hinting at? I don't like it, Olga, I don't like it one bit," Harry said. "I wish I could have a cigarette. No, don't worry, I'm not, repeat not, going to slip. It's socially irresponsible. What an example to Elfi!"

"Elfi's asleep. You know, Harry, I think maybe you *should* have a cigarette. Listen to what I have to tell you."

Olga Carter-Fox had been telephoned personally by Burgo Smyth that afternoon while Harry was in the park with Elfi. It was a call whose message she had not yet fully digested. She had tried in vain to reach Millie to pass on the horrifying news about the discovery in their childhood home, but her telephone remained obstinately on answer. Olga had therefore postponed telling her husband, but she did not think she should do so any longer. Even if John Barrymoor was so far referring only to her mother's revelations before her death, the media explosion on the subject of Franklyn Faber must come soon.

Olga switched off the television. Why on earth had she thought she wanted to watch her sister, with her successful career and her wonderful lover, receive a prize?

"Darling," she said, "Burgo Smyth rang me up this afternoon—" Painfully, Olga noticed on her husband's face that look of hope with which a junior politician wontedly greets the news that a senior minister has been trying to make contact. Swiftly, Olga Carter-Fox put an end to those expectations.

As it happened, by switching off the television at that juncture, Olga did not miss watching Millie get her prize. For Millie Swain did not receive an award for her performance as Viola. Exactly as Charley Baines had predicted, it was Randall Birley who scooped the awards from *Twelfth Night* both as director and actor. Clearly, the judges had found Best Actress to be one prize too many. For that matter, Charley Baines did not win either, but he consoled himself that Su Waggoner had also been pipped at the post by an ageing raffish actor named Charles Paris playing Davies in *The Caretaker* (with words, many but not all of which were supplied by the author).

For Jemima Shore, however, the drama of the evening was not over. It was Helen Troy herself, on stage growing from a small tramp to a delicious star, who presented Randall Birley with his Best Actor Award. As Helen Troy began to speak—"My friend, my very dear new friend"—there was a rustle behind Jemima. For a moment she feared that it was yet another demonstrator. But the protest, if it was a protest, was of another sort. The noise was caused by Millie Swain pushing her way out of the row, under the cover of the heavy applause for Randall Birley, or was it for Helen Troy? Or for what was perhaps a new combination?

It was quite a while after that the ceremony, at last, at very last, drew to a close. Yes, thought Jemima, you could say with Randall Birley that award ceremonies were boring if you got (or gave) an award and even more boring if you didn't. She could not blame Millie Swain for exiting, even if it was hardly politic under the curious eyes of the whole theatrical world and television.

Cy Fredericks was bustling past her with Mrs. McGee—a homely but not undignified figure in a tartan skirt and waistcoat—on his arm: "Jem, my gem, come with me, we are all going to the Ivy, you remember." Cy had not actually mentioned this plan before, but he was obviously in need of company if the party would otherwise consist of the McGees and himself. Jemima was prepared to go along with him for want of anything better to do, when she felt a savage grip on her upper arm.

"No, you are not!" said the voice of Randall Birley in her ear. "You're my prize. I'm going to take you home."

CHAPTER 13

PASSION

VERY EARLY ON MONDAY MORNING, THE TEAM OF WOMEN CLEAN-
ers—all related or connected by marriage, all Asian—entered
the Irving Theatre. As usual, they entered by the Stage Door,
unlocked by the cleaner in charge, Mrs. Patel senior. Because
the team cleaned backstage first, it was some time before the
body of Hattie Vickers was discovered.

When the team went towards the front of the house, Mrs. Patel
found the communicating door shut but not locked, and she thus
did not need to use the code to open it. This was unusual, but not
unknown. Mrs. Patel could remember previous occasions when the
code had not been necessary. She had no way of realising that it
was Hattie Vickers, not Mike, who sometimes made the mistake out
of nervousness; but Mrs. Patel had certainly never pointed out this
lapse in security to the theatre management. It was never part of
Mrs. Patel's plan to make unnecessary enemies.

Hattie lay, as she had lain since her fall, wedged between two
seats in the stalls. In the hours when she had slipped slowly from
unconsciousness into death, Hattie had remained motionless as

though held in a red plush-lined tomb. Later it would be discovered that she had broken both hands in her fall (trying in some pathetic way to ward off the inevitable?) as well as suffering such terrible injuries to her head that there was never any question of recovery. Hattie Vickers had thus been dead for well over twenty-four hours when the cleaning team arrived.

Nevertheless, the first instinct of Mrs. Patel senior was to try to shake the body awake. She put her hand on the huddled form. Mrs. Patel did so rather gingerly because she assumed Hattie was one of the homeless who had infiltrated the Irving. Experience had told her that the homeless, even outside the Irving, could be quite vicious when disturbed.

At the same time Mrs. Patel knew her duty: "Wake up, please! I am asking you, please, to wake up."

The tangled mass of hair, spilling everywhere, told her that the sleeper was female, well probably female. When there was no reaction Mrs. Patel, more boldly, touched the hair itself, first one straying piece to which she gave a gentle yank, then the hair on the sleeper's head. The place where she touched the head felt slightly sticky, as though something had congealed. It was not until she saw her fingers—blackish-red in the low lights of the auditorium—that Mrs. Patel realised what she had found: not a sleeping form but an extremely dead one.

Even then, with that extraordinary self-control and personal dignity which had enabled Mrs. Patel to see her huge family through many vicissitudes, Mrs. Patel did not scream. She rose up and taking her youngest daughter-in-law, a sensitive creature, by the hand, led her away. Mrs. Patel junior had not seen the corpse, but felt the occasion was owed the tribute of her tears. She sat sobbing discreetly as Mrs. Patel senior telephoned 999 from the theatre payphone just outside the stalls.

The dead body of Hattie Vickers remained exactly where it had fallen. The fact that Mrs. Patel senior had led a life of difficulties in two countries meant that she was not unacquainted with British police procedures. She knew that it was important not to touch anything before the police came, otherwise trouble ensued—trouble for the Patels, that is. Trouble might come their way in any case (undeserved trouble had happened before now), but Mrs. Patel would do her best as usual to protect them all. After her first tentative exploration, Mrs. Patel had left the body quite alone in its position which mimicked sleep. Her reddened fingers, were, however, scrubbed and scrubbed again, regardless of what anyone might say.

Paradoxically, at about this time, you could have mistaken Jemima Shore, lying half-asleep in her huge, pale, disordered bed, for someone who was dead. There was a particular abandon about the way her body lay, death and gratified desire producing roughly the same effect. And indeed desire had been gratified, very much so. Something dangerous which had existed between herself and Randall Birley from their first meeting had detonated. The result was an explosion of violence, of sexual energy, from Randall, from Jemima, then from Randall again.

"I want you like this—am I hurting you?—and like this, and like *this.*"

"I want you like *this*—I don't care—and again, yes, again . . ."

"And like this. Darling."

They slept a little. Jemima woke to find Randall's dark head on her arm; for a moment in her confusion, its blackness puzzled her. Ned . . . she put the thought from her, and a moment later Randall too was awake, taking her, and she was able to put the thought very far away indeed.

Now that he was gone, Jemima lay for a long time luxuriously in her bed, letting sleep come and go. After a while she remembered his last words as he kissed first her breasts, then her shoulder. Randall had efficiently pulled the soft lace-covered duvet across her, rescuing it from some strange corner of her bedroom where it had ended up.

"So I won, you were my prize, the only prize I wanted." He picked up one of the dizzy strappy high-heeled shoes she had worn to present her Award. Jemima, who loved a virtuous opportunity to buy shoes, really amazing shoes, had decided that it was her duty to give the viewers a treat.

"Perhaps I should take one of these as a souvenir," said Randall lightly.

"Give me my shoe, my shoes."

"If I give them to you, will you put them on for me?"

"One day."

Jemima pondered briefly her words "one day," and then drifted back to sleep. When she woke again, it was time for coffee, and in Midnight's disgusted opinion—he did not like rivals, any rivals—time for food. Jemima put on her robe but nursed her coffee back in bed. The sheer animal happiness of having enjoyed sex and still more sex the night before had not faded; the imprint of it all on her body, the bruises, would probably take even longer to fade, but about that she felt grandly reckless. At the same time, she was beginning to ponder Randall's last remarks: "I won you, my prize . . ."

A pleasantry? Yes. All the same, "Was I won? Do I want to be won? I think it's me who's supposed to give the prize," she thought wryly. On the whole, Jemima Shore did not want to be anyone's Garrick Award.

Yet in his other declarations—those there had been before by mutual agreement they fell into bed—Randall had been wonderfully ardent and yet unpossessive. "I could have a real passion for you. What would you think of that? You might not like that. Passion can be dangerous." He had used the word, alluded to the threatening bond she had felt between them from the start.

Well, what did she think of that? Jemima looked at the high-heeled shoes still lying on the bed where Randall had left them. One day, she had said. Yet she agreed with Randall about passion, and its consequences. Ned's particular mixture suited her, in spite of her grumbles: passion, including most satisfying physical passion, when he was there, coupled with long periods of absence, during which she was out of his sight and thus out of his arms (and she had a suspicion out of his mind too) for all the faxes which screamed their way across the world to debouch from her machine.

"But I rather hope not this morning," thought Jemima guiltily. And the fax seemed to sense her reluctance and remained tactfully silent. She did not plan to feel guilt about what had happened with Randall—in that respect she and Ned, so often apart, carefully respected each other's privacy—but all the same a loving fax at that particular point might have brought her perilously close to the tinglings of guilt.

She turned her thoughts back to Randall Birley: Randall and the question of danger. In particular, a more prolonged passionate relationship with Randall could be dangerous. Given that she had sensed that from the start, wasn't that what had drawn her to him . . . Jemima's honest self-interrogation was interrupted not by the fax but by the telephone.

It was Cherry. "I just got back from Nice—more about that later—in time to see you last night. Those were wicked shoes! What? Yes, yes, what you said was fine. What *did* you say? I couldn't stop looking at your shoes. I thought that was the point. And *did* you get to meet Randall Birley?"

Jemima knew she had to apply herself to the task, never easy, of telling Cherry enough but not too much. She could begin—if not continue—by telling the truth. "Yes, I did meet Randall Birley. But then I met him before at the Irving Theatre, with his—" she hesitated, "with Millie Swain. On Friday. We went to Gino's."

"I'm dying to see *Twelfth Night*." Cherry allowed herself to be distracted. "I hear it's terrifically upbeat, all that sixties pop music at the end, you leave the theatre singing."

Hattie Vickers of course did not leave the theatre singing. Nor did the shaken (but outwardly calm) group of Mrs. Patel and her helpers. Not many people witnessed the departure of Hattie's small body on a stretcher, face covered, one little skein of hair dangling beneath the blanket. Just as few people had witnessed the arrival of a police car, then another police car, followed by an ambulance.

The West End, around the Irving Theatre in its side street, was quiet and curiously listless of a Monday morning as though still hung over from the ritual enjoyments of the weekend. The story of Hattie's death did not make the early editions of the *Evening Standard,* which carried an inspiring headline on the subject of the election: LAB-LIB: NEW POLL SHOCK. The small print indicated that 67 per cent of those polled replied, "Don't Know," when asked whether they thought the Labour-Liberal alliance was helpful or otherwise in the present international situation.

Another discreet arrival and departure later that day was that of the Foreign Secretary, Burgo Smyth. He visited the Prime Minister, Horace Granville, at Number Ten Downing Street. A great deal of telephoning—awkward, ghastly telephoning—had preceded this meeting. But both men knew that the telephone discussions must finally culminate in a personal meeting.

"I won't insult you, my dear fellow, by saying that you probably need to spend more time with your family." The Prime Minister spoke with that mixture of gaiety and briskness which Burgo Smyth knew he reserved for really difficult situations. Smyth had after all sat in the Cabinet long enough beside Horace Granville, first as his colleague, latterly as his subordinate.

There was no doubt that H.G. had great personal charm and a good deal of it was probably genuine. "After all, why shouldn't he be charming?" thought Burgo with a spurt of anger that broke through the exhaustion currently—perhaps mercifully—dimming his inner reactions. "Inherited wealth, no wife, never felt the need apparently, poor fellow, *lucky* fellow, not even queer when he was young. I can never get used to 'gay' (what's gay about it?), no hint of that, no scandal anywhere, and a devoted sister to look after him. I should have had a sister like Miss G.—" He conjured up the image of the Prime Minister's sister, a quiet, pleasant, well-mannered Scotswoman who conveyed the air of a superior school matron. "That would have saved a lot of trouble."

Horace Granville leapt up. His spare figure and thick fair hair which had passed imperceptibly from blonde to grey, coupled with

his characteristically energetic movements, contributed to an air of
youthfulness. Compared to H.G., Burgo felt weighed down, old and
finished. Whereas H.G. would never be finished. If he lost the
election, he would retire to his estates in Scotland, his lovely Adam
house in its elegant park, the rare books in his library—and his
trees, those forests about whose fortunes Burgo Smyth had been
rather too often kept informed. For Burgo Smyth on the other hand,
the end of his political career was death itself, not only political
death, but the end of the only life he had ever wanted.

"How is Teresa by the way?" asked the Prime Minister.

Burgo shook his head. "Not well. That is, the same. I
haven't . . . I haven't bothered her with all this yet. My children
think it's better to tell her everything at one time."

H.G. had always been extremely courteous to Teresa Smyth. He
was invariably courteous to women, the chivalry of his manner to
the new Labour leader Helen Macdonald being a joy to certain
Tories, since she found it infuriating; that is, it teetered on the edge
of patronage without ever quite falling into the trap. But in those
long-gone days when Teresa had sometimes laboured to fulfil her
role as a minister's wife, with occasionally embarrassing consequences, H.G. was one of Burgo's colleagues who had always
treated her kindly. He was grateful to him for that. Now he wondered just what else, if anything, he was going to have to be grateful to H.G. for.

"Limit the damage, limit the damage!" cried the Prime Minister.
His step was so light and springy as he paced up and down the
huge formal room that he gave the impression of taking part in
some old-fashioned measure. "You'll resign, I understand. Pity, pity,
but there it is." Then with even greater cheerfulness the Prime Minister threw in the afterthought, "No House of Lords for you, my
dear fellow, no peerage. So unfair, you've certainly deserved it.
When I think of the types who are going to get peerages and go to
the House of Lords. Whether we win or lose."

Burgo Smyth could think of those types too. Curiously enough,
thinking of them enabled him to endure stoically the casual way the

Prime Minister had disposed of his final dream. A secret dream, that
in the House of Lords one day he would still find some kind of
political arena. After all, the members of the House of Lords were
not exactly subject to the same pressure to preserve stainless reputa-
tions; no electoral challenge for them. At this point Burgo had no
idea whether he would have to face prison for his offence; he was
unquestionably guilty of covering up a death. But even people who
had been to prison had a perfect right to sit in the Lords on release;
it was one of the British anomalies that you could not strip away a
peerage as you could strip away a knighthood or other decoration.

That had been Burgo Smyth's wild hope, after all the service to
his country and his party. With a cheery wave of his long-fingered
hand, H.G. had put an end to that secret longing too. It was unreal-
istic and had always been so. "Limit the damage, limit the damage."
And he Burgo Smyth, who had for so many years and in so many
turbulent countries done just that, he, Burgo, *was* now the damage.

"You've got a really splendid majority," said the Prime Minister;
he might have been congratulating his Foreign Secretary on his fine
head of hair. "At least you had a splendid majority last time. This
time round I think yours is one of the really safe seats in the country. Well done. With all those trips, it can't have been easy to keep
in touch. Or perhaps they prefer reading about us in the newspapers. I sometimes think that about my lot. Of course my sister is
wonderful there, better than any wife—" But even the Prime Minister's natural exuberance faded as he realised the implications of
what he was saying.

He returned to briskness. "So we shall have a seat to play with—
your seat—to win or lose after the election. Reward some good
fellow who doesn't deserve to lose but is going to. Get him back.
You will resign shortly after the election. Exact timing to be discussed. I've been on to the Home Secretary of course. Sandra will
be as helpful as possible. Which cannot be, alas, *very* helpful. Resign
for personal reasons, whatever you like. I'm afraid the full inquest
will eventually make it quite clear what those are, but, as we both
know, that can't be avoided. I understand the inquest will be for-

mally opened, and immediately adjourned, on Friday morning. That's the latest we can hope for. Besides, on Friday the Press will be busy proving they were right all along about the election. The real inquest may not be for some time. And by then," H.G. gave Burgo a darting smile, "you'll no longer be Foreign Secretary. Not even a Member of Parliament.

"To be practical," he went on, "your seat. Your dear good girl, now what a bright future *she's* got. Alas, they tell me she'll be lucky to hold that seat. Let her have yours? But no, that wouldn't be quite right. Your boy was lucky, wasn't he? Very lucky." Burgo did not know whether H.G. was referring to Archie's unfortunate brush with the neo-Nazis being papered over, or to his selection for a safe seat. He noticed that H.G., whose liberal credentials were impeccable, did not predict a bright future for Archie.

"Your seat. Let's see, what shall we do with it? Whom shall we reward? Some nice, loyal chap who will just have lost his own seat. For example, I also hear that Harry Carter-Fox can't possibly hold Bedford Park."

"The Carthorse!" exclaimed Burgo. "For God's sake. That we should be so lucky as to lose him. If the electorate get rid of him, every committee he's on will take half the time." (Had Olga Carter-Fox heard this, she might have revised her opinion of Burgo Smyth, at any rate as a future protector of her husband.) Burgo's response was automatic. He had forgotten for the time being the Swain connection, as the politician in him became once more dominant. Yet he had spoken to Olga Carter-Fox only recently, as he felt in honour bound to do, following the discovery at Hippodrome Square: that sulky brooding Olga Swain whom he had never liked even when she was a child.

"Oh, I should rather miss him!" cried the Prime Minister. "No one can accuse us of being a party without a conscience with him on our backbenches. Conscience, yes, yes. What a nuisance consciences are, aren't they? But some people have to have them, don't they? Otherwise where should we be? No, we can't afford to ignore the conscience factor, can we? Under the circumstances."

Throughout this light-hearted tirade, the Prime Minister had
continued to walk about, occasionally peering out of the deep windows at the various structures of the British Establishment which
the views provided. Burgo Smyth realised that he had always been
maddened by H.G.'s apparent inability to keep still, never more so
than now. But of course, like so much of seeming inconsequence
about Horace Granville, this habit of peregrination served its pur-
pose. In this case, his restlessness protected him from direct eye
contact with Burgo Smyth, as he pronounced the exact steps by
which his political execution was to be carried out.

The death was to be self-inflicted. Like a kamikaze pilot in the
service of the Japanese emperor at the end of World War II, he was
expected to commit a form of suicide. Burgo Smyth knew that; he
accepted that; he had in a conscious or unconscious sense been
expecting this moment for almost the whole of his effective political career. He still paused to wonder at the cold-blooded cunning
of Horace Granville who would accept the sacrifice of his safe seat,
at one and the same time as stopping the mouth of the late Imogen
Swain's family by promising it to her son-in-law.

When Burgo replied, he did so with great formality. "I'll do whatever you say, Prime Minister. I began this meeting by apologising
for all the distress I am giving and shall be giving to the cause we
both serve. I should like to end it by apologising again. To you
personally. You have shown many kindnesses in the past—both to
me and to my wife." Burgo Smyth stood up, towering heavily over
the slight dapper figure of the Prime Minister; he prepared to ex-
tend his hand. But, like an eel, H.G. slipped away from the closeness and in an instant was to be seen at the drinks tray, pouring
from a cut-glass decanter full of pale gold-coloured liquid.

"Malt whisky. Local. Made in my constituency. But of course my
sister always insists we pay for it and it costs a fortune." He handed
Burgo Smyth a beautiful and weighty tumbler. The Prime Minister
sipped. The Foreign Secretary took something not far from a swig.
On doctor's orders, he had not drunk whisky or any other spirits for
a long time; as he tasted the elixir, he decided that whatever his

future held, it was going to feature whisky once again. Suddenly, to Burgo Smyth's astonishment, H.G. put down his glass and, stepping towards him, put his arm around his shoulders, reaching up slightly to do so. He's going to hug me, thought Burgo Smyth, he's really going to hug me.

"My dear Burgo, I'm so terribly, terribly sorry," said Horace Granville gently. For once in his life he sounded absolutely serious. "I keep thinking how for thirty years you must have dreaded this moment. The anguish you must have felt. Following the—accident, how you must have longed to put the clock back."

For the first time since that midnight encounter with his children and Jemima Shore, Burgo Smyth felt his self-control faltering, that iron self-control on which (like Mrs. Patel the cleaner) he had prided himself throughout his career. By this time the Prime Minister had delicately stepped back, and his glass was once more ensconced in his hand. Burgo's voice when he answered was unusually husky, but he managed a kind of smile.

"Putting the clock back! Yes indeed. Don't we politicians always wish we could do that?"

"You must have felt great love." H.G. sounded almost wistful.

"I felt great passion. Not always the same thing."

"Ah yes, you're probably right. I wouldn't know about that. Or so my sister tells me. Passion, I mean, not love. I tell her I would be perfectly capable of feeling passion if only the right woman came along. It would serve her right if I *did* fall violently in love, at my age, and insisted on getting married. Then where would she be?" The frivolous mask was back.

"Thus putting the clock back, Prime Minister?" murmured the Foreign Secretary in the same vein. He took another long drink of the magic pale liquid in his heavy tumbler.

CHAPTER 14

AT THE CENTRE OF THE WEB

OLGA CARTER-FOX CONTEMPLATED THE WOMAN SHE HAD ONCE known as Nanny Forrester. Her first reaction was surprise at how spry her former nurse was: not yet an old woman, although she remembered her thirty years ago as a middle-aged gorgon. But the former Nanny Forrester was gone; she was now apparently to be called Glenys.

"Since we are more like friends!" said Miss Glenys Forrester with a little laugh. She poured Olga a second cup of coffee out of a bone-china coffee-pot, painted with tiny roses and forget-me-nots. A plate containing sugary biscuits matched exactly and so did the cups, with handles so spindly it was difficult to hold them.

Then Miss Forrester twinkled even more archly, "Especially as I'm going to be able to vote for Mr. Carter-Fox on Thursday. What a surprise to find I was in your constituency after all these years! At the time I just couldn't help dropping Mr. Carter-Fox a wee note, reminding him of the connection, and a card for you. Then of course there was my problem with the Town Hall, everyone there is so dreadfully left wing. Mr. Carter-Fox did what he could, but I suppose I had hoped for some tiny personal touch from you, Olga . . ."

She rattled on in what was a parody of amiability, just as Olga remembered her: "Still you must have so many responsibilities. Just one little girl, Elfrida, isn't it? I loved the photo—more like Lady Imogen, I thought, than you. The eyes, anyway. But isn't it terrible when they lose their teeth and they *will* smile to the camera? I bet you and Mr. Carter-Fox had a good laugh about that photograph."

Then Glenys Forrester returned to the subject of their new friendship. "Certainly, I don't expect you to call me *Nanny* any longer. I haven't been called Nanny since I left you. In my next post I was called Glenys. Mrs. Arkwright considered Nanny to be quite old-fashioned. And later I called the Arkwrights themselves, Jack and Josephine Arkwright, you know, the Arkwright Foundation, they do so much for charity, I was asked to call them Jack and Josephine. Wasn't that surprising?"

Olga wanted to say, "Since those were their names, it would have been surprising if they had asked you to call them anything else." But she bit back the childish impulse. She was here, in this horrible, stuffy, over-furnished West London flat, drinking weak milky coffee and eating sweet biscuits, only because she was desperate. Nevertheless, Olga was reminded how much she had always disliked the late Nanny Forrester, now her friend Glenys. Fortunately, it seemed the dislike had not been mutual.

"Of course Olga, you were always my little pet." Glenys Forrester spoke in a sentimental voice which Olga also remembered from the past, in those days applied to kittens in baskets, baa-lambs with blue bows, and flower fairies. "That's what I told the Arkwright boys, and all my other families. Olga Swain was quite the best behaved little girl I ever looked after. Not that deep down you didn't have a temper—your little black clouds we used to call them—but your manners were a joy. Millie was quite another matter. What a little liar! As I always told your mother.

"And how is she?" Glenys Forrester hardly varied her cosy tone. "Of course I don't believe all I read in the newspapers." She pursed her lips. "But really, some of the things she says in public! And badgering our poor Prime Minister all the time. As if he didn't have better things to do."

Then a curiously avid expression crossed Glenys Forrester's face. "So what's he like?" she added.

Olga was startled. "H.G.? Very good manners. As you would expect." It seemed an appropriate thing to say to a former Nanny.

"No, no, not the Prime Minister. Randall Birley. Does he come to your dinner parties? I watched *Rebecca*, I wouldn't move from the set. I told my friends, now just don't telephone me on Sunday nights . . ."

But Olga Carter-Fox had not dug out Nanny Forrester's change-of-address card (hitherto purposefully ignored by her) to talk about Randall Birley. She thought it best to come right out with what she did want. "Nan—Glenys. Something extraordinary, something horrible has happened. How can I put this? I'm afraid it will be a great shock to you. It was a great shock to me. It's to do with the old days at Hippodrome Square. It's to do with the house itself."

"The *house*—" It was Glenys Forrester's turn to look startled. She put down the delicate coffee cup she had been endlessly sipping. Olga knew that she would be even more astonished at what was coming next—astonished, and no doubt legitimately horrified. Olga had to press on while she still had the advantage of surprise.

"Glenys, I wonder whether you would talk to someone about the old days, and how you left us so suddenly. The fact is that I have someone with me, someone outside, Jemima Shore, you know, from television, Jemima Shore Investigator."

"Here? Television cameras here, oh Olga, what on earth, I don't understand, an interview—" Glenys Forrester touched her hair. "I must make some more coffee." You could almost have said she bridled. The hair style had smartened up since Olga's childhood and there was evidence of a blue rinse.

"Not actually on television," Olga explained patiently. "You see, Jemima Shore's helping us, Harry and me." Olga judged it better not to mention Millie. "This is all absolutely confidential." And there was another thing Olga judged it better not to mention to Glenys Forrester: she was fairly sure the former Nanny would end up having to talk to the police.

But she, Olga, could fight this thing better—this thing, whatever you called it, this scandal—she could fight it better if she at least knew the facts, the ancient facts. She could hardly persuade Nanny Forrester to trim her story. That would be quite wrong, against the law, no doubt. Olga was conscious of her responsibilities as an MP's wife. Nevertheless, forewarned was forearmed, and there was nothing wrong with probing the mind of her former Nanny. As Glenys Forrester, excited as well as mystified, agreed to talk to Jemima Shore, Olga Carter-Fox blessed the magic persuasive powers of television.

Glenys Forrester did not scream or faint or do anything dramatic when Jemima Shore broke the news that a skeleton had been discovered in the cellar of Hippodrome Square. Jemima referred as euphemistically as possible to "an accidental death," and an equally accidental discovery. She did not try to cover up Lady Imogen Swain's involvement, but she simply did not mention any other names. At first Miss Forrester said nothing at all, merely pursing her lips again into that narrow line which reminded Olga vividly of the tyrant of the Hippodrome Square nursery. Then she flushed visibly beneath her pale powdery skin, but it was not until Glenys Forrester spoke that Jemima and Olga realised she was not so much shocked as intensely angry.

"That wicked selfish woman! I'm sorry, Olga, but your mother was one of the most selfish mothers I ever had the ill fortune to work for, never a thought for anyone else, no consideration whatsoever. *And* a wicked temper when no one was looking. That's where you got your little black moods from. Sweetness and light to her friends, but very different where the nursery was concerned." Miss Forrester paused for breath, then returned to the attack as the full enormity of what she had heard struck her.

"How dared she do that? With decent people and little children in the house?" The angry flush deepened. "So that's why—everything locked up and sealed off. No one allowed in the cellars, some talk about damp, flooding, all lies of course. And the smell of paint! The smell of paint everywhere! It made me feel quite ill, and my poor little girls too. Why was there so much paint? She had the whole hall and dining-room repainted after one year, after all the trouble she'd taken with the previous colour, endless coats and varnishes. Now we had all the pots all over again, the smell of paint everywhere, and she never made a fuss, she, Lady Imogen, who was always so fastidious about smell, about anything like that."

Jemima Shore thought about those baffling open tins of paint, the old dried paint sloshed about in the outer cellar. She could imagine no better mask for some more sinister odour than the smell of fresh paint . . . nor apparently could Lady Imogen Swain. She must have done that herself if Burgo Smyth never visited the house again. His idea, her idea? Since Smyth had not mentioned it, possibly her idea, the brilliant notion of a woman whose great interest in life in those days, judging from her Diary, had been interior decoration—apart from parties and of course sex.

Glenys Forrester was now in full flood: "And when I started to ask questions—well, naturally I did, I had my little girls to look after—just like that, three months' pay instead of notice. And off I was asked to go. The girls were heartbroken." Miss Forrester stared at Olga as though daring her to contradict her. "I knew it was all wrong. But of course I thought it was all about . . . *other* things, never mind."

"It's a long time ago," Jemima said gently. "What other things?"

"If Olga doesn't mind—no, why should you? As Jemima says, it's all a long time ago. Lady Imogen's *behaviour*, I should call it. A married man too! With such a nice wife. I sometimes saw poor Mrs. Smyth at children's parties. Naturally, I never said anything, I was just specially nice to the twins. And how well they've turned out, haven't they? Archie Smyth, a proper young Englishman, not enough people like that now in the Conservative Party—"

"So you knew all about it? Lady Imogen's affair. And that was why you thought she asked you to leave." It was the persistently gentle but relentless voice of Jemima Shore Investigator.

"Of course I knew all about it," Miss Forrester retorted. She added witheringly, "You can't keep things like that from a Nanny, you know." Jemima Shore had absolutely no difficulty in believing that. "Even though I was on my nursery floor," Glenys Forrester continued, "and never let my little ladies go where they weren't wanted."

"I understand." Jemima's response was deliberately warm. "But a death in the house—I take it you wouldn't have known anything about that at the time? Beyond being surprised at the fresh paint."

"No, no, not a death, God save us!" Miss Forrester gave an artistic shudder. "But I knew there was something fishy, very fishy in that house. The way I was asked to leave so suddenly. It was all wrong. My instinct told me that. A Nanny's instinct is *never* wrong."

"Now, do you remember someone called Franklyn Faber coming to the house?"

Miss Forrester frowned. "The name is familiar. Why is it familiar?" Jemima did not enlighten her. "But no, I don't remember him, and I should say that we didn't have people like journalists coming to the house. Lords and ladies were more likely. And you may say where Lady Imogen was concerned, more lords than ladies." The prurient note was back.

Jemima drove Olga Carter-Fox away from the depressing red brick house, built at the turn of the century, where Miss Forrester had her flat. She put on a tape of Jessye Norman and Kathleen Battle singing a negro spiritual, to eliminate the need for conversation.

Olga was silent, staring ahead. As they approached Shepherd's Avenue, Olga said, "Stop the car. I've something to tell you. I can't say it in front of Elfi. It's way after four o'clock. The *au pair* will have fetched her from school."

Jemima switched off the glorious voices.

"I've learned something from visiting that ghastly woman. To think she was put in 'sole charge' of us, as they used to call it, dreadful phrase but accurate where my mother was concerned. Be that as it may . . . this is something about that night. The night he must have died. Something I knew all along but didn't know I knew it."

Olga looked at Jemima for the first time. She appeared to be extraordinarily tense and her dark eyes had that fierce expression which Jemima had noticed on their first meeting in the Irving The-atre. "Jemima, my sister Millie went downstairs that evening. I think it must have been that evening. She saw something. It's nonsense what Nanny Forrester said about our never going downstairs. That's what brought it back to me. Everyone tells lies. Including Nanny Forrester. She used to go to bed, in her own room, with the door open, and snore like an elephant. A sherry or two probably helped. She slept like a log; you could hear her a mile off. And then we used to go downstairs, something we were strictly forbidden to do. Which made it an adventure."

Olga sighed, "How pathetic! When I think of Elfi, downstairs every night and we love to see her. Well, mostly we love to see her." Olga smiled. "But for us, Millie and me, to go downstairs and spy on our mother was a great adventure."

"What did Millie see? And how did you know?"

"Millie saw *something*: Madre and a man. I suppose it must have been Burgo. Millie adored Burgo. Several times Millie and I saw Burgo and Madre kissing. We thought it was horrid—sucking noises—we had to try not to giggle. Once he put his hand—well, you can imagine. We thought that was rude. At the same time Millie still loved Burgo. But that night it was different. I don't quite know what Millie saw. 'The man fell down. And Madre was angry.' I remember that Millie was very frightened."

"But the next day Madre said it was all a horrid dream. Some-thing that Millie had made up, because Millie was always telling lies in those days. And Millie must forget all about it. And if she didn't, she would be sent away to a school for bad girls, and never see Madre or me again.

"And we had to forget about Burgo too. Burgo coming to the house. Because he was never coming back." Olga's voice became extremely quiet. "And I suppose he never did. I never saw him again until I was married to Harry. And then he just said, 'Little Olga! I can't believe it. Little Olga grown up into a fine lady!' As though there had never been anything else between us, not my mother, not my childhood, not our ruined childhood." Olga gave a little sob and covered her eyes.

"I'll be in touch," said Olga hurriedly. Then she opened the car door and jumped out before Jemima could say anything. Jemima watched her tall, slightly heavy figure scurrying down Shepherd's Avenue towards her home. She wanted to call after her, "Do you realise what you've just said? That your mother *killed* Franklyn Faber, and Millie watched her?" Everyone tells lies . . . If this was the truth, it made Burgo Smyth an accomplice to murder or manslaughter, in terms of the law. But it also made him a chivalrous man who had acted to protect his mistress, in part at least.

Out of habit, Jemima bought the late edition of the *Evening Standard* in Holland Park Avenue before turning in towards her own flat. The election still dominated the news but, wrestling with this latest twist in the Faber Mystery, she barely glanced at the headline. In any case, she was dispirited by the way the Tories were once more drawing ahead. Then she saw the name of the Foreign Secretary: he was getting a particularly high rating for his handling of the inflammatory East European situation. Burgo Smyth was praised for such qualities as "unflappability, security, stability." Horace Granville on the other hand was widely seen as "lightweight" and "uncommitted" (to politics). Stable, secure! If only they knew. But she, Jemima Shore, was not about to tell the world: which is when Jemima realised she sounded as sanctimonious as Nanny Forrester.

What Jemima did not notice until she was inside Holland Park Mansions was an item on the back page of the paper in the STOP PRESS. The word "theatre" caught her eye. It read, in smudgy type:

THEATRE DEATH FALL: Stagehand Henrietta Ann Vickers, 23, fell to death in Henry Irving West End theatre.

There was the item in all its sickening brevity. Jemima felt a horrible lurch in her stomach as if a physical blow had been dealt her. There were no further details—she combed the rest of the paper—and those that were given were not necessarily accurate. Stagehand indeed! Poor Hattie Vickers. But the actual death must be true enough. The cause of death, a fall, was also most probably accurate and the name of the theatre was correct.

Poor Hattie Vickers indeed: an image of her, with her cloud of honey-brown hair and her pretty honey-coloured skin, came before Jemima's eyes. Along with the image there returned a memory of Hattie's distressed chatter, her terrible day and so forth, on the evening Jemima had gone to the Irving.

Another death. Imogen Swain in Hippodrome Square and now Hattie Vickers at the Irving. Actually there were *three* deaths if you counted the death of Franklyn Faber, so recently revealed. Death three times over: what was the nature of the web which wove them together? Was there such a web? And if so, where and who was the spider?

Right at the centre of the web there had to be Imogen Swain; that was incontrovertible. Franklyn Faber had died in her house, either accidentally or as a result of some action on her part. Jemima decided to list some of the many questions which remained unanswered about all this.

First question: what is Faber doing in Hippodrome Square in the first place? The short answer is, keeping the appointment he mentioned to Laurel Cameron. Faber is not a friend of Lady Imogen's, if Nanny Forrester is to be believed, and the nanny undoubtedly keeps a beady eye on the comings and goings in the house. Even more to the point, Lady Imogen's name never features in Jemima's media researches on the subject. But Franklyn Faber *is* a friend of Burgo Smyth, a close friend since Oxford days. And Imogen Swain, according to her diary, knows that Franklyn Faber can ruin Burgo.

You might think that Faber has gone far enough already, abstracting documents from Burgo's briefcase, involving him in a secrets trial, but there has to be something else. Back to the lawyer Laurel Cameron and her interview with Jemima: quoting Faber's own words that last night, when he seems to have an appointment, "They're trying to make me a fall guy, Laurel" . . . "Not prison, if it's a question of prison," and "I've been betrayed, I never thought it would end with a betrayal." Laurel Cameron simply assumes that it is a general betrayal by "the Establishment" and goodness knows that is a plausible scenario, and not because Laurel Cameron generally does discern these betrayals in her cases. But the discovery of Franklyn Faber's body at Hippodrome Square alters the scenario. The appointment must be with Imogen Swain. And the betrayal has to be much more specific.

Logically, the person who had "betrayed" Franklyn Faber (in Faber's opinion) has to be his old friend Burgo Smyth. What then was the true deal between them? Jemima recalled Laurel Cameron's vituperative remarks to her (which for reasons of libel, had fallen on the cutting-room floor); Burgo Smyth talking in court about trust betrayed—that word again—and so forth, yet leaving unexplained the question of how Faber got hold of the document so easily. Supposing, just supposing, that Laurel Cameron is in this second instance perfectly right. Supposing Burgo Smyth has been in cahoots with Franklyn Faber, for some reason unknown, but then betrays him and allows him to take all the blame?

A phrase in Imogen Swain's Diary floated into Jemima's mind. She had of course not been able to destroy it, as ordered by Imogen's heirs. Or rather Jemima had destroyed it technically, shredding the little volume in her office. But she had copied it on the photocopier, that silent late twentieth century spy. Jemima unlocked her safe and searched for the entry. She found it:

"February 3: . . . He's never loved anyone like me, not Tee. That's just because he thought an MP should be married. I'm the first woman he's ever really loved. He never understood about loving women before he loved me. His shady past, we call it!"

Burgo Smyth and Faber: an early romantic connection? was it possible? a masculine love affair? well, why not? Burgo Smyth then marries the decent Teresa to keep himself on the conventional straight and narrow path, only to find himself swept away by passion for Imogen Swain. So, pursuing this train of thought, does Burgo Smyth tacitly connive at Franklyn Faber's snitching of the documents? As for Franklyn Faber's need for ten thousand pounds, which puzzles so many people who know him, including his lawyer Laurel Cameron, you have to remember that before the 1967 Act, closet homosexuals with a public position (Faber is a leading campaigning journalist) are hopelessly vulnerable to blackmail. This fits with Imogen Swain's Diary once again. Faber knew something which could really ruin Burgo and bring about his "political death."

So, however approximately, Jemima felt she might have the answer to the first question: Franklyn Faber is in Hippodrome Square at the request of Imogen Swain. An appeal? a deliberate trap? In the absence of the other Diaries, difficult to know. And there Faber dies, no question about that, not to be discovered for thirty years.

The second question is of course: how did Franklyn Faber die? Jemima decided to leave that aside for the time being. At least the concealment of his corpse was not an issue; Burgo Smyth had admitted to doing it, with the connivance of Imogen Swain.

So fast-forward thirty years. Imogen Swain begins to lose her memory, or, to be more accurate, reverts to her embarrassing memories of the past, hitherto well buried. And she has letters, Diaries . . . then she dies. Apparently accidentally.

Yes, that is the third big question: how and why did Imogen Swain die? You might begin by asking *cui bono?*, one of the few things Jemima remembered from frustrating Latin lessons at school. Who benefited? One obvious answer was Burgo Smyth, whose guilty secrets—sexual secrets of one sort and perhaps also another—she was beginning to spill. Yet Jemima could not help doubting whether Burgo Smyth himself had the opportunity to carry out such a deed let alone the inclination, which was another matter altogether. For one thing, given the Special Branch who had to guard him, even to arrive at Hippodrome Square unrecorded would have presented considerable logistic problems.

The younger generation was another matter. Sarah Smyth had paid visits to Hippodrome Square on her father's behalf. As for Archie Smyth, he was definitely not a character of whom one could safely say that he wouldn't harm a fly. Had they been out to protect their father? Politics was one of the worlds where the bubble reputation, that evanescent thing "a good name" was all important.

At this point Jemima stopped. She had an inkling that her thoughts had taken her down an important path. But she was brought right back to the subject of the Diaries. Where were they now? Millie Swain had entrusted them to Hattie Vickers at the theatre; there was general agreement about that. How had they disappeared? Who had access to the cupboard or safe apart from Hattie herself? Who had stolen them and why? Had they been destroyed by now? Above all, how had Hattie Vickers come to die: another very convenient demise? It was time—not before time—to make a call she had been meditating ever since the death of Imogen Swain. She had to talk to Chief Detective Superintendent John Portsmouth.

Jemima reached for the telephone. "Pompey," she began, "do you fancy a drink? two drinks?"

"I've heard it said that drink loosens the tongue," Pompey responded cautiously.

"My point exactly. And two drinks will loosen two tongues, mine as well as yours. Remember the Faber Case? You gave me some help with my research, we had a jar or two then. Now, I want to put a scenario to you. So you'll have to do some more homework, legwork rather, for me, get the police to help you, that is me, with my enquiries. Two deaths, Pompey, one quite recent, one very recent, an old woman and a young woman, see what you can sniff out . . ."

CHAPTER 15

ONE OF US

THERE WERE TEARS AT THE IRVING THEATRE THAT EVENING. A COM-
pany meeting was called to announce the death of Hattie Vickers. There were of course no drinks, given the nature of the
occasion and the performance ahead—no public drinking anyway.

Jemima Shore's meeting with Pompey of the Yard took place at
the Groucho Club a little later. The venue was Pompey's choice.
He had a fondness for spotting literary celebrities, to report back to
Mrs. Portsmouth, discerning the most unlikely faces—Salinger?
Surely not—in the smoke-filled ground-floor bar. At this Groucho
meeting there were drinks but no tears.

At the Irving, Charley Baines was choking back sobs and Millie
Swain cried openly. Roz, the company manager, was ill (and had
been ill before Hattie's death with the same flu which had stricken
Mike at the Stage Door). But in any case Randall, as director, star
and founder of the company, would always have dominated proceedings. The meeting was held onstage and that lent a certain
gruesome element to the proceedings. The Safety Curtain was

down, but that did not prevent the feeling pervading the cast that Hattie had lain dying in the stalls not far in front of them. The cheerful inner set showing the Illyrian court, and including a good deal of unspecified blossom of a vaguely psychedelic nature, did not help either. Nor for that matter did the vivid outer curtain in front of which Millie would shortly play the first scene with her Sea Captain: "What country, friends, is this?"

To denote a stormy scene far removed from the harmony of Illyria, a mediaeval map had been adapted in a pop-art style, showing a tempestuous wave-ridden sea where various huge and threatening monsters were visible. In one corner the legend "Here be dragons" could be seen. In another, the designer had the happy conceit of putting a large erect naked Cupid with his arrow, and the legend, "Love Conquers All," in case people had difficulty understanding what this production of *Twelfth Night* was all about.

On the fringe, at the Addison, the legend had been in Latin: "Amour Vincit Omnia," or what was thought to be Latin. But on the transfer to the West End, the producer's beautiful Japanese wife, never normally known to speak, had objected. Nobody grasped what her point was but everyone hastened to agree with her in case they were committing some unspeakable offence by Japanese standards. (Only Charley Baines had the cynicism to whisper to Hattie Vickers as it happened, "Besides, she's the producer's wife.")

Only later was it discovered that the objection by the producer's wife had been to the incorrect spelling of Love in the French manner instead of the Latin "Amor." By this time the curtain legend had been changed to English at considerable expense. But, English or no English, the painted monsters of the deep seemed to point more clearly to Hattie's fate than the priapic Cupid.

Randall Birley did not show a great deal of emotion when he addressed the company, but his voice was uncharacteristically flat as if he were making an enormous effort to show leadership by not breaking down. Only when Randall alluded to the police was the full extent of the horror understood by the company.

"The police!" burst out Kath Lowestoft, who played Maria and, like Charley Baines, had counted herself a friend of Hattie's. Kath had huge surprised blue eyes which gave the impression of being quite circular. She dabbed at her tears with a piece of Kleenex and focused this alarmingly intense gaze on Randall once more. "Not the police! Oh poor, poor Hattie. She hated the police and things like that, authorities."

"For God's sake, Kath, don't you understand? It's not to do with her. It's to do with us." The acerbity beneath Randall Birley's measured tone was evident. "We all have to talk to the police. Anyone who knows anything about this ghastly—," he hesitated, "this ghastly *tragedy*, has to tell the police anything they know."

"But it was an accident," persisted Kath, eyes watering again. "Wasn't it?"

"Randall," said Millie Swain softly but clearly, "poor Mike at the door is terribly upset. I think you should talk to him. He keeps saying it's all his fault, he should have done the locking up on Saturday night, not left it to that poor little girl. His words. I kept telling him no one can help having flu." Charley Baines noticed that Millie was not standing close to Randall, nor did her body language indicate any particular closeness between them (compared to meetings in the past). He guessed that the incident of Randall's arrival with Helen Troy the night before had not been forgiven.

"He was sitting there crying, big Mike crying, when I came in. Just staring at his bloody television and howling." This was Alice Martinez, a sparkling (if possibly too mature) Olivia; the den mother of the company. Alice Martinez had acted a great deal with Randall in the past and there were those (including Millie Swain) who assumed there had once been a romance between them, despite the age gap. Whether the rumour was true or not, Alice Martinez had a sweet nature which made her universally popular, even with Millie.

"What's he so upset about? Will someone tell me?" Kath again, whose particular grief seemed to express itself in persistent questioning. "He was always foul to poor little Hattie. Pretended not to recognise her, thought she was a visitor, asked who she wanted to see, stupid tricks like that."

"It's called guilt, Kath." Charley Baines put an arm around her shoulders. "He feels he should have been the one to cop it, not her. Or rather he feels he could have taken care of himself better than Hattie could—let the bugger have it, words to that effect."

"You see, Kath, I'm afraid the police don't think it was an accident," Randall explained. " 'Cannot rule out foul play,' that's the message. That's why we all have to talk to them, tell them anything we know."

"Including where we all were on Saturday night?" Millie Swain's voice was carefully expressionless but it was clear to several of the cast, including Charley Baines, that her main interrogation was directed at Randall Birley. "Apart, that is, from all being in the theatre."

"Are they thinking that she surprised someone—some homeless person?" suggested Kath, sounding more tentative. Then her blue eyes welled up again. "Oh how ghastly! Mike's absolutely *right* to be upset. Hattie was so little and Mike's a hulk to put it mildly. He really could have seen the bugger off."

"How did this lethal homeless person get in?" asked Charley Baines abruptly. "Has anyone thought about that?"

"I suppose the police have," murmured Alice Martinez.

Suella Martin, one of Olivia's ladies-in-waiting, who was black, muttered something to the tall dark-haired man standing next to her who was playing Sebastian (he *did* bear quite a decent resemblance to his stage twin, Millie Swain).

"Did you say something, Suella?" asked Randall sharply; his charming matinée idol manner was singularly lacking today. Suella Martin stared back at him but said nothing.

"Well, I've got a comment on all this," went on Charley Baines as if no one had spoken. "I can buy Hattie leaving the outer pass door open when she went to the front of the house, although she wasn't supposed to do that. But I know that she did it at least once, told me that she didn't want to cut off her retreat. Her retreat!" He laughed mirthlessly. "But supposing, just supposing this wasn't a violent member of the homeless community—"

"The homeless *what?*" asked someone, possibly Suella again, *sotto voce.* Someone else laughed.

"Don't laugh," said Millie Swain. "It's not funny. Charley is quoting our present Prime Minister. He actually used that phrase on telly on Sunday morning. Christ! The homeless community. Vote Labour on Thursday or you're all *insane.*"

This was manifestly not a popular statement with the rest of the cast. As a matter of fact, of those who were registered to vote in London, and intended to use their vote, a good proportion was probably going to vote Labour, especially given the new alliance with the Liberals. But there was an uneasy feeling that a political discussion at this juncture was disrespectful to Hattie.

It was also distracting. But Charley Baines decided not to be distracted. "Supposing *not* the lethal homeless, nor even that well-known brute, the single mother," he went on, daring anyone, including Millie, to interrupt. "Supposing it's one of us?"

"I think that's absolutely appalling—" Alice Martinez was trembling as she spoke. But Charley was relentless.

"You see, I've been thinking about the keys. Whoever did it knew exactly what to do about the keys."

"Which was?" The curt question came from Randall.

"You told us the theatre was found locked. So the murderer must have known enough to lock the Stage Door from outside and then post the keys back in. The cleaners presumably had their own keys."

"How do *you* know all this? While we're on the subject." There was something unpleasant about Randall's tone.

"I know it because Hattie and I were good friends. And once, she got spooked about locking up and I went with her. And she explained it all to me. That's how I know about the Stage Door too, because I told her she shouldn't do that, it could be dangerous." Charley's voice began to break. "And it was."

He pulled himself together and, in a truculent tone to match Randall's, added, "And I spent Saturday night in Joe Allen's till far too late, getting completely pissed, as any one of a hundred people, who were not similarly pissed, will tell you."

"It's still appalling—" Alice began once more. This time it was Kath who interrupted her.

"I just have to say this. I do. It's true that Hattie was worried about something, very worried. Oh God, I can't believe it," she wailed. "You see, Hattie was this terrible worrier about things, she did have a therapist, but if the therapist was away—it was because she hadn't got a family, not a real one, her adoptive parents were both dead, and she felt too insecure to look for her real parents—"

"But not too insecure to talk about it," put in Charley rather sadly.

"Honestly, Kath, what's this got to do with it?" asked Randall. "I'm sorry, I know you're upset, God knows we're all *devastated*, but sooner or later we've got a show to do."

"Kath, you must tell all this to the police," said Alice more gently.

"I will! I will! But I wanted you all to know in case someone else remembers, remembers anything at all."

"I don't even begin to understand what you're saying" came quite loudly from one of the men in the cast.

"Hattie was frightened. That's what I'm saying. She knew something that frightened her." Kath turned towards the director and star.

"Randall, don't *you* know what it was? I have this feeling—"

"You're upset, Kath, it's understandable that you have feelings, this feeling and that feeling," was all that Randall said. He still did not sound friendly.

"I don't know what it was," went on Kath. "She never quite got round to telling me; several times I thought she would but she always backed off. And yes, I will tell all this, all of it, to the police," Kath ended sullenly. "And anyone else who's interested."

Millie Swain moved to Kath's side and hugged her.

"We all need to do something positive. That's the only way. We'll have a sort of benefit. On election night. We'll take a collection for Hattie. We'll give it to something she would like. In her name. I don't care what the management says. Fuck the management."

"Save the Whale?" suggested Alice. "She had this sticker."

"Bosnian children?"

"Something to do with adoption? Adopting Bosnian children. That would be positive."

"Shelter—the homeless?" But there was undeniably something awkward about that last suggestion, and shortly afterwards the meeting broke up.

Jemima Shore's meeting with Pompey of the Yard at the Groucho Club was more satisfactory in the sense that drinks flowed (whisky for him, white wine for her) and the atmosphere was, generally speaking, cosy, unlike that at the Irving Theatre. Nor did Pompey deplore, as he had done in the past, what he called Jemima's feminine instinct. Jemima preferred to call it simply her instinct, or, if he preferred it, an imaginative quantum leap of the mind.

The forces of public feminism, or the enquiring mind of Mrs. Pompey, or some combination of the two, had taken their toll on Detective Chief Inspector John Portsmouth. Quite a time had elapsed since he had first collaborated with Jemima, over the case of a missing child, in which a television appeal had played a beneficial part. Experience had taught them to trust as well as respect each other. In some cases a nod was as good as a wink; in other cases, more explicit confidences had to be made, but each knew they would not be betrayed. In short Jemima was, in Pompey's opinion, close to being "one of us."

"It's possible," said Pompey judiciously after he had listened to the scenario outlined by Jemima: the connection her instinct or her leaping mind had made between the various aspects of the Faber/Swain Case. His expression did not change when she referred to the discovery of the skeleton at Hippodrome Square. He merely bent forward and picked up his glass. For the time being Jemima did

not mention the name of the Foreign Secretary in connection with
the discovery, merely reporting what she had seen with the Smyth
twins, which in any case would shortly be the subject of a statement
to the local police. But she had the impression from Pompey's
watchfulness that he might—in his capacity as a senior member of
the Royal and Diplomatic Protection Unit—have some inkling of
what would shortly happen to an equally senior member of the
government.

"There is a connection," went on Jemima, "there has to be. Three
deaths, one a long time ago, two more recently."

"A thing I can tell you," pronounced Pompey, glass (once more
empty) in his hand. "I've done my checking. The old woman—did
she fall or was she pushed? The answer, so far as the police are
concerned, is that she fell. Nothing suspicious there. No tell-tale
injuries incurred before death, of the sort you have to find if somebody gives somebody else the heave-ho. No telltale fibres, nothing.
She could have staggered and fallen, she could have wanted to fall
and then staggered, but there's absolutely no evidence of a shove."

"Suicide? The inquest didn't say so. Accidental death was the
verdict."

"Difficult to prove and not much point in proving it. A lot of
alcohol in her body, late at night, stormy, low balcony, confused
old lady. Death wish is maybe a better way of putting it. And by
the way, her family is not without connections. Son-in-law an MP,
that do-gooder who's always bellyaching about us poor policeman:
don't want to tangle with *him.* Holy Harry, they call him." Pompey
was unaware that Harry Carter-Fox's pious nickname was something the police shared with his irreverent sister-in-law, Millie
Swain.

"Ah. No murder, then, not on that occasion. Apparently." Jemima
paused, then, "The Diaries," she said more forcefully. "Pompey, the
clue has to be in her Diaries. And where the hell are they? Hattie
Vickers had them, lost them, but had probably read them and that
must be why she was killed. I have this strong instinct—no, Pom-

pey, no cracks—" Pompey looked at her reproachfully. "They must contain the clue."

"The girl in the theatre, now that was murder." For the time being Pompey would not comment on the Diaries. He had accepted that Jemima was about to hand over her copy of the single volume she had retained, even though it had been a gift from Lady Imogen, and that she did so of her own free will, having come to the conclusion that it contained evidence related to the case of Franklyn Faber, something which had apparently not occurred to Jemima before. "No question about that," continued Pompey. "No suicide there. Plenty of bruises, not all caused by her fall. I've talked to a mate on that one, which was altogether trickier than finding out about the death of the old lady."

"Originally a good many people stood to lose from those Diaries," Jemima murmured. "Listen, Pompey, you know the real Smyth connection."

He looked at her sharply. Jemima gazed back with her most guileless expression, the one that would have been familiar to followers of her television programmes, when Jemima was bent on eliciting a particular answer from an unwilling celebrity.

"I just meant the fact that Burgo Smyth inherited Hippodrome Square under Imogen Swain's will, although I believe he's planning to give it back to her daughters, or at least not take up the bequest, whatever it is you do in those circumstances. But, as you know, the young Smyths had the key. I suppose Olga Carter-Fox was too frightened of Burgo Smyth, thinking of Holy Harry's career, to object. The young Smyths hardly wanted news of their father's affair being broadcast."

Jemima stopped. "My God, Pompey, that must be it. What Sarah Smyth said to me that night. She was in midsearch. The treasure-hunt they kept talking about. The Diaries must be back there."

"Put by exactly who?"

"At this point I've no idea. Sarah Smyth must know. That scary *Archie* Smyth must know. When I find them, and when I've read them, I'll know. But I'm beginning—" Pompey looked at her directly.

"Jemima—"

The guileless expression returned. "I'm beginning to realise the importance of the Diaries, was all I was going to say."

To herself, Jemima was thinking: a treasure-hunt and Randall Birley. Who had the perfect opportunity to get hold of Lady Imogen's lethal packet? Randall Birley could all too easily have got hold of the key: borrowed or stolen from Hattie, who adored and trusted him.

"*When* you find them?" countered Pompey. "I think I'll have another whisky if you don't mind. And is that Edna O'Brien over there? Otherwise Mrs. Portsmouth will be most disappointed. So far it's been a thin evening, literary-wise."

"That's Jeanette Winterson," said Jemima, hoping to honour her promise to Pompey. After all the literary-minded Mrs. Portsmouth had to be placated, she recognised that, but at the same time, mischievously, she did not mind baffling her old friend.

She had mistaken her man. "Ah, yes," said Pompey knowledgeably, *Oranges Are Not the Only Fruit.* Mrs. Pompey loved the series, bought the book. Actually she gave a talk about it at her group. It's called 'Another way of looking at things.' " Then he turned his attention back to the problem in hand. "Now, tell me, tell me honestly please, just how are you going to find those Diaries?"

"Pompey." Her voice was as urgent as she could make it, the guilelessness abandoned. "My hunch is that the Diaries are somehow back there, in Hippodrome Square. The last thing I want to do is obstruct the police. In fact, in that traditional phrase, I really do want to assist them in their enquiries. I've been frank with you." Well, she had—at long last.

"Help me, help me now," Jemima begged. "Give me the contact. Make the call. Help me to get into Hippodrome Square. Yes, I can get the right authorisation. After all, the interested parties—all four children, Swains and Smyths—have at one time or another implored me to find the Diaries—" And the letters, if they still exist, she added mentally. But that was too complicated to add to the equation at this point. Cherry had checked on copyright for her; the copyright of the Diaries rested unquestionably with the Swain sisters as Imogen Swain's legatees, whereas the copyright of the letters rested with Burgo Smyth, still very much alive if beleaguered. It was only their physical possession, the objects themselves, which belonged to the Swains (because they happened to have ended up in the keeping of their mother).

Jemima thought, If he asks for another drink, the answer's yes.

Pompey asked for another drink.

CHAPTER 16

DECISION NIGHT

T TOOK JEMIMA SHORE THREE DAYS TO GET THE RELEVANT PERMIS-
sion to enter Number Nine Hippodrome Square—until Thursday
night, in fact. For several interested parties in the matter of Imogen Swain's Diaries, it was important that this was Polling Day in
the British General Election of March 1993, the decisive day, in
the phrase generally preferred by the morning's Press.

DAY OF DECISION was the headline for the *Daily Express* (who ran
an opinion poll reporting neck-and-neck results, with the Tory neck
slightly ahead, but appeared to have tired at last of the phrase
"neck-and-neck" in its headline). The *Daily Mirror*, arguably more
democratically, blared out, YOU DECIDE! above another neck-and-
neck poll also with the Labour-Liberal Alliance just slightly behind.
The *Sun* preferred a shorter message, or at any rate shorter words;
YOU TELL US! The *Sun* also announced that for its special Election
Issue, the price of each copy would be slashed to 5p "in celebra-
tion." It was not clear yet what the *Sun* felt it had to celebrate.

The weightier papers could not resist the opportunity of giving
the government a good talking-to, despite the fact that their owners

favoured the Tories by inclination. This was assessed as a cheering phenomenon by the Labour-Liberal Alliance, on the grounds that anything that was not against them was for them; more impartial observers were not so optimistic. Mack McGee took the unusual step of writing a signed article in the *Telegraph,* a paper he did not actually own, about government responsibility and the preservation of moral standards (which meant family standards in any Tory newspaper). But the rumour in the corridors of McGee's own group, was that Mrs. Mack McGee was behind the articles; maintaining her rigid Presbyterian standards even in the luxurious atmosphere of the south, and worried by Helen Macdonald's unmarried status.

"Why hasn't the Labour lassie got a husband?" she was supposed to have enquired plaintively. Cherry reported this story to Jemima. She said it had to be true because it came from Dulcie, a young woman who sometimes served at the McGee dinners in Westminster Place. These dinners were always popular because they were deliciously cooked by Mrs. Mack herself, and Dulcie, who was part of Cherry's growing female network, nearly always had something interesting to report.

"You remember Dulcie, Jemima, Cy fancied her, asked her to Glyndebourne without realising she was the person who served his office lunch, just thought she was a rather glamorous young woman who happened to be passing by with a portion of Chicken Kiev . . ."

"So what happened to the Chicken Kiev?" snapped Jemima. She could not help envying Cherry's extraordinary contacts while constantly benefiting from them herself.

"Oh, they took the whole thing with them to Glyndebourne in the car. Cy thought it was a miracle, an instant picnic. Miss Lewis was furious." Cherry mentioned the name of Cy Fredericks's personal secretary. A recent attempt by Miss Lewis to get free of Cy's demanding employ by marrying a man in Australia had ended in disaster when Cy continued to telephone her with his needs regardless of her marriage—and regardless of the difference between British and Australian time; Miss Lewis had returned in a distinctly sour mood.

"Did anyone at the McGees have the guts to point out that our male Prime Minister is also unmarried?" asked Jemima, realising that she could not win any discussion about office politics with Cherry.

"Yes, someone did. The Prime Minister himself pointed it out. H.G. was there, trilling away about his trees, according to Dulcie."

"And what did Mrs. Mack say to that?"

"Said 'Hoots, mon' if you believe Dulcie, dug H.G. in the ribs— this may actually be true—and told him she was working on it with his sister. 'It's never too late for a man (or mon),' she definitely said that."

"Sexist," said Jemima bitterly. "Two leaders, both alike in dignity, both unmarried, and look how differently they're treated. One needs to be married, to have her very own Labour Denis Thatcher, whatever that would be, and the other doesn't. After all, nobody has ever dug up an atom of scandal about Helen Macdonald."

"Not even us." Cherry was tactless enough to remember the preliminaries to Jemima's first interview with the Labour leader.

If you were thinking of moral turpitude, there was of course the question of Burgo Smyth. Even at this late stage, Jemima felt the struggle within her surge up again, as decency fought with the instincts of investigative journalism—and, more importantly, the instincts of a Labour voter. Yet it could not be right, could it, to pillory Burgo Smyth for an adulterous affair thirty years earlier? The tacit cover-up of Franklyn Faber's death which followed from that adultery was another matter and for that he would now be ruined, when he should have been ruined then. But since this was Polling Day, it seemed that Burgo Smyth would be ruined following the General Election . . .

This might be the Day of Decision for the country, but Jemima had made her decision early on Sunday morning and had stuck to it. The electorate would vote on policies (in so far as they ever did) not on the personal shortcomings of the Foreign Secretary. It was just irritating to hear of Mrs. McGee's denigration of the admirable, pristine albeit unmarried Helen Macdonald under the circumstances.

The last Party Political Broadcasts on television had taken place in the preceding days, after some extraordinary wrangles as to how much time the Labour-Liberal Alliance should be allowed. Helen Macdonald, in her last broadcast, was thought by her supporters to have done extremely well ("anything that's not against us is for us") although even loyalists were divided on the wisdom of her fireside chat with her eleven-year-old goddaughter on the grim educational future awaiting her under the Tories. ("Why a godchild, for God's sake? It just rubs it in that she doesn't have children of her own," was a typical comment. Others would have sagely preferred a god-*son:* "OK, OK, so she doesn't have one, but surely one could have been found, mixed race would have been helpful there.") Of the Tories included in the last broadcast everyone, including Labour supporters, had to agree that Burgo Smyth was the star. Dignified, charming, fatherly without being condescending on this occasion, he had definitely improved his act. When on earth had he made the programme, wondered Jemima. Whenever it was recorded, his appearance, in contrast to H.G.'s over-whimsical, lacklustre approach, was another pill for Jemima to swallow.

Jemima raised the subject with Olga Carter-Fox. Olga declared herself as being frantic in her house between bouts of canvassing and caring for Elfi (her *au pair* had chosen this precise moment to leave for a better-paid job looking after one of Elfi's friends, contacted via the school pick-up). But she was agreeable to signing a paper allowing Jemima to take charge of her mother's Diaries, saying firmly that she, not Millie, had been named as executrix of her mother's will. "I always end up doing that kind of thing," she remarked in her deep voice, signing her name in a diminutive, repressed script.

Jemima mentally contrasted it with the handwritten fax she had received from Sarah Smyth, in answer to one of hers, hoping that her entry into Hippodrome Square, escorted by the police, would not be felt to conflict "with any interest of your family." Even in haste—and as a candidate Sarah Smyth had every reason to be frantic at such a time—Sarah Smyth's writing was beautifully flowing and completely legible. She declared herself well satisfied on behalf of her family with anything Jemima might choose to do in the house, without committing herself to any precise involvement: a politician's letter.

On the telephone Sarah said to Jemima in a voice without emotion, "I feel completely drained on this subject, you know. I've failed Dad or he's failed me. A bit of both. For the time being, I'm just trying to hold my seat. The horror will come later. For now, do what you like."

Jemima did not speak to Archie, but she did speculate what his handwriting would be like. Could he write? But these were prejudiced thoughts . . . then she saw that Archie Smyth had signed the fax beneath his sister's signature. But his handwriting was so small, smaller even than Olga's, that she had not noticed: A.B. Smyth, she read.

"Don't you hate him? Burgo Smyth?" Jemima couldn't resist asking Olga. She had a feeling that Olga wanted to prolong the interview a little longer, if not on this precise subject. But Burgo's broadcast had been the subject of polite chit-chat when they first arrived, part of the course of this unpredictable election.

"As a politician I admire him," replied Olga carefully, in her MP's wife voice. Then she added in quite a different tone, "As a man, I hate him. Or rather I hated him as a child."

"Who?" asked Elfi. "What child? Hate is horrid. I'm not allowed to say hate." Her large soulful eyes, so like those of her grandmother Imogen Swain, gleamed with pleasure.

"How can you admire him as a politician—now?"

"*Who?*" Elfi's voice was rising. Jemima, who had arrived armed with chocolates (for Olga), applied one to Elfi's little O-shaped mouth.

"We don't eat chocolates in this house." Olga spoke as if by rote. But she made no gesture towards removing the large chocolate-toffee her daughter was chomping happily.

"What difference does it make? To him as a politician, I mean. All that. Harry is such a good man, but where has that got him? Is Burgo Smyth such a terrible Foreign Secretary just because of what happened in the past? They wouldn't tell you that in Europe, not in all those dreadful unhappy Balkan places. Look what he did in Georgia, look what he's done for us. He had a bad past. So what difference does it make?" It was the question Jemima had been asking herself. Even so she was shocked at the measure of despair in Olga's voice. Then she saw to her dismay that Olga Carter-Fox had buried her face in her handkerchief. She was crying.

Olga gulped, "It's nothing, pay no attention, I'm just so bloody exhausted."

"Bloody! Bloody!" echoed Elfi in ecstasy, chocolate finished. She gave a little skip and clapped her hands. "Mummy said bloody!"

Olga stopped sobbing, scrunched her handkerchief and said to her daughter in a loud, cold voice, "Elfrida, go upstairs. Go into your bedroom. Shut the door." Immediately and without protest, Elfi Carter-Fox left the room. They heard her laborious child's foot-steps climbing the steep staircase, and upstairs a door was carefully shut.

Olga began to cry again. "It's all too much for me. Harry's going to lose his seat. I know he is. He can't help it. All that redistribu-tion, immigration, in spite of all he's done to help people, help *them*, help everybody. Holy Harry, my sister calls him. But I'm not at all holy. And I feel so guilty. I've been just as bad as my mother."

"Olga, you're crazy, I mean you're *not* crazy, you're definitely not losing your memory—"

"No, not that way. My memory is fine, all too good. You see, Jemima, I've been having this—this affair I suppose it was. Except it's over now. With a married man, a married man who has two little children, and a nice wife. In Harry's local Conservative office. His agent's brother. He came to help out. Oh God, what a mess. It's all hopeless, of course, and it's well and truly over. I ended it, the night Madre died. Except I didn't know she was going to die. That was just a horrible coincidence. But I went out, left Elfi, the moment the *au pair* came home, I shouldn't have done that. The *au pair* was never all that reliable and of course Elfi did come looking for me. I had to see him, Chris, this man, tell him it couldn't go on. Listening to Madre's ravings about her sordid past made me determined not to go the same way.

"I'm not sure it was even love," Olga sobbed. "Just sex. As for Harry, well, he worries so much, he's always worrying, and that's not easy in those ways, shall we say it doesn't exactly promote romance. I won't say more—you can imagine. But he's a good man," she ended violently, as though Jemima had contradicted her.

Jemima had not contradicted or even answered Olga. Who was she to point a finger at poor Olga Carter-Fox? She had made no move to contact Randall Birley, and what had that encounter been about if not "just sex?" He had telephoned her twice, leaving messages on the machine, then signed off on the note, "You know where I am." He had made only a brief reference to the death of Hattie Vickers: "A dreadful thing happened here, you may have read about it."

Jemima had put this together with a call out of the blue from a certain Charley Baines, who introduced himself as "Sir Toby Belch at the Irving Theatre. I saw you at the Garrick Awards but you didn't see me, worse luck." He went on, "You're an investigator sometimes, aren't you? Kath Lowestoft—that's Maria—and I think you should know that Hattie Vickers was hugging some kind of secret which frightened her. We've tried telling the police but they don't want to know." Then he mentioned the benefit for a Hattie Vickers Memorial which would be given on Election Night. But Jemima had other plans for that evening.

Yes, Jemima knew where Randall Birley was: at the Irving Theatre, at least he would be there until 10:30. But there had been a picture of him in the paper escorting Helen Troy out of the Ivy restaurant after a late night rendez-vous. His arm was around Helen

Troy, who was otherwise virtually extinguished by her Chaplin-esque black hat, but still indubitably a star. Baz Bamigboye of the *Daily Mail* was the first to put into print the rumour that Helen Troy might star in the film of *Twelfth Night* in place of Millie Swain (there was no comment from Millie). No, Jemima would not be calling Randall Birley. Nor would she be pointing a finger at Olga Carter-Fox.

Besides, she was busy coming to terms with what Olga had just told her. So Olga's mysterious outing that fateful night—the one which Elfi had referred to reproachfully during Jemima's previous visit—had no more sinister explanation than the guilty conscience of a frustrated wife. Jemima realised that at some level she had retained a suspicion about Olga; had that suspicion now to be dismissed?

"I must go to Elfi." Olga sounded calmer. "And I've got to organise a babysitter so that I can be with Harry at the Town Hall for the count. Forgive me."

Jemima wanted to say: forgive yourself. Instead, she patted Olga on the shoulder and pressed the open chocolate box into her hand. "One more little one won't hurt Elfi," she suggested. Jemima had done worse things in her life than silence Elfrida Carter-Fox by stuffing her with forbidden chocolates.

Jemima Shore was let into Number Nine Hippodrome Square, according to arrangement, by the policeman on the beat who had the task of keeping an eye on the house. A skeleton had turned up there, even if the fact was not yet generally known. PC Carr was a stolid taciturn young man, but Jemima did not object to his silence or his stolidity. She took him to be a young man who had his orders and intended to follow them.

PC Carr drew her attention to the taped-off basement area: out of bounds. But Jemima had no wish to go down to the basement; she had been there. Furthermore, whoever had hidden the Diaries had done so in a hurry, and done so before the basement area was opened up.

Then PC Carr gave Jemima an unexpectedly charming smile. "It's quite like the telly, isn't it—*Prime Suspect*. I love it, though it's not much like life around here, I can tell you. But I think you look rather like Helen Mirren." On that happy note, he left Jemima to her task and resumed a position outside the house in the square. She could see his hat and shoulders for a while, outlined in the street light; then he moved away.

She was alone. For a moment, Jemima was genuinely frightened. The house was so dark, so immense, so cavernous. Suddenly, to her fraught imagination, it was also full of ghosts. She was aware of all the tragedies which had taken place there, including one death and the long death-in-life of a deserted woman. She even thought she heard a creak upstairs and something like a footstep, but she knew that could not be so. The noise probably came from next door; these old houses might be imposing, but they were not necessarily well built. Think of all those cracks in the walls she had noticed on her visit to Lady Imogen. Jemima looked at her watch. It was ten o'clock.

Voting had just finished. The politicians—all of them, even Burgo Smyth—would be in their constituencies, awaiting the count. Millie Swain (and for that matter Randall Birley) were still on their own kind of stage, taking their bows. There would shortly be a collection in the name of Hattie Vickers, announced by Randall Birley according to Charley Baines, who had admitted that the precise destination of this sum was still the subject of argument. Burgo Smyth, Sarah, Archie, the Carter-Foxes, Millie and Randall, all on their respective stages.

Jemima decided to move fast. She ran up the first flight of stairs. That sense of distant light footfalls somewhere above still haunted her. But that was common to any experience at night in an empty house, as she told herself. At first she thought she would not venture into the large decayed first-floor drawing-room, the room where she'd had her encounter with Lady Imogen, playing her Miss Havisham role. Sarah and Archie Smyth must have searched the drawing-room, according to what she had gleaned from their "treasure-hunt" conversation the night of the discovery of the skeleton. But then she noticed the door was ajar. Jemima went in.

Shutters had been drawn across the long windows, since the frayed strips of taffeta, all that remained of the curtains, were inadequate. But the shutters were warped, one of them did not fasten, and in any case, for some strange reason, the shutters had been fashioned to leave a gap at the top of the window. The glow of the street lights gave some illumination, which was just as well since she could not get the lights to work. Jemima shone the large practical torch she had brought with her, and its beam picked up some glass. The photograph of Lady Imogen as a society beauty getting married was lying upside down. The other photograph of Lady Imogen and her sulky dark-eyed daughters was on the floor, some way away, with the glass smashed. A little marquetry desk was open: and its drawers empty. There was nowhere else where a hefty packet of Diaries could be concealed. Jemima went out on to the landing and looked at the staircase. Was this the staircase where Franklyn Faber fell accidentally? and died?

At that moment she heard it again: an indisputable light movement above her head. She was not alone in the house. The question was, what to do about it? She had to take a decision, rather as the rest of the country had been exhorted to do by the daily papers. The *Evening Standard* had been unable to resist the same headline, DECISION DAY. For her, it looked like being Decision Night.

Jemima found that she was no longer frightened. The visceral terror which had seized her when she entered the house had vanished. Having lived alone all her adult life, she was not even particularly scared of the dark. And the dark in this case was only partial; there were still some light bulbs in the house, for example in the light on the upper staircase. The telephone was probably still working—Sarah Smyth had used it on Saturday—although she was at this point a long way from the nearest instrument.

As irrational fear faded, a prudent rationality took its place. If there was a person upstairs, taking care to tread extremely softly (but unable to control the sound in an old house), that person was hardly likely to be an innocent bystander. That person, a deliberate and stealthy intruder, could on the contrary turn out to be dangerous.

Jemima took her decision. She would go upstairs. But as she put her foot on the first step of the second staircase, which would lead her up to the upper floors, she hesitated. There was now silence again in the darkness above her head and she was probably responsible for the faint creaks around her. Another run at it: that was the only solution. Slightly breathless, Jemima arrived at the second landing and pushed her way through the half-open door into a large bedroom. She felt for a switch, and a dim pink-shaded light on the wall actually worked. Then she saw the huge dark mass in the centre of the double bed and in spite of herself screamed out: "Oh my God!"

Something long and black uncoiled itself from the heap, followed by what was unquestionably a white paw. Her scream found its echo in an answering yowl. Jemima, heart thudding with a mixture of relief and sheer rage at her own foolishness, realised that she was gazing at Joy (or Jasmine), one of Lady Imogen's cats. A softness brushed her legs, and Jemima looked down. Here was the second cat, Jasmine (or Joy) gazing up at her with an expression that could be construed as imploring—or defiant.

Joy *and* Jasmine, Lady Imogen's precious "girls." How on earth had they got in? The kindly neighbour was supposed to be harbouring them. The cats seemed unfazed, perfectly at home, as well they might be, having lived for so long in this house, and no doubt this bedroom. Knowing the ways of cats, Jemima guessed that they were spending a lazy period in their old home before going next door to be fed in the morning.

Quite light-hearted in reaction, Jemima turned to the drawers before her. They were open and empty. The second cat joined the first on the bed. Together, the pair paid her no more attention.

All along, Jemima had imagined that the nursery floor would provide the answer. When she reached it, she found that here at least the doors were shut. The first room had a narrow bed in it with an iron bedstead, and the atmosphere was extremely stale. Was this the former room of Nanny Forrester? If so, she had certainly lived to enjoy more luxurious circumstances. A bulb (which did not work) hung from a flex in the middle of the ceiling, without a lampshade.

The second room was bare, whatever its original function, and also without light. There was only one other room, apart from a poky lavatory of an old-fashioned sort, and a dismal room which contained a sink and a half-bath (for children? how unbelievably spartan!). This was the nursery. This was the room from which Lady Imogen had fallen. Jemima could see the balcony, the doors to it closed. The light in the middle of the nursery ceiling, which had a broken shade, did work. A hand mirror with the glass cracked and splintered—that traditional unlucky symbol—lay in the middle of the floor.

The pictures on the walls were a curious mixture. There was a series called "Flower Fairies" by Margaret Tarrant (Jemima could remember having those in her own little bedroom) and several posters of some pop star she also dimly recalled, conventional in black leather jacket and sporting a guitar. The room was full of cupboards, with drawers below, none of them open. But Jemima did not have to look far. In a basket-work chair by the window was an airline bag zipped shut. She opened it. She was looking once more at the Diaries of Lady Imogen Swain. She sat down in the basket chair and started to read.

A long time later—Jemima had no idea how long—she heard footsteps on the staircase. This time there was no mistake. These were human footsteps and they were approaching the top floor. She thought she knew who it was, who it must be.

Jemima was still holding one of the Diaries when the latest entrant to Number Nine Hippodrome Square came through the nursery door.

"Ah," said Jemima Shore coolly. "You. I was just reading about you." She pointed to the Diary and read aloud in a voice which she was proud to note did not tremble. *"Saw his children again today at dancing. Archie is such a little white mouse."*

She gazed at Archie Smyth, the little white mouse who had grown up to be a man standing in front of her with a gun in his hands.

CHAPTER 17

STRANGE RENDEZ-VOUS

"YOU'RE WRONG," SAID JEMIMA SHORE. "THAT WON'T SOLVE ANY-thing."

Archie Smyth stepped farther into the room. He put the gun on a basket-work table. Then he sat down on the only other piece of furniture, a very small carved wooden chair. His long limbs stuck out from the chair like Gulliver's in the land of Lilliput. He put his head in his hands.

"I think I'm going mad. I thought—I would frighten you. Don't worry. It wasn't loaded."

"You did," replied Jemima with some feeling. "You frightened me very much. Not when I saw you, not with your gun, but *before* I saw you, when I heard you coming up the stairs. Before I knew it was you."

She added, "Archie, here are the letters. Take them. Destroy them. Don't read them. You asked me to help you. Remember?"

Jemima did not tell Archie that she had found one special letter, folded very small, inside one of the early Diaries. It must have been an early letter, perhaps the very first? After the first night together?

After the first afternoon together? It was entirely covered with three words over and over again: "I love you I love you I love you I love you" and lastly "I love you forever."

Treasured for thirty years, this was the letter of a young and passionate man to the first woman in his life. What connection did he have with that sad ruined statesman Jemima had seen on Saturday night? She should not have read the letter. She looked around for a match. A Swan Vesta box stood by the fireplace, which still contained a gas fire, although with its elements much broken. There were two matches in the box. One would not strike. Jemima used the other to burn the letter.

Nor did she tell Archie the single most affecting line in all the Diaries. It was quite short.

"Today Burgo Smyth rang and asked me for lunch. Said he'd been plucking up the courage ever since that evening at the Barrowcloughs. Told him I'd think about it. He's so dishy. I think I'll go."

Over thirty years, Jemima had wanted to cry out to the woman writing laboriously and lovingly in her Asprey's Diary with her fountain pen, "Don't go."

Inspecting Archie's slumped form, Jemima was suddenly reminded of the time. "What the hell are you doing here anyway?"

"What does that mean?" Archie showed a trace of his old truculent manner.

"Why aren't you busy being counted in as a splendid new Tory legislator? That's what I mean."

"Our declaration is not until tomorrow. It's a big constituency, rural. That was the point. That was going to be my alibi. I worked it out. I'm not as stupid as everyone thinks I am, you know. It's a quick journey, I do it all the time, I use the M25, then the back roads, clear at this time of night. My car is not exactly slow and I keep a look-out for the police, although the last time they stopped me it was no problem—actually I made record time—"

"For God's sake," Jemima interrupted him impatiently, "spare me the macho boasting."

"Sarah didn't know," said Archie sullenly. "She got me to sign that fax. She did know the letters were here; Randall Birley arranged it. But she'd no idea what my plan was tonight. Please believe that. Sarah's great on truth and justice and all that. Even if it ruins Dad."

He got up. "I've no intention of reading the letters. That sort of thing disgusts me. My father! I'll take the Diaries too. And I'll destroy them unread, I assure you. This time I really will destroy them. I don't care who they belong to."

"It's too late." Jemima did not move. The pile of small blue Diaries lay at her feet, and one was on her lap. "I've read them."

"Well, you'll bloody well have to keep your mouth shut, won't you. Because you won't have any proof."

"I mean: I've read them. And I know what happened, all those years ago. I can't keep my mouth shut. You see I know who killed Franklyn Faber. And another death as well. You may not like what I'm going to say, Archie, but at least your father was not and is not a murderer. Not in the clear about everything, I'm afraid, not by some standards. As for your verdict, it rather depends what your personal standards are."

She thought of the crucial passage in Imogen Swain's Diary: *"Bur told me everything. He trusts me. He doesn't trust anyone else. Not even Tee knows this. Well, she wouldn't, would she? Just sits in the country. No support, ever. Bur told me all about F.F. and him at Oxford. I knew that before, knew that he and F.F. had a sort of affair, knew that F.F. was queer, but Bur wasn't. He just lacked confidence, he said, that awful mother, etc., etc. But they did get involved. F.F. was madly in love with Bur, can't blame him for that I suppose. He just likes beautiful young men. But now F.F. is being blackmailed, needs a lot of money, he says. So he's been putting pressure on my poor darling Bur.*

"Bur has done something very silly. I don't quite understand, except it was very silly, reckless, he says. Bur is reckless sometimes. He let F.F. have a document to sell, let him steal it, sort of put it in his way. It was an arrangement between them. Nothing really wrong because Bur said the facts should have been known anyway. But he had to do it, otherwise F.F. might have said awful things about him and Bur at Oxford. Bur said—

The Diary broke off. When it was resumed on another page, the handwriting was perceptibly larger and more frantic.

"Bur just rang. He's desperate. F.F. says he's going to tell the truth. He won't go to jail for Bur, he says. Why not? It's all his fault. He says Bur has betrayed him and if he goes to prison, he'll take Bur with him. Just because Bur had to think about his career. Of course he did. Bur is important. He's a politician. F.F. is nothing, a nobody, journalists aren't important."

There was another gap, then: *"I've got to help Bur. I don't care what I do. I'd kill for Bur. I will kill for him. Nothing in the world matters except my darling Bur."*

There must have been a call. There must have been a call that lured Franklyn Faber to the appointment at Hippodrome Square. Perhaps the promise was a rendez-vous with Burgo Smyth in his mistress's house. The word "rendez-vous" had been used in Faber's last note addressed to his flat-sharer John Barrymoor. Then there was the reference to Captain Oates, which had seemed to point to suicide (providentially from the point of view of Burgo and Imogen Swain): "As Captain Oates said in a very different kind of storm, I may be some time." Now Jemima realised that it had merely been an indication of a potentially long (and tricky) visit.

Jemima had continued reading. At one point she gave a slight gasp; otherwise she was quite still.

At last she had put down the Diary. She had read the crucial entry. So that was it, the truth. The truth at last.

Given that she now knew what happened when Franklyn Faber got to the house, it hardly mattered how he had been brought there. She wondered, briefly, how much of this Archie Smyth needed to know before deciding that there was no point in any further cover-up concerning Burgo.

"Your father was a homosexual at Oxford," she said. "Or at any rate he had a homosexual affair. With the journalist Franklyn Faber. Later when Faber was being blackmailed over his homosexual tastes (this was all pre-Wolfenden, don't forget) and needed a great deal of money, he turned to his old friend to help him. Your father was a very junior minister. They concocted a plot. There was genuine public interest in a particular document relating to arms sales: both your father and Faber wanted it made public. But by letting Faber steal the document and sell it, they imagined they would kill two birds with one stone.

"The theft duly happened and the sale. It was a set-up. The papers made a great to-do. What neither of them reckoned was that there would be a prosecution. But the money Faber had received was the problem. Nothing very high-minded about money! It looked like being fatal to his case. The judge gave a hostile summing-up. And at that point Faber panicked, threatened to betray your father if he didn't come clean, explain what really happened."

"So then?" said Archie, "supposing all this is true?"

"So then Franklyn Faber was brought to this house—nothing to do with your father—by Imogen Swain. And he was killed."

"She killed him! I knew it. That dreadful woman, that slag."

"I didn't say that. I merely said that your father didn't kill him. He was an accessory after the fact, in the legal phrase, but not before it. Look Archie, I'm going to make a call. Then I want you to let me take the Diaries away, to where they belong. You can drive me in your magnificent Porsche." Jemima could not resist adding sardonically: "After all, I shan't have any trouble with the police, shall I, not in your tender care?"

The front of house of the Irving Theatre was still lit up when Archie Smyth deposited Jemima in front of the glass doors. The last of the audience was trickling out: the Benefit Performance of *Twelfth Night*, longer than usual, because of Randall Birley's spirited appeal from the stage at the end of the play.

Archie said nothing as he drove away, just as he had been silent in the car all the way from Hippodrome Square to the West End. Jemima even wondered if he had taken in the import of what she said. A kinder explanation might be that he was totally shocked—and that was probably the true one. Jemima watched him roar away in his Porsche (he was not too shocked to do that) to what was no doubt a glorious future as a Tory MP, provided he didn't get caught for speeding once too often. Not all policemen could be guaranteed to be indulgent of that kind of thing: rather the contrary. But for the time being, if the late polls were anything to go by, Archie was set for the kind of future his father had once had.

Jemima picked up the airline bag and walked around the corner to the stage door. There was a considerable crowd of autograph hunters gathered, and the autograph they really wanted was that of Randall Birley. One woman, looking middle-aged, was clutching a large photograph of the star playing Romeo. Standing near her were two much younger girls in jeans and anoraks, giggling secretly. Jemima wanted to say to them, all three of them:

"Do you really want to know what he's like? I could tell you. I could tell you what he's like when he makes love. And other things. You might not like all you heard. You might not like what's going to happen now, inside a dressing-room at the Irving Theatre."

Instead, she passed on up the steps to the Stage Door. She knew exactly where she needed to go. Jemima had memorised the place from her previous visit, which she thought she could recall in every detail. But she was unprepared for the bark which came from the little room beside the Stage Door where someone was watching television. That man: Mike, if she remembered right. But "that man" confounded her expectations by greeting Jemima with a smile.

"Jemima Shore, just seen you on telly, you gave him hell, I'll say that for you. I was quite surprised." Who or what? Some repeat. She looked over Mike's shoulder and saw that by now, for better or for worse, the results of the election polls were being discussed by a panel.

"What's it look like? The election?" she asked urgently.

"What does it ever look like?" The Stage Doorkeeper sounded particularly robust. "They're going to win again, aren't they? They always do. Bloody government. I can tell you something. I wouldn't dream of voting for them. I wouldn't dream of voting for anyone. You won't catch me voting. Bloody government . . ."

Jemima slid away. She did not need the man's directions, and his political ramblings at this point were hard to take because they were almost certainly correct.

There was no Hattie Vickers to guide Jemima this time. She had to make do with a large rough-and-ready poster in the corridor which included an informal photograph of Hattie, slightly turned away, laughing over her shoulder, a thick hank of hair curtaining her face. Tonight's Benefit was announced. Donations, she noticed, were to be given towards a bursary at a drama school. Heated exchanges had not only preceded this decision but also followed it. In the course of them, Alice Martinez, favouring Save the Whale, and Kath Lowestoft, favouring Bosnian children, had fallen out so violently that their relationship as stage-mistress Olivia and stage-maid Maria had suffered considerably.

Jemima, looking at the poster, imagined a small, pathetic, prattling ghost at her side. And that gave her courage.

There was a noise of revelry in several of the dressing-rooms as Jemima passed through the square of corridors. The Benefit had brought in many admirers of *Twelfth Night* (or Randall Birley) who were not condemned to linger at the Stage Door. But there was no noise coming from the dressing-room she sought. She went directly to it and opened the door without knocking—she was after all expected.

"Are you going to say something like 'the game is up'?" asked Millie Swain.

CHAPTER 18

LOVE CONQUERS ALL

MILLIE SWAIN LOOKED AT HER. AS SHE LOUNGED, ONE LONG LEG dangling over the chair, her expression was almost insolent.

"You needn't tell me about my mother's Diary. I can tell *you* what it said without having read it. The Diary said I stabbed him. With her knife.

"It was that ornamental knife, incredibly sharp, our father brought back from Malaya or Burma, some place like that. She kept it in her bedroom as a kind of protection. She once let me feel the blade, otherwise we just looked at it with awe.

" 'That knife has killed people,' Madre used to say. I was ten years old, I was big for my age, I was strong—and I suppose I struck lucky where I hit him. He fell and I think he must have struck his head on the marble mantelpiece. There was blood, lots of blood. Why did she have that knife there, on that table? To kill him, she told me. And why? I don't understand."

"He was blackmailing Burgo about homosexuality at Oxford," said Jemima. "I've read that too by now. Illegal of course. Dangerous stuff."

Millie pushed back the dark hair styled to be both boyish and sexy, which had made her—many thought—the perfect Viola.

"Once Hattie reminded me, I remembered it, every single detail. Before that, there was only some kind of horror, a fear that was always with me. I came down from upstairs, our ghastly Nanny was asleep, snoring away, and I thought Olga was asleep too. I watched them, Madre so little, but not with Burgo. With another man. Faber, I suppose. She was crying and his arm was around her. I thought . . . I thought he was her lover, and that she was betraying Burgo. Isn't it odd? I was madly, childishly in love with Burgo. So handsome, my Prince Charming. I used to imagine that I would marry him when I grew up. Madre would die and I would marry him.

"So I saw this man, he put his arm round Madre for some reason. Arguing with her perhaps. And I ran in. I took the knife, her knife, and stabbed him . . . the rest you know. What happened to that knife, I wonder," Millie added suddenly. "Did the Diary say?"

"Your mother says she washed it and washed it before Burgo came. Then she buried it in the garden some time later."

"Where I suppose it still is. Ah, well."

"I don't think Burgo had anything to do with that, just helped her with the body, which obviously he had to do. But she got the cellar blocked up, from outside that is, handled it all by herself. She was quite proud of all that, how she was managing," said Jemima. "At that point she was so sure that it wasn't forever, the separation, that it couldn't possibly be forever."

"But it was." There was a short silence. "Would you believe me, Jemima," Millie went on, "if I told you that I remembered none of that? I repressed it all; I think that's the phrase. Olga knew or guessed something had happened. I used to have nightmares . . . but it all got covered up under the general convenient blanket of 'Millie's lies' . . ."

"I believe you. You were only a child. But that's not why I'm here, Millie, the *other* deaths—"

"She—Madre—was going to blow everything right up in smoke.

She was going to broadcast to the Press about Burgo. I couldn't let there be a scandal," said Millie sharply. "This was my big chance, wasn't it? Not only on stage, of course, but with him, with Randall. I couldn't lose him, as Madre lost Burgo. It simply wasn't possible. He's my whole life."

Jemima, recalling some of the phrases in Imogen's Diary, thought: Like mother, like daughter. That seemed to be the lesson from this hideous tangle, not the cherry message of the curtain of *Twelfth Night*: Love Conquers All. Except that as it turned out, Imogen Swain had never been a murderer, which was more than you could say about Millie. Lady Imogen's cover-up had possibly been as much to protect Millie as to protect her lover. At least one should give her the benefit of the doubt. And Burgo too had acted to protect the child as well as himself.

"You've killed three times. In the name of love." Jemima, who had intended to sound aloof at this point, realised that she sounded what she felt: angry.

"*Three* times?"

"Your mother?" In spite of Pompey's pronouncement, she had to test it.

Millie seemed genuinely astonished. Then she laughed; it was not a pretty sound. Her lovely musical stage voice had been abandoned for one more like the harshness of her sister Olga.

"Oh, you think I killed Madre? My dear, I can assure you that was simply not necessary. Madre killed herself all right. A horrible scene it was. And yes, I was there when she did it. I went back after the theatre, I was furious with her. It was easy. I helped myself to the extra key in the bowl when Olga wasn't looking and let Olga think she had the only key. I had to come back and confront her. Suddenly I couldn't bear it any more, this dreadful pretence that she was a young woman, a beautiful woman with a lover. *I* was the young woman with the lover and she was wrecking everything I'd worked for.

"We went first to the drawing-room and I tried to put away her photo, the bride. We struggled. So I grabbed that terrible false picture of her with both of us, the devoted mother we never had, and smashed it. Nothing she could do about that. Then we went to her bedroom. I picked up a mirror. After that, the nursery. I took her, I led her, quite gently. Firmly. And I said, 'Madre, look it's empty. There are no children here. And Madre,' I said, 'Burgo is not coming back for you. He's never coming back for you. You're not a Beaton Beauty any longer. You're old, Madre, wrinkled, a horrible old lady. It's over. If you don't believe me, look, look in this mirror.' I turned the mirror and showed her her face. She screamed. She ran to the balcony, it was very windy, but she managed to open the doors and she flung herself over. 'Burgo.' Her last word was 'Burgo,' Not 'Millie.' Not 'Olga.' 'Burgo.' "

"Do you think that makes you free of her death?"

"Oh no, I'll never be free of Madre, I know that now," said Millie. The insolence had gone.

"But Hattie, poor little Hattie."

"She was going to betray me. She told me. She read the Diaries. She shouldn't have done that. She taunted me. She said there was something horrible in it about me. I pretended not to know what she was talking about. But that's when it came back to me. In all its horror. And she said she would show them to Randall—she was in love with him, you see—and then he would be disgusted by me and our relationship would be over. And then he would turn to her. And after that, she deliberately let them be stolen, or stole them herself."

"It wasn't deliberate, except in so far as Hattie was Randall's pawn." Like a few others, Jemima thought. "Randall stole them. Your beloved Randall. And put them back into Hippodrome Square so that Sarah Smyth could find them."

Millie ignored the reference to Sarah Smyth. She simply smiled. "Hattie—poor little fool. As if Randall would ever turn to anyone who couldn't be of use to him. Helen Troy—all the time Helen Troy was waiting for him. And I was a poor fool too, I didn't know that."

"All this, for love." Jemima took a deep breath. "He wasn't worth it."

"How would you know?"

"I would know," said Jemima.

Millie gave another of her smiles, terrifying because they were mirthless. "Ah, I see. Another rat, like him, only a she-rat."

"I'm not particularly proud if it, if that interests you. But it enables me to tell you that he wasn't worth it." She went on more fiercely, "Keeping Randall Birley was not worth the casual death of Hattie Vickers. No love affair could ever be worth that. Nothing was worth that, the death of a human being."

Millie looked at her speculatively. "About that, you wouldn't know." It was a statement, not a question; once again she was almost insulting in her calmness. "I wouldn't have thought passion was your thing. You're *detached*, aren't you?" She made it sound like a disease, like leprosy, as scornful as Archie was of a "caring" MP. "No, not sex, I don't mean sex, I'm sure you're terrific in bed, but actual passion for another human being."

Jemima saw no reason to answer the taunt. "What happens now?" was all she said.

"What do you think? No, don't worry, I'm not going to kill myself, jump off any balcony. And I'm not going to sit like bloody Patience on a monument, never telling my love. Not for me the life Madre lived—silence, hope, despair, and nothing. I'm going to confess to the police. That's what I'm going to do. It should be a good scene, shouldn't it? And the trial even better. I shall tell all. How I did it all, absolutely all, for Randall Birley."

Jemima considered her. "Must you? Another ruined life . . ."

"How little you know about it. That sort of thing may ruin lives in politics. But in show business, just wait and see . . . Watch our Randall survive even this and with one bound be free, unlike Burgo Smyth. Randall will be the hero, if you like, of a *crime passionel*. So much more satisfactory, the theatre than politics, don't you think?"

Jemima Shore thought of Millie Swain's bitter words, as she watched the election results until the early hours of the morning. She had forced Cherry to come around and share a bottle of pink champagne.

"At least our champagne is pink even if the country is once more turning blue," she said to Cherry. It was true. Remorselessly the map of Britain went bluish, then bluer. It was not a landslide. The margin was narrow. But it was a victory. Britain remained blue in principle. By the time H.G. was eating his proverbial hearty Scottish breakfast cooked by Miss Granville (did ever a spare man put so much food away?), Helen Macdonald had become the latest in the long list of Labour and Liberal leaders to act the gallant loser.

As the champagne flowed, Jemima confided to Cherry something of the story, hoping that she was the one person whose gossip Cherry would honourably protect. About Randall Birley, however, she told Cherry nearly everything.

"You really fancied him."

"Yes, Cherry, that's exactly what I did do. Purely physical, I have to admit. A fantasy fulfilled. But Ned comes back in two days' time. He's *not* a fantasy. And now please pass the champagne. Damn, it's getting low. No more pink, I'm afraid. Still, it hardly matters now. Oh God, Cherry, there goes poor old Holy Harry."

On the screen Jemima saw Olga at defeated Harry's side, fighting back tears. At least there was no sign of Elfi; she must be safely in bed, sated with chocolate.

Jemima told Cherry, "Harry Carter-Fox, a decent if pompous Tory, has just lost his seat."

An hour later Sarah Smyth also lost her seat on the third recount. Jemima watched her and admired the sangfroid with which Sarah, blonde hair impeccably groomed even at three o'clock in the morning, flashed her strong white teeth in a smile and waved cheerfully. "I'll be back," she was saying. Her huge blue rosette was exactly the right colour to complement her smart pale blue jacket. You might have thought that no scandal threatened—or would ever threaten—her family.

The Right Honourable Burgo Smyth held his seat by one of the biggest majorities in the country. How long he would be allowed to stay there, Jemima wondered. She did not know the careful timing set out by the Prime Minister: Burgo was to resign as Foreign Secretary in a few days "for personal reasons" and give up his seat after a personal statement in the new House of Commons. In the course of time, Harry Carter-Fox, the conscience of the party, would be selected for this seat, with a little discreet pressure from above.

The next day, around lunch-time, Archie Smyth was elected with a passable majority (although considerably down from that of his more Liberal-minded Tory predecessor). "A new member very much on the right wing of the party," said the television commentator. There were some Nazi salutes in the Town Hall, and a scuffle when the neo-Nazis were ejected by angry Tory workers.

Afterwards Archie Smyth telephoned his mother at the house in the country. As usual, Mrs. Dibdin, the housekeeper, answered the telephone.

"Dibs, I want to speak to Mum. I won, I won, I'm in."

"I saw you on telly and told your Mum. Now she's asleep, fast asleep in her bedroom," said Mrs. Dibdin. But it was not true. Teresa Smyth was lying awake, not quite sober, but sober enough to be terrified. What was frightening her was the prospect of her son, he too, vanishing from her into the political world. She was as yet unaware that her husband, for better or worse, would be leaving it.

About the same time Millie Swain went voluntarily to Bow Street police station and made a statement. On this occasion Randall Birley did not escort her as he had done when she attended the coroner's court. He was busy with Helen Troy, giving a Press conference about the coming film of *Twelfth Night*. The money was promised; even before the film was made the Oscar nominations were surely half-way there. Yes, thought Jemima, Millie Swain had been right: you could indeed say that show business was more satisfactory than politics.

Jemima understood anew the force of Millie's cynical saying when she had a drink with Randall Birley. She asked to meet him, against her better judgment, because there was a question she had to ask, to satisfy her curiosity. Randall agreed to slip away from the morbid excitement of the Press and the unsolved question of what happens to A Hit when its leading lady is arrested for murder on her own confession. (That was certainly A Happening in its own right, as many discovered that they had discerned violence in Millie Swain "ages ago.") Would Kath Lowestoft take over the part of Viola? Would Suella be given her big chance? Would Helen Troy deign graciously to step on to the London stage in preparation for her role in the film?

Jemima met Randall in a small, rather dark bar near the Irving, which she liked because its background music was an eternal tinkling Vivaldi rather than something more aggressive. Despite the semi-darkness, she noticed heads—mainly female—turning at Randall's entrance.

Jemima asked the question which was still unanswered in her mind. Why had Randall put the Diaries back in Hippodrome Square to be conveniently and secretly destroyed by the Smyths? A plan that had gone wrong with the unexpected and grisly discovery of Franklyn Faber's skeleton.

"Why did you do it?"

"To protect her."

"To protect *Sarah Smyth*?" Jemima thought you might just as well protect the railing in Hippodrome Square. Both seemed to her impregnable.

"A plot. It seemed harmless enough at the time. Archie Smyth thought it up; he's the sort of person who loves plots. An overgrown schoolboy. And Sarah went with it, to get rid of the scandal. For one thing there was no question of my keeping that bag. I had to get it out of the theatre and fast. Millie was—how shall I put it?—in and out of my dressing-room. And my flat." There was a brief, embarrassed pause.

Randall resumed briskly, "I broke into Hippodrome Square and deposited the bag. There was an old cat-flap at the back, which I got through by breaking down the wood around it, all fairly rotted. The whole house was rotten, you know." In more than one way, thought Jemima. But she did not interrupt him. Jemima understood at last the explanation for Joy's and Jasmine's presence in Number

Nine. Perhaps even now they were resident there, languorously lying on Lady Imogen's bed, the last inhabitants from the old sad regime.

"Actually, I rather enjoyed doing it!" said Randall. He began to laugh and then stopped. "Not so funny now, with that poor little girl dead, is it? I never even read them, the Diaries—please believe me. I wasn't that interested. Hattie tried to tell me things about Millie but I stopped her. If only Millie had accepted that! It's an awful thing to say but I always knew Millie was, somehow, violent, unstable, beneath that disciplined exterior. That made acting with her—and other things—quite exciting. As for the Diaries, I just knew they contained things damaging to Sarah's family. That was the point to me: Burgo Smyth and the Smyth twins, no one else. I've always helped Sarah. She's always helped me. We're allies from way back. Sarah understands me, no questions asked. In my own imperfect way, I suppose I love her."

Jemima gazed at Randall's handsome face. For the first time— freed of her fantasies because they had in a sense been fulfilled— she saw weakness there, or if not weakness, vulnerability. Poor Randall Birley! He who was not Heathcliffe nor Max de Winter but simply the repository of women's dreams of them. It was an odd thought, but Jemima could imagine the attraction of Sarah Smyth with her certainties; Sarah even had a maternal quality, probably from looking after her inadequate brother for so long.

"Do you find that surprising?" Randall smiled. "As children we always said we'd get married."

"A Tory MP for a wife! Bad for your image," said Jemima waspishly.

Randall stared at her blankly. Jemima had the odd impression that he'd hardly taken in Sarah's independent political career. He had helped her to help her father, but in his narrow concentration on his brilliant career (and it was brilliant, no question about that) he had not considered the importance of her politics any more than he had considered those of Millie Swain.

It was not a very satisfactory encounter. But after it matters improved, at least for Jemima Shore. Ned actually returned on schedule, as promised.

"Did anything sort of much happen while I was away?" asked Ned. He did not look at her. It was a odd, awkward question from the normally ebullient Ned. Who told him about Randall? thought Jemima. Someone told him something. Maybe it's just intuition, his *manly* instinct. Of course, he's used to dealing with unsatisfactory witnesses.

She put her arms around Ned. As a result her voice was muffled as she replied, "Nothing sort of much."

Ned turned, and looked at her. "Anything I need to worry about?"

"Definitely not." Jemima did not lower her arms. "Listen, Ned, are we going to go back to our old ways and make love right now or are you going back to Singapore?".

"Actually, both," said Ned. He sounded more sheepish than uncertain. "I've been meaning to tell you. Darling, it's true that I do have to go back, but there's this wonderful hotel on this island and I thought, Jemima, you might come too, our long delayed holiday . . . ?"

"First things first," said Jemima Shore, tightening her hold. "In other words, Love Conquers All."

"*Omnia Vincit Amor,*" murmured Ned, who prided himself on being a classical scholar.

The telephone rang. Ned made an instinctive gesture towards it. Jemima stopped him.

"Leave it. It's *my* telephone. And it's on answer. I know who it is. It's Cy Fredericks."

Sure enough, after a moment, Cy's mellifluous voice boomed from the machine.

"Jem, this really is a *most* exciting proposition . . ."

By this time neither Ned nor Jemima was listening.